Sarah Goodwin completed the BA and MA in Creative Writing at Bath Spa University. *The Blackout* is her fourth novel to be published with Avon, following several years as a self-published author. She lives in Cornwall with her family and a very spoiled dog.

Also by Sarah Goodwin:

Stranded
The Thirteenth Girl
The Resort

THE
BLACKOUT

SARAH GOODWIN

avon.

Published by AVON
A division of HarperCollins*Publishers*
1 London Bridge Street
London SE1 9GF

www.harpercollins.co.uk

HarperCollins*Publishers*
Macken House
39/40 Mayor Street Upper
Dublin 1
D01 C9W8
Ireland

A Paperback Original 2023
1
First published in Great Britain by HarperCollins*Publishers* 2023

A catalogue copy of this book is available from the British Library.

ISBN: 978-0-00-859157-1

Typeset in Sabon LT Std
by Palimpsest Book Production Limited, Falkirk, Stirlingshire
Printed and bound in UK by CPI Group (UK) Ltd, Croydon CR0 4YY

Trust your instincts. Be scared, be rude, be smart. Be safe.

Chapter One

2022

I nearly broke my ankle running downstairs to the door in my heels. Normally I don't rush to get it but Cat was already in a party mood and singing along to the rhythm she was beating on the door and playing on the buzzer. Clearly pre-drinks at mine were following pre-pre-drinks at hers.

I could already hear Mrs Clarke shuffling around in the flat upstairs. It'd be another letter to the council if I wasn't careful. For all the good it'd do. I kept telling her I was a private renter, that the flat hadn't been council for years now, but she still sent her letters. I got a copy of each one from her too, on tartan bordered notepaper. I could imagine her already scribbling away.

To whom it may concern,

My downstairs neighbour, Megan Fellows, is a vile chav and probably one of the dole scroungers I keep reading about in the paper. One of her friends woke me up at ten by screeching god awful 'music' at the front door. I could barely hear Gardeners' World – despite having it on at five times the normal volume! Please discipline her forthwith, ideally with eviction, unless hanging is an option?

P.S. There were two bottles of wine in her recycling last week. TWO! I know because as usual I looked through the bin before the lorry came. Can I have her sectioned for this rampant alcoholism?

Well, at least I recycled, unlike her. Between the two other flats in the converted Victorian I much preferred Mr Barrett downstairs. He was partially deaf and had a fat tabby cat called Pudding, whom he chewed out at ear-splitting volume at least twice a day. He also went on holiday to Spain four times a year and always brought cigarettes or wine back for me. In return I cut his hair for free and took care of the cat while he was away. I also invited Pudding in whenever he hauled himself up the stairs to my door to scream for salmon chunks. It made the flat feel less lonely. Though he did sometimes paw at the door to Damian's room as if he wondered why my brother wasn't coming out to give him belly rubs.

It was Damian who'd moved us to the flat, out of the place he got us when I was a teenager. Back when we had to leave our old estate, because of me. Though after the move he'd put it down to not wanting to live with Mum and her terrible taste in men. Probably to make me feel better. Not that all of her boyfriends were bad, but once you've had your telly carried off by debt collectors twice, it starts to get really annoying.

I let Cat in and she twirled past me into the stairwell, heels clattering on the cracked Victorian tile. The unmistakable smell of weed followed her in, mixing with her flowery perfume.

'It's party time!' Her nose wrinkled and she sneezed. An enormous sneeze for such a little twig of a person. It echoed up the stairs like someone had put a firework through the door. 'You've not had that cat in your flat, have you? I'll kill you if this eyeliner runs.'

'No, he's not been in,' I promised, though he had, all morning in fact. He'd also peed on the sofa, which I had just finished scrubbing down and squirting with Febreze. I was hoping Cat wouldn't notice the lingering smell.

I knew from experience that shushing Cat only made her louder so I did my best to waft her upstairs to my flat as quickly as possible. She looked incredible as usual. If anyone else dressed like Cat they'd either be laughed off the street or carted off and committed. That night she was all wrapped up in a pink faux sheepskin coat, so frizzy and fluffy it looked like candyfloss. When she threw it onto my sofa I winced, thinking of cat piss. Then I saw that underneath it she had on a spaghetti strap dress made of silver lamé, with candy pink thigh-high socks and silver ankle boots. Pink and silver makeup had her looking like some kind of space Barbie.

I'd tried to make my go-to little red dress into something a bit more fun and original for the night. I had a little black beaded bag fastened to my wrist for my purse and phone, plus some of those seamed, vintage-looking tights. I'd even spent half the afternoon trying to get my hair into a sort of 1920s up-do, which had become more and more half-hearted with each failed attempt. I'd also tried to pull off some red lipstick. But beside Cat's effortlessly eye-catching look, I felt like I was wearing a last-minute gangster's moll costume. The kind you find in a plastic bag at the supermarket two weeks after Halloween's already over.

'You look hot.' Cat grinned from the arm of the sofa. 'Very Velma Kelly. Hey, can you put my keys in your bag? They'll scratch my phone in my pocket.'

'Oh, shut your face,' I said, catching her keys and popping them in my bag, where they could scratch my phone instead. 'I look like GCSE Drama Velma Kelly at best.'

'You don't know how to take a compliment, that's your trouble,' Cat sighed. 'Look at your legs, they're fantastic in that dress. I always say so and you never believe me.'

It was true. She even called it my leggy dress. Not to be confused with the 'titty shirt' which was the one button-up I had which miraculously gave me cleavage. I'd die before I threw that shirt away. It was one of a kind.

Cat heaved herself off the ugly mustard-coloured sofa which came with the flat and teetered to the kitchenette on her heels. The silver dress was backless and her shoulder blades wiggled as she danced on the spot, filling a glass from the bottle of vodka on top of the fridge. It was clearly not her first one of the night. Cat usually drank as she got herself dolled up. It was a key part of the process and possibly how she managed to pull off her over-the-top looks without worrying about stares and comments.

'Help yourself, why don't you?' I said, without much heat.

'I always do.' Cat brought me a glass of my own vodka with a wink. The glasses fizzed as she splashed in some off-brand Red Bull.

'Cheers!' She downed her glass and went back for another.

'Easy, or we won't even make it out before you're asleep on the floor.'

'Have you seen the price of drinks recently? You gotta load up before you hit the town, Meg, or you'll be coming home poor and still sober.'

She brought me another glass, so I reluctantly downed the first. I had to agree with her. We'd not been out in a long while, not like properly out, just down to the pub or out for a cocktail or two and home by ten. But I'd noticed the prices creeping up on me every week in the supermarket and even at the bargain store when I went in for the big bottles of shampoo. They'd gone up by three pounds. Never mind the cost of bleach and developer and the dye. It wasn't like I could charge much more either. Most of my customers got me round because they couldn't afford or couldn't manage to get to a 'proper' hairdresser. I wasn't about to start price-gouging old ladies for their blue rinses or single mums for three number-2 all-overs and a root touch-up.

'Stop worrying so much, you'll get a faceful of wrinkles,' Cat said, tapping me on the forehead with one sparkly talon. 'You know I can give you a lil bit of Botox if you want – sort those out for you.'

'Fuck off,' I said, shoving her lightly. Cat giggled, swaying from the push, vodka and 'Charging Bull' slopping down her wrist.

'I mean it – I've got some in the flat. One of my regulars decided to ease off the old injectables so she can look happier at her wedding. Or if that's not your thing I can do you a lovely Brazilian, some extensions – on your head, obviously. Though who knows, that might be the next hot trend – "pubic extensions, by Cat Walker".'

Cat struck a fashion advert pose and dissolved into giggles at the look of horror on my face. I could never tell if she was being serious or not when she came out with this stuff. She loved winding me up, had done ever since we met at college. I was doing hair and she was there to study travel and tourism, then IT, and then settled on becoming an aesthetician. She still did a bit of the computer stuff on the side, fixing things for people and jailbreaking used devices. Which reminded me.

'Before you get too pissed, can you take a look at my phone? It's losing battery so fast, I'm having to keep it on charge most of the day.'

'That's probably not helping,' Cat pointed out.

I got the phone out of my bag but realised Cat had gone for the one on the shelving unit across the room. Damian's phone, almost identical to mine except for the worn stickers on my case. He'd left it behind the morning of the accident and I hadn't moved it since. Like most of his stuff it had just sat there, waiting for him to come home.

'It's dead,' Cat said, turning it over in her hands.

Embarrassingly I felt my eyes start to well up. I tried not to think about my brother when other people were around. Even Cat. No one wants to look at grief, do they? Especially not over a year after it happened. I was meant to be OK now. But how was I ever meant to be OK with losing the one bit of real family I'd ever had? Not even in some foreign country with the army like I was afraid of, but on leave in his hometown. Run down by a fucking cyclist. Dead at twenty-eight. One day soon I'd be older than my big brother – the thought made me tear up more and I put a hand over my mouth as my lips spasmed in a sob.

'Aww, babes.' Cat was on me in an instant. She put her arms around me. 'It's my fault, I should've realised. Shhh . . . it's all right. Hey, why don't I order us something in and we can just chill out, OK? We don't have to go anywhere – hey, in this outfit I bet I could get the pizza for free.'

She was trying to make me laugh and normally it would've worked, but not just then. I needed a distraction.

'I need to go out.' It came out like a silly little bleat, but I did mean it. Damian wouldn't want me to hide away and cry over the past, over him. Especially not on a Saturday night. He said as much when he got accepted into the army. Told me, 'If I get merced out there, you better not hang around the house all day in your pyjamas for ages – you get one week, then it's back to work, back to normal – no slacking.'

Only it wasn't that easy, was it, Damian? It was just so fucking random. So unfair. He'd been to see a film in the centre, catching up with his mates before he left. Then wham. He probably never saw the delivery bike coming. Just went down and stayed there until the ambulance came. But he had to have felt it, not just the collision but the injuries. The internal bleeding, the fractures.

It had been a year and still I was finding it hard to let go. How could you when it was that sudden, that brutal? When someone you loved was snatched away from you? That left a mark, a stain on you. A hole you couldn't fill, no matter what.

But at least his death wasn't my fault.

I felt something dark opening up in a corner of my mind, something I was careful never to touch or even look at. That was happening more and more lately. As if losing Damian had weakened the soil of my soul, letting things best left buried poke through.

I backed off from Cat and gulped down my drink, letting the alcohol drown that feeling out. 'Do you have anything else on you?'

Cat pulled a face. 'I thought you didn't do that stuff? What happened to "Cat, you never know what's in it"?'

'Tonight I don't care what's in it – have you got anything or not?'

Cat looked shifty. 'Not on me, no. Besides, I don't know that it's a good idea, Meg. Wait 'til later, OK? See if you still feel the same and I can sort something.'

'This is meant to be taking my mind off it.'

'I know. But you don't need a pill for that, you've got me.' Cat gave me a squeeze.

I didn't want to wait but I knew Cat wasn't going to give me anything right then and there. Probably wouldn't hand over anything more than paracetamol tonight, period. She was right, I never touched anything stronger than weed. Hadn't ever popped a pill or laced a joint. Until now I'd never felt the need, never needed to forget badly enough that it seemed like a good idea.

It was her idea, tonight. One year to the day since Damian died. I'd gone to his grave that morning and spent all day curled up with Pudding, watching his action films. Cat wasn't going to let me spend the night alone in a silent flat. But it looked like she wasn't going to let me get too messy either.

No, Cat wasn't going to give me anything. But even if she didn't I was going to get fucked up. No matter how much the drinks in town cost. I just wanted to forget about everything for a few hours and dance like I had nothing to bring me down. No future to worry about and definitely no past.

10

Chapter Two

Bristol on a Saturday night was like a whole other country. I hadn't been there for a while, keeping mostly close to home where the streets got quieter as it got darker. The opposite was happening in the centre. In the daytime that part of town was just office workers, coffee shops and one or two lost tourists. At night out came the kebab vans, the crowds and flashing lights. The only crossovers were the seagulls, always present and hunting for spilled kebabs or dropped croissants indiscriminately.

The streets were full of people, spilling off the narrow pavement and into the road. Not that there were fewer cars. Taxis, buses and ride shares came past pretty steadily, honking their way through. Bikes with boxes of takeaway on the back shot through red lights and made me feel ill just looking at them. They looked so harmless, but in seconds one of them had taken my brother from me.

I almost told Cat to forget it and take me home, but the idea of being stuck with my thoughts convinced me to stay. I was out-out and had decided I wasn't going home again until the sun was well and truly up. By then I'd be drunk enough to avoid hours spent watching the light change on the ceiling.

After a while I started to get into the mood a bit. By the time we reached the row of clubs I was glad Cat had suggested we go out. Being out with her was an all right mood lifter. Once we were part of the crowd I started to feel like my old self again, ready to have some fun. There was music from twenty different clubs making the pavement hum under my heels and I found myself smiling at all the girls in tiny dresses and the guys drenched in Paco Rabanne. It was like stepping back in time to before Damian, before everything changed.

In the dark it was easy to believe that we weren't in a chilly British town centre, but out for the night in Ibiza. Though I was already freezing my tits off and couldn't feel my feet. But maybe that last part was because of the bottle of vodka we decimated back at my flat. I was still swaying a little from the bus as we queued outside Tea Party, the girls-only club. It was new and Cat said it would be just the thing for a good night out. No creeps allowed.

Cat in her fantastic pink coat didn't seem bothered by the cold. I'd not wanted to wear my tatty pleather jacket and was now really regretting my choice. The smell of hot chips was making my mouth water. I could already imagine the relief of kicking off my heels at the end of the night, sliding my feet into fluffy slippers and opening a steaming box of fries with Cat. That was if she didn't make one of her fried egg sarnies. But that could wait until after we'd danced ourselves ragged and drunk enough to fill the weird, dark holes in my head.

The line moved quickly and soon we were inside. Cat checked her coat in with a girl dressed as a doll, who was on her phone and looked really bored. Tea Party had a very girly aesthetic: pink walls, glitter over everything and giant teacup booths like the ride at the fair. On the dancefloor I could see several big pink teddy bears being bopped around by the crowd. At the bar Cat bought the first round from a waitress in an Alice in Wonderland costume. The shots came in cups from a child's teaset and our pornstar martinis were in cupcake-shaped tumblers. Not as nice, I thought, as having them in a proper glass. Jesus, was I getting old?

Cat saw my expression. 'Bit cringe,' she muttered, but downed hers anyway. I followed her. The drinks were at least good, though for the amount they'd cost I could've bought another litre of vodka and at least two bottles of the post office's best wine.

Drinks done, Cat towed me out into the throng and started doing her usual thing – hopping up and down and swinging her elbows at anyone in a two-foot radius. I went for a more self-conscious hip wiggle. The place was fairly packed with all sorts of girls, from the ones who had to be using fake IDs to a hen party in their fifties. The music shifted between the current charts, kitsch country, 90s club beats and 80s pop. No wonder Cat loved the place – they might as well have hooked her phone up to the speakers.

We danced on and off, breaking for drinks when one of us was desperate for a lean on the bar. That was until I ran out of cash and Cat's card got declined. I would've used my card but I knew from experience that if I started paying by debit I probably wouldn't stop until my card got declined as well. I ended up pouring my change out like when we were students and asking how many shots this could get us – hoping for an even number. The bartender – now a woman dressed as a teddy bear, complete with ears and nose – sighed and poured us three Sambucas. While she was pawing the coins off the sticky bar we downed the drinks. Cat claimed the extra shot while I was wincing away the taste of mine. Then we returned to the dancefloor for a final lap. It wasn't that we intended it to be final, but Cat tried to do a slutdrop and tipped over, knocking a girl down and getting tangled in another girl's legs. After that it felt like the right time to go.

'Lemme get cash out for chips,' I said, limping along with Cat on my swollen feet.

'Nu-uh. Don't give out on me now – that was a warm-up.'

'We've got no cash and I'm freezing. Can we just go home?'

'And waste a pill? No way.'

'You took a pill? You said you didn't have any.' I glared at her but she just rolled her eyes.

'I don't have any *now*, I took it right after we left Tea Party. Should kick in by the time we get to Triangle.'

'That's a gay club, Cat. And it's gone two. They'll be shut by the time we get there.' I had to double-check the time on my phone, juggling my purse in the crook of my elbow. The drinks at mine and the long bus ride had really cut into our time, which had passed quick as a blink in Tea Party. I couldn't really remember how many drinks we'd had there, but the ground under my feet was rolling from side to side.

Someone shouldered past me and I staggered, nearly falling over. My phone slithered out of my cold fingers and before I could finish saying 'Fuck' it had smashed onto the ground. Not for the first time, as the scrapes on the case showed, but for the last. When I picked it up the screen was black and no amount of hammering the power button could make it turn back on. Fantastic. Now how were my clients going to call me? I'd have to stay close to my laptop and wait for messages there, at least until I could get down to a second-hand place and find a phone I could afford.

'Oh, Meg,' Cat said, looking at my phone and quickly confirming that it was fucked. 'Come on, I'll buy you a drink.'

'Your card's maxed,' I pointed out.

'Pssh,' she spluttered. 'I'll get someone else to buy you a drink then.'

'I just want to call it a night, OK?' I said, slightly sharper than I intended. My relaxed buzz was wearing off. I was thinking about all the pictures on my phone – Damian's last birthday, the day we went paintballing, the night we got slaughtered and he tried to teach me how to army crawl in the park. I could get them back off the cloud but until I got a new phone they'd be locked away somewhere. Suddenly I wanted to cry.

'OK, let's find a bus,' Cat said, putting her fluffy arm around my frozen shoulders. 'We'll get you home and find some chips on the way. Like, good chips. Not town centre van chips.'

My laugh sounded wet but thankfully chased the

tears away. Together, like we were in a three-legged race, we shuffled towards the bus stops at the end of the street. Away from the clubs it was much quieter, or at least the other sounds of the town could reach us. The revving motors and honking horns of late-night drivers making the most of the almost empty roads outside the centre. Screeches and yells of fun and threats from side streets. A sharp wind came whipping down the road, bringing Styrofoam trays and plastic beer cups with it. I hugged my arms around myself.

'Here, get in,' Cat said, holding the sides of her coat open.

I put my arms around her and she wrapped it around both of us, hissing when my cold arms brushed against her back.

'Should've brought a jacket, silly cow,' she muttered, then giggled when I pinched her.

We waited like that for a while. Cat started to shift from foot to foot, alleviating the pain her boots had to be causing her, as high and pointed as they were. She started chanting under her breath, slurring slightly as the words bled together.

'Busbusbusbusbusbusbus,' like she was trying to call a cat out of a bush instead of summoning a ride home.

I was already mentally on my way to bed, going through the route in my head. Get on the bus in the centre, all the way through town to the big ASDA, where it turned sharply to follow along the canal, through the industrial estate where we went to that one rave, ages ago. Then over the train lines, up past the station, around the crazy roundabout and up the massive hill to the estate. At least we'd be sitting down and warm. Even if I was starting to feel really sleepy. I hadn't drunk like this in a while and the shots were catching up to me.

'Bus!' Cat suddenly exclaimed, right into my ear. I staggered out of the protective circle of her coat.

The double-decker bus bumped to a halt, brakes squealing. A rush of hot exhaust momentarily chased the chill off my skin. The queue moved up slowly, until finally we were the next to board.

That was when I went to get the ticket out of my purse and realised it wasn't there. Not just the ticket but my purse was gone. The only things in my bag were my busted phone, two sets of keys and the driving licence I'd used to get into the club and not bothered to put back. Where was my purse? Then I remembered I'd had it tucked under my arm because getting it in and out of the bag on my wrist was a pain. Had I dropped it? I had a flash of the guy who'd bumped into me and shut my eyes for a second.

'Oh, you motherfucker.'

'What?' Cat asked, twisting around.

18

'That fucking guy stole my purse. My ticket.'

'Single ticket, three pounds eighty,' the bus driver chimed in.

'I don't have any money.'

'Then you need to get off,' he said, waving me towards the door.

'No, I'll get one for both of us,' Cat said, staggering forward and tapping her card on the reader. I knew it was useless but the driver confirmed it for me.

'Card declined,' he said, now looking done with the entire exchange. He waved to the door again. 'Get off.'

'Cock,' Cat muttered, probably louder than she'd meant to. She was searching her pockets for forgotten money and coming up empty. 'Can we not just get on? Pretty please? It's so late.'

'No, now get off, other people waiting.' The bus driver beckoned the guy behind me, who'd been sighing so hard the back of my neck was now warm. He slid past me and showed his ticket, prompting the rest of the queue to start pushing past us.

'Oh, nice – none of you worry about it, all right?' Cat called. 'No, I insist, keep your hands off your wallets.'

'Get off the bus!' someone shouted from the back.

Cat gave them the finger.

We fought our way back off the bus and watched as the rest of the queue boarded and the prospect of heating and seats closed its doors and trundled away. Most of the passengers ignored us, though a couple sent glares through the glass and one put his fingers up at Cat. Probably the guy who'd yelled before. I felt like crying again. My face was hot with humiliation and fury at the guy who'd swiped my purse.

'Oh shit, I could've done the pay thingy with my phone,' Cat said suddenly, looking at a poster advertising this move into the twenty-first century.

'With what money? Your account's empty,' I pointed out. 'We can get the next one. Maybe that driver'll let us on.'

'Uh . . .' Cat was patting her pockets. 'Where *is* my phone? It must've fallen out of my pocket. It could be anywhere.'

I tried to remember when I'd last seen it. 'I think you left it on my coffee table.'

'Oh . . . right.'

I sighed. Cat had no phone and no cash. I had no cash, no card and my phone was busted. It looked like we were walking home. Perhaps the miserable walk would keep me from thinking about things I didn't want to. Even if the evening was a disaster, at least I wasn't spending the anniversary of my brother's death all alone.

Chapter Three

17:30

Five hours until the blackout

I left buffing the hall floor 'til last that Friday, as a sort of end-of-the-week treat. Technically I was meant to do it when I finished stacking all the chairs and moved on to the bathrooms, but it was my favourite bit, so I liked to savour it. It was a good way to end the week, a nice little relaxing job.

If you'd have told me a year ago that I'd have a 'favourite bit' of cleaning anything, let alone a junior school, I'd have told you to get lost. Only in more colourful language. Just like with everything else 'colourful' from back then though, I'd left that behind or squashed it right down. Unlike Megan, Sally Flint did not swear. Not out loud anyway.

Sally Flint was polite, helpful and as boring as plain porridge. Sometimes I felt that dullness spreading down inside me. Like every day I was becoming a bit more Sally and a bit less myself.

Still, that wasn't necessarily a bad thing. What was so great about being myself? That idiot had brought me no end of problems, with her mistakes and her terrible choices. If she withered away under Sally's beige anorak, that was only for the best. Though sometimes I missed her. The girl I'd been before. Bad, mad and sad as she was. She was at least not alone. She had people, even if she didn't deserve them. I shook my head and told myself not to go down that road.

I needed a distraction, something to drown those thoughts out. The buffing was as always an excellent excuse to wear headphones, the machine being so old and so loud that eagle-eyed Janet agreed to let me listen to music whilst I used it. Probably she was hoping to avoid a lawsuit if it fucked my hearing up. So I got out the spray bottle, plugged in the buffer and brought up Cat's playlist on my phone. It wasn't a perfect distraction, because it made me think of her, but it mostly did the trick. It was a way back to better days.

Cat's musical tastes were so eclectic that every new song was a surprise. Just when I thought I'd heard them all, a new song would come on. From club tracks to ballads and old rock music to soundtracks from musicals and Disney films. Cat saved every song that ever meant something to her and we'd spent so much time together that most meant something to me.

I let the music drum those thoughts out of my mind. Internally I switched to after-work mode and cluttered my thoughts with chore planning instead. I needed to go to the shop and restock on some food and things for the weekend. I wasn't looking to come all the way down to the village tomorrow, and on Sunday nothing would be open. Except the church. Could I afford to leave off buying eggs on the chance that there'd be some at the gate to Simmons Farm? They were always cheaper than the little shop but if they didn't have any out I'd be eggless until Monday. I wanted to make one of Cat's fried egg sandwiches over the weekend. Just a little something to make me feel less alone over the two days before I came back to work.

Fuck knows why the shop had to shut on a Sunday. No one was going to have a fit if they did business while everyone was in church. Well, almost no one. A couple of diehards like Mrs Sable would have something to say. But then again it wasn't like she or any others of the churchy type needed to work anymore. They were happy with things as they were, Churchcliffe was practically stuck in the Victorian era.

The only thing missing was the original church, which had dropped off the cliff years ago. There was a black and white picture of it in the school reception area. In the background you could just see the lighthouse in the distance, poking up like a mushroom.

Some people probably dream of living in places like Churchcliffe. That's why there are so many programmes about rich couples of a certain age buying five-bedroom homes with 'land for horses' and an outbuilding for unspecified home businesses. Not that Churchcliffe would appear on a show like that. It wasn't two hours from London by train, boasting excellent connections to international airports and railways. It barely had a bus service. There was nothing to attract anyone who didn't have to be there.

A tap on my shoulder made me jump. I let go of one of the safety handles and the buffer juddered to a stop, wobbling back and forth at this rude interruption. I removed a headphone and turned around to find Janet there, ham-hock arms folded across her chest, hands and wrists still scalded red from cleaning the kitchen.

'Sally, can you stay a bit later and sweep the leaves off the playground? Douglas had to leave early to visit his ma and I've got to be home in fifteen minutes to put the tea on before Colm gets in.'

'Sure,' I said, because it wasn't like I could say

anything else. Janet didn't do options. They were just orders phrased like wheedling little favours.

'Thank you, petal,' she said, already dashing out of the hall.

'Uh, Janet?' I called out, bringing her to a stop. She looked back at me with a glare which clearly said that unless I was a sausage in need of frying, she didn't want to know.

'Do you have my pay for this week?' I asked.

Janet looked at me with an air of disappointment. She always acted like it was rude to remind her that I didn't scrub toilets and clean up spilled poster paint for the sheer thrill of it. After slapping at her anorak pockets for a moment she found the crumpled envelope of notes and waved it at me before leaving it on the upright piano.

As a point of pride I waited until she'd left before scurrying over to count it. Seventy-five pounds for the week. When I worked at a makeup counter in college I made more in a weekend than I do now. And that was for less work and all the lip-gloss I could carry. Still, I couldn't complain. For starters Janet would just get someone else in if I made a fuss. She annoyed the hell out of me but she'd been a good sport about my lack of ID and National Insurance number. Which was probably something the governors would be concerned about. This being a school and all. She never even did a criminal records check. I'm not actually sure she ever asked for my last name. Which doesn't matter really since it's fake, like my first. Sally Flint. Sally, off a memorial bench at the station, and Flint for the stones studding half the buildings in the village.

With the money in the back pocket of my jeans I buffed the rest of the hall. The music on Cat's playlist changed from lyric-less dubstep to an upbeat bit of pop-punk. I remembered that song, beat for beat. One of the tracks we'd danced to at the club the last time we went out. Though Cat must've added it before then. Just a coincidence, but I thought I'd deleted it last time I heard it. After quickly skipping over it I put the buffer away and stowed my phone in my rucksack by the back door. I didn't feel much like listening to it anymore.

I took my time locking up the last few doors of the school and making sure the lights were all off. All done for another week. In my own anorak I crossed the playground to the groundskeeper's shed and let myself in. The huge push-broom was wedged behind buckets of vomit sand and grass seed. I had to really yank on it to get it out and staggered back into a stack of boxes. A plate covered in cigarette ends fell off the top and broke. Bloody Douglas. I kicked the bits of plate into a pile and scooped them up in a plant pot. He could deal with those on Monday. He wasn't meant to be smoking anywhere on school grounds. Definitely not in the shed where he kept the petrol for the mower.

As I was putting the pot on his work bench I noticed the packet of cigs half-hidden under a newspaper. There were only six left but I pocketed them anyway. I wasn't going to chance my only source of income by stealing from work, but this didn't count. Douglas couldn't report me for taking something he wasn't even meant to have. That's if he noticed them missing in all that mess. Judging from the collection of biscuit wrappers and dirty mugs, he'd been hiding out in his shed a lot during the work day.

Outside I quickly zipped my coat up. The sky had been pale grey as I cycled in to the village for work but it was bruising up quite badly. Heavy dark clouds were coming in from over the coastal side of Churchcliffe, threatening rain. I only hoped it wouldn't start until I'd finished up here, done my shopping and arrived back at the cottage. I'd cycled out to Clifftop Cottage in the rain more times than I could count over the past twelve months and it sucked every single time.

The playground was bordered by several large oaks which had been busily shedding leaves all day. Douglas swept them up every evening and there were always more by morning. I thought it was a waste of time to keep picking them up but apparently it was a slipping hazard. The head teacher, Mrs Graves, was the grown-up version of one of those teachers straight out of university who do excellent paperwork and wet themselves at the first sign of classroom disruption. The kind of teacher I used to torture at school. Mrs Graves seemed to have memorised the health and safety manual and regurgitated chunks of it as memos to 'The Janitorial Team', which was just the three of us: Janet, half-deaf Douglas and me. So far she'd requested colour-coded mops and sponges, non-toxic cleaning fluid which worked about as well as water, tamper-proof plug sockets that I had to uncover one by one to use the hoover and, of course, the daily sweeping of leaves. God forbid a child step on one and their parents sue for millions.

I took the broom to the furthest corner of the playground, where a faint hopscotch grid was still visible on the pitted concrete. By the end of my first row I'd accumulated a mound of leaves and had to stop and scoop them into a clear plastic sack. I repeated the process in broom-width sections up and down the playground. By the time I'd done it four times the first section was scattered with leaves again.

I looked at the bags of leaves I'd already collected, then at the area I'd swept, which looked exactly like the section I had left to do. There was literally no point to this. It was Friday. By Monday morning this playground would be smothered in leaves again. I could feel a storm blowing up even as I stood there.

The Head was just going to have to pop an anti-anxiety pill, fill out a risk assessment form and cope.

'Eff this,' I said, muttering the censored curse under my breath as if there was someone there to hear me. Then I went and put the broom away.

Even a year ago I'd have left the broom on the playground and gone home, never to return. When I quit my Saturday job at the makeup counter it was over a customer being a rude arsehole over a lipstick she said we used to do but now didn't. Like it was my problem. She threw the 'new' one at me and demanded her 'signature shade'. I threw it back, harder and told her to shove it up her arse. Then I grabbed my bag and left.

I'd become a self-employed hairdresser specifically to avoid working for idiots who didn't know their arse from their blow-dryer. Damian always used to say I had a problem with authority. Which wasn't true. Authority just had to have a clue. Not like he could talk either. I think the first time he listened to anyone else was when he joined the army. Before that he was more of a handful than me. He'd once spat on a teacher, thrown a chair at the Head, then climbed out of the classroom window and run off. It was a point of pride for him that he was the reason the whole school got window restrictors installed. Though he wasn't there to see them. He was expelled before the work was done.

Anyway, that was then. This was not a Saturday job to get money for weed and earrings. I needed cash for things like firewood, tinned soup and electricity credit. Not to mention top-ups for my stupid pay-as-you-go phone. Even my limited internet use went through that shit faster than fire burned logs. At least rent wasn't a concern. Squatting had its perks. So I stowed the broom, locked up the shed and took the bags of leaves to the bins before retrieving Cat's aunt's bike and riding off to the shop.

As I freewheeled down the hill towards the centre of Churchcliffe I looked over at the iron-coloured sea beyond the fields. Sticking out over it was the ragged cliff, rust-coloured where the dense clay had been steadily shearing off into the sea. The whole cliff was riddled with wounds from slips and slides. The odd fencepost or chunk of rubble were all that remained of the ancient church and the few farms that went over the edge. Like plates being dragged off with a tablecloth by a shitty magician.

On a cliff above the headland that still stuck out bravely into the sea was a single cottage. It used to belong to the lighthouse keeper's family, before the lighthouse was automated and the cottage became a holiday let. It hadn't even been that for a while now, according to Mary in the shop. Just an abandoned little hovel on the cliff. Although lights were coming on in the village as the sky darkened overhead, there weren't any on at the cottage. Because I wasn't up there to switch any on.

It had belonged to Cat's aunt, who'd died around eighteen months ago. It now technically belonged to Cat. There wasn't much to the place; just a squat little bungalow with wide single-glazed windows and thick stone walls that the wind had taken most of the paint off. It was damp, barely modernised and at night mice scrabbled around behind the kitchen cabinets. But it was the only place in the world that I felt safe.

From this far down I couldn't see the Simmonses' farm, my one and only neighbour. They were over the other side, hidden from view by the slope of the cliff. Safe from erosion, for now, but the cliff edge on that side would get it eventually. The lighthouse was visible though. It gave a weird glow to the storm clouds overhead, a yellowish tinge like chemical clouds of poisonous gas.

The edge of a bit of woodland snatched the cliff from view. A roll of thunder sounded in the distance. I started to pedal, shooting down the road as fast as two wheels could take me. There wasn't much chance of outrunning the rain. The storm was blowing in and it was headed straight for me.

Chapter Four

18:30

Four hours until the blackout

I had to get off the bike to go past the church. It wasn't a respect thing – there were cobbles there and riding over them was almost impossible. I wheeled it past the outdoor planters, still full of dead geraniums. In a few weeks they'd be replanted with ivy and mini-holly bushes for the winter. Just like they'd been last year.

I wondered, wheeling the heavy old bike along, if I'd still be around next spring to see them change back. The idea filled me with a weird mix of emotions. Partly restlessness and a yearning for escape, but also hope. Perhaps by next year things would be different. I'd be different. Perhaps by then

I'd finally feel safe. Perhaps then I'd feel worthy of what peace this place had to offer.

Mrs Sable was coming down the front steps of the church in her beige mac, carrying a box of cleaning supplies. I waved but she didn't wave back. As she tottered over to her cottage I noticed she was wearing slippers. Not a good sign.

I heard a scuffling noise on the pavement and turned to find Robbie bounding towards me. When he got close enough he threw himself at me and slobbered all over my hands. His owner, Davy, came puffing up behind him – curly hair in disarray and mud all up the legs of his jeans and over his wellies.

'Sorry,' he said, after subduing the Labrador. 'He got away from me.'

'No worries, he's a good boy, aren't you?' I took one hand off the bike and rubbed the dog's big flat head.

'You wouldn't be saying that if you'd just chased him the length of two fields and caught your jeans on a stile,' Davy said, showing me the flapping edge of a rip in the thigh of his jeans.

I laughed. 'Better get home and change, you'll be giving everyone an eyeful.'

'You're not going to offer to sew them up for me?' he asked, though he knew full well I would do no such thing.

'I could cut them down into hot pants for you?'
I offered.

'Bit chilly for this time of year.'

'I thought postmen wore shorts all the time, even in winter? Besides, do you want to be warm or do you want to look good?'

'You're a leg woman then, I knew it.'

I slapped him on the arm and Robbie jumped up at him, demanding some attention. I decided I'd sacrifice some of my weekly shop budget on gravy bones for him. Davy and Robbie were my only visitors up at the cottage. Davy brought the post round to me, though it was always junk. He usually brought the dog with him for the walk. I'd summoned the courage to ask him to stay for a cuppa once or twice but only in the summer when we could sit on the rusty garden bench. Though I suspected he'd sit out there in a snowstorm, in cut-off jeans, if I asked him to. He was that kind of guy – always trying to make me feel comfortable. He reminded me of Cat, just a little. They both had that same instinct that seemed to push them towards fucked-up people. The need to make things better for them, to cheer them up and chase the darkness away.

He also asked me out, just the once. We were saying goodbye and he said there was a music night on at The Beacon, the only pub within thirty miles. I said I was a bit busy and he acted like he believed that I was ever anywhere approaching 'busy'. I had no idea if he went to the music night anyway. I spent my evening using nail-free adhesive to go round the front door, step one in making the cottage secure. Only one door in and out.

Looking at him now, his eyes twinkling and a flirty look to him, I realised he was about to ask again. Panicked I started to say, 'I'll leave you to it' just as he said, 'Would you like to go for a drink tonight?'

We both froze and he chuckled awkwardly. 'You go.'

'I meant, I've got to get to the shop before it closes,' I said. 'Another time, yeah?'

'Sure.' He smiled. 'You know, they overcharge in that shop. If you need a ride to the supermarket just let me know. The selection's better and so are the prices. Or if you ever need anything else in town—'

'Thanks . . . I'm good though.'

I passed him and was just feeling the weight of the awkwardness settle on my shoulders when he called from behind me.

'You know, if you want me to stop asking – I will, right?'

I turned back. He looked soft and confused, sharing more than a passing similarity to Robbie. The same big brown eyes and pleading eyebrows. Only he didn't just want a pat on the head and a biscuit. He wanted me to let him in. Something I couldn't do, not yet anyway.

'I know,' I said. 'I mean it – another time.'

He brightened, nodded and turned around to lead Robbie home. Though the dog looked back at me once as if wondering why I wasn't going with them. I was wondering the same thing.

I wasn't lying to Davy. I didn't want him to stop asking me out, mostly because I wanted to say yes, one day. I tried the first time but it was the same then as it was now. I wanted to say, 'Yes, that would be great' but I couldn't make the words come out. I couldn't get them past the lump in my throat at the thought of getting into a car with him and going somewhere, anywhere. Even a trip to the supermarket. He still felt practically a stranger and part of me insisted that I couldn't trust him. Even though I knew he was nothing like the people I was running from.

Not that it mattered. Even if I could find it in me to trust Davy, he was better off not knowing me. The real me. If he knew the kind of thing that lurked in my past, well . . . he wouldn't even be speaking to me, let alone asking me out. He'd probably turn me in.

I wheeled my bike around the corner and tried to forget the whole exchange. Maybe I should have told Davy to move on. Maybe next time I would.

After chaining my bike up at the post office shop I grabbed a wire basket and went straight to the reduced section. Whatever they had was going to be the basis of my menu. Not that I was much of a cook. Cat used to make fun of my 'speciality dish' – packet rice with meatballs and pesto. But then she almost burned down her mum's house with a chip pan so she could hardly talk.

They had slightly dented tins of chicken soup, ravioli and potatoes in water. A few squashed boxes of stuffing mix, three jars of jam covered in sticky residue and a loaf of bread that was going hard. I took everything but two jars of jam and the potatoes. I used to love tinned ravioli as a kid. We couldn't afford the pasta shapes for kids, the tins with cartoon characters on them. So Damian used to pretend he was buying special 'Postman Pat Parcels'. I fell for it every time.

I filled the basket with the rest of my shop. I got the eggs, fuck it. I was having that fried egg sarnie, even if mine wouldn't be a patch on Cat's. She used to make the best fried egg sandwich you've ever had. Fried white bread, runny yolk, two slices of burger cheese and HP sauce. She used to do this stupid posh voice as she waved the bottle at me, 'Will you have a dollop?' and I'd always say, 'Just a half if you please.' I felt a stab of regret as I put a bottle of sauce into my basket. Cat's voice in my head was as clear as if she was right beside me.

'Can I have a bottle of vodka too, please, Mary?' I asked at the till.

Mary turned from trying to squint-read the back of a vape box and eyed my basket, then put her glasses back on and had another look. With a sigh she stepped over to the display of bottles tagged with day-glo starbursts and speech bubbles.

'What brand?'

'Whichever's cheapest. Oh, and I need some credit on my electric key.'

'Now you tell me.' She stepped back and waved a hand impatiently for the plastic key. Her rings, all seven of them, flashed under the fluorescents. I doubt Argos had ever made a bit of bling Mary didn't own. Some of it was the exact stuff my mum used to wear. Some of it changed but she always had a big locket on, the size of a matchbox, with all her kids' and grandkids' pictures inside. Like in films where the guy opens his wallet and it unfolds to show about eighty pictures. I knew this because she showed them all to me the first time I went in the shop during her shift. Each and every one. I only went in for a pint of milk.

I watched her struggle with the machine, impatiently sliding the key in and out as she fumbled with the buttons. We were going to be here a while.

'I saw your mum coming out of the church,' I said, as she finally keyed in the amount I'd placed on the counter in notes.

'Let me guess, she had her slippers on.'

'She did.'

'I already had Ida and Harry from the surgery over to tell me the same thing.' She sucked her teeth as she squinted at the display. 'She's not gone funny. She ordered them from a catalogue and won't shut up about it. They're so comfortable, she says, they've got grip on them so's she can walk on ice, you could step on them and she wouldn't feel it. She won't wear anything else.'

Mary dropped the key on the counter and scanned my shopping before looking at the alcohol again. She plucked down the smallest bottle of vodka and waved it at me.

'That's eight pounds,' she said.

I couldn't afford it. I knew that. Not with needing new gas cylinders for the camping stove and the electricity prices going up again. But the thought of passing a whole weekend sober in the mood I was in was unthinkable. I nodded and Mary swiped it.

'That everything?' she asked.

'Yup.' I handed over the notes and all too quickly I was down to almost nothing for the week ahead, once I allowed for gas canisters. I usually bought some seasoned logs too for emergencies but I'd have to rely on whatever I could get from the woods around the village and hope they dried out before I needed them.

'You work at the school, don't you?' Mary said suddenly.

'Yes?' I wondered where she was going with this. Was she about to ask something difficult like where I'd come from and why?

'Do you work any hours on Saturday? Only my niece just left for university and I've got the afternoons to cover.'

She must've seen me wavering because she reached out and patted my hand with her bedazzled one. 'Cash in hand, like. Just until she's home for the summer.'

'I can do that. Just let me know when you need me to start.'

'Tomorrow then,' she said like it was obvious. 'Come in at ten and I'll get you trained then you take over from one to six.'

'Great,' I said, mentally calculating how those five hours of extra minimum wage were going to improve my budget. Not a lot, but they'd give me some breathing room. Besides which I might be able to get some expired stuff off Mary to save on my shopping. Or at least some broken pallets for the fire. Amazing what difference a year could make to my thoughts. Firewood and expired tins of soup. Things I'd never have spared a second on before.

Outside I shouldered my backpack, now stuffed full of shopping. A second bag weighed down the fraying basket on the bike. I'd rescued the bicycle from a bramble patch behind Cat's aunt's cottage and it was old and heavy framed. Loaded with shopping I could barely cycle at walking pace. It was going to be a long ride back up to the cottage. I checked my phone, thinking some music would make the journey pass quicker. But listening to Cat's playlist had sapped the last of the ancient battery. It was dead. Typical.

The first drops of rain began to fall as I left the village. By the time I was on the hill, thighs and lungs burning with the strain, there was a constant drizzle trickling down on me. My anorak was soon slick and a cold dribble found its way down my neck.

The rain always reminded me of Cat and not in a good way. The smell of wet, crushed grass and the sounds of water splashing brought me back to that night. A night I never wanted to think about, but which always found its way into my head. Miserable and wet through I found myself struggling to hold back tears. As much as I wanted to blame the impending anniversary of my departure from Bristol, the truth was that I thought about her every day. Even now, a year later. Just as Damian was never far from my thoughts. I took my memories of them with me everywhere.

Finally the sign for Simmons Farm appeared, a new landmark. They'd put it in a month ago and the sheep-shaped sign now marked the home stretch of my journey. It had already been vandalised by Churchcliffe kids with nothing better to do. So it was a headless sheep which loomed out of the mist. Reg Simmons was probably fuming about it. Cheap old git that he was, it was unlikely he'd take the ruined sign down though. As I passed their gate I checked and found the little shack empty; no eggs or veg. Even the cash box was gone. Maybe he'd taken it in because of the vandalism.

I wheeled the bike over the gravelly track towards the cottage, eager to get inside and out of the rain. Not that it would be much warmer or even drier inside. The cottage had a bit of a damp problem as there was no gas for the heating, thanks to a landslide disrupting the supply. But I could get a fire lit and hunker down for the night. Thank God the shower unit was electric. The storm could do what it liked once I'd had a hot shower and a bowl of soup.

The light on the bicycle flashed lazily as I wheeled it along. I wasn't too worried about being able to see. This track was a dead end, petering out towards the lighthouse. No one but me and the occasional maintenance worker ever used it. I'd only seen him once or twice in a whole year. The lighthouse was automated and probably controlled by a computer thousands of miles away. So when my foot slid into a rut I didn't immediately think anything of it. It was only when I looked properly that I realised it wasn't a hole in the track but a tyre tread. A fresh one.

Frozen in place I peered into the darkness. Someone had been this way, towards my safe place. The maintenance van? Someone lost, perhaps, or turning their car? Or someone who was there for me?

Chapter Five

19:30

Three hours until the blackout

For several long minutes I stood in the rain and peered into the darkness. The only sounds I could hear were the splashing of raindrops and the churning of the sea at the base of the cliff. There were no lights around except the distant glow of the lighthouse. Even though I ought to have been able to see the glowing windows of the Simmons place from where I stood. There were no lights on. Unusual but not unheard of. They sometimes left for whole days to go to equipment and livestock auctions. Sue'd mentioned it once when I saw her restocking the eggs.

They didn't drive this way though. I assumed they had an access road that took them down the other side of the cliff. Beyond the gate there was just a muddy trail and I'd only ever seen them use a small tractor buggy thing on it. Not the type of thing you'd drive into town.

Indecision had me in its grip. There was no sign of headlights and I couldn't hear an engine. Was the car that had made these tracks gone, or parked in the dark where I couldn't see it? I eased the bike forward a little and the light flashed, revealing nothing on the track ahead. I could see by the lamp though that there were two sets of tracks, coming and going. Whoever had driven up here had gone back the same way.

Most of me was sure that I had nothing to worry about. That the tracks were just left over from some tourist getting led astray or teenagers looking for a spot to park up and smoke. But I knew all too well what assuming the best led to. I wasn't going to take any chances. Who was to say someone hadn't driven off and walked back across the field? Or that the car hadn't dropped someone off at the cottage to wait for me?

With the lamp switched off I wheeled the bike cautiously towards the cottage. When I reached the gate I left the bike leaning against the wall and crept up the path. I was alert for any sounds, anything out of place. When the security light snapped on overhead I nearly yelped. The light was blinding, illuminating all corners of the front garden and the side of the cottage. The only shadows were where the cliff cut away a few steps from the back door. Below, in darkness, the sea roared.

There was nowhere for anyone to hide in that light. Not to mention the whole cottage was alarmed. I'd lived on nothing but stale bread and coffee for months to pay for it, but it hadn't been optional. Every window and door was rigged. No one could be hiding inside without the whole place going off like the primary school music club, wailing and clanging as one.

I went back for the shopping on the bike and let myself in, deactivating the alarm. The shop bell over the door chimed as I swung it open and closed. A low-tech fall-back for if the meter ran out, which I made sure almost never happened. Even with the knowledge that the alarm was still functional I checked every room before I started to unpack the shopping. Lounge, bathroom and hallway were all clear. The bedroom was last on my list, because I was fairly sure that if someone had gone in there, I'd already know about it. The alarm wasn't my only line of defence.

Everything was in the cupboards before I realised I hadn't picked up any cat food. I knew I should've written a proper list. Poor Duzzy. I wondered if he'd eat a gravy bone. Though it wasn't like he didn't get

47

fed at home. He was one of the Simmonses' many farm cats, a fat-cheeked orange tom scarred from boxing other cats. The Simmonses' cats weren't pets and mostly ran wild but only Duzzy had made a habit of stopping by the cottage. Despite my lack of cash I usually got a packet or two of whatever was cheapest. Having him around was good for me. He was pretty much the only regular company I had.

Mr Simmons saw me petting him on my wall one day shortly after I arrived and told me, 'That one's duzzy.' It was ages before I found out that was just local slang for 'stupid'. By then the name had stuck and I'd already fed the cat so he stuck around too. No one seemed to care that I let him in occasionally to spoil him. He reminded me a bit of Pudding, the fat tabby from back home. It was nice, having someone to talk to whom I didn't have to be on my guard around.

A thick roll of thunder overhead made me jump. The storm was gathering in tightly, and even a city girl like me could feel the charge in the air. I waited, counting, and soon the windows flashed with lightning, followed by a louder crack of thunder. I thought of the steep drop down to the dark sea and shuddered. I'd seen my fair share of collapses in the past year, including the one that took the garden shed, which had been only metres from the cottage. Chunks of soil and rocks that were there one morning and were gone the next, replaced by empty sockets like pulled teeth. The cottage was only barely holding on to the cliff; every storm was a threat. If I'd had anywhere else to go, I'd have left. As it was I went to light a fire to keep the chill at bay.

When I'd come to the cottage a year ago I'd only meant to stay a month or two at the most. It was a bolthole, a panic room teetering on the edge of a cliff. It didn't even belong to me. As of Cat's death I had no idea who it did belong to. It wasn't like anyone would be lining up to claim it in the state it was in. Even so I knew I couldn't stay there for ever. Yet I hadn't moved on. Worse, I'd formed roots: created a name, found a job, developed a crush. I told myself that I was just considering my next move but the truth was I didn't have one. Like everything else on the clifftop I was stuck in place, waiting for the day something happened to me. I couldn't even claim I deserved any better. My conscience wouldn't let me.

With a fire in the grate I changed out of my wet clothes. As I towelled my hair dry I glanced at the bedroom door, firmly shut. How long had it been since I'd practised? A month? Two? I was letting my guard down but I couldn't seem to stop it. I'd been neglecting my exercise regime too – all those runs and cold-water swims at the rocky shore.

I'd started out doing it every day. A combination of training and punishment. Now they were few and far between. I knew I should run through a drill but I was just so tired. One more night wouldn't make any difference.

I heated some soup on the camping stove. A year in and I still hadn't replaced the gas cooker with an electric one. It wasn't like I could just go and buy one second-hand and pop it on my handlebars to get it home. All my money had gone on security and I had no idea when I'd be able to afford a new cooker. That was if I found a way to order one without a debit card. I was on my last mini gas canister though. I'd need to buy some more tomorrow, maybe in the gap between training at the shop and my first shift.

With the bowl of soup on the coffee table I wrapped myself up in Damian's sleeping bag and some blankets. The heat from the fire was welcome but not enough to combat the wind that was making the single-glazed windows shiver. Even the flames were wavering as the wet sea wind swept down the chimney. The walls were oozing damp and stank like a forgotten swimming kit. It was going to be a long, cold night.

What I needed was a distraction. Some way out of my own head and the memories the wet weather always brought out. I'd finished a book the previous night and the cheap paperback was already burning

50

in the stove. I selected a new one from the pile by the sofa. Only two left. I'd have to hit up the 'little library' in the church annexe and get some more. I didn't feel bad about using them as extra firewood. God knows there were always too many on the trolley. Someone in Churchcliffe had a serious mystery habit and someone else couldn't resist a three-for-a-fiver deal on cosy romances. Between those and a steady supply of old classics, A-level readers and gardening books, I was saving quite a bit on fuel.

Without phone reception, 4G, a TV or even a radio signal up here, books were my only reliable source of entertainment. I'd never really been a reader before I found myself at the cottage. I was always more of a podcast girl – listening as I disinfected my kit or walked across town to meet Cat for a bitching sesh over coffee. I suddenly remembered an afternoon hanging out with Cat after college. There was nothing to do while waiting for the bus other than get takeaway coffee and doss about in the local library. We ended up reading aloud to each other from a pile of old romances, snorting over the rude bits and the flowery language. A clear image of Cat in an emerald green boiler suit came to mind, tears on her cheeks as she mouthed the words 'turgid member'. The small smile that raised froze on my face as the image was replaced with the last one I had of her. Her face covered in tears from fear and pain instead of laughter. I shook my head, trying to escape the images.

Unfortunately the latest book, about spirited wartime nurses, couldn't lighten my mood. My thoughts circled back to the tyre tracks outside. I told myself not to freak out. That over a year had gone by and I'd not so much as seen my name in the paper. No one had come to the cottage, or my workplace. I hadn't even had a letter or a threatening email. They weren't looking for me. Or, if they were, they weren't even close to finding me. Yet I couldn't let it go. Someone had been up here recently and I had no idea why. Was it just an innocent passer-by or someone on the hunt?

Sometimes I felt as if I'd been looking over my shoulder for longer than a year. Which in a way I had. Not as much though. It was only at certain moments that I worried that what I'd done way back when would catch up to me. It was a different kind of fear too. Not of escaping an attacker but of being found out. Of having to face what I'd done. However you looked at my life, I didn't deserve to be let off. Sooner or later, justice would come for me.

Maybe that sense of impending punishment was why I went through my nightly checks with more thought than I'd spared for several months. First the alarm system, fully armed, then the five locks on the front and back doors, all done up. One of the first things I'd done was nail the windows shut with glue between the frames. Later on I'd stapled wire over them, straight into the wooden surround. The guy who came to fit the alarms didn't comment on it but he gave me some funny looks, though that might have been because I waited outside for him to finish. I didn't care. Although it was boiling in summer, the alternative didn't bear thinking about.

Before settling down to bed on the less saggy of the two old sofas I plugged in a nightlight. It was a cloudy pink plastic seashell, glowing in the darkness by the kitchen door. Just enough light to see by in an emergency.

Thunder rolled overhead as I slid my hand under the sofa cushion and gripped the kitchen knife underneath. No lightning had preceded it this time though. Perhaps the storm was moving away or dying down? Maybe it was just circling back. I was too tense to read and too wired to sleep, but at least lying still allowed me to listen more carefully to the sounds outside. Though all I could hear was the wind moaning and buffeting the walls.

I lay there and listened so hard that I hardly dared to breathe. Slowly, though, exhaustion began to take over. It had been a long, long week of work, cycling to and from town and preparing the cottage for winter. Despite jerking awake a few times at imagined voices, I eventually slipped into sleep.

Chapter Six

2022

The only good thing about the long walk ahead was that Cat was there. If you're with your best friend, no situation can be completely shit. Just mostly shit. Even when the situation is walking bloody miles home in the small hours. In heels. With no jacket and an empty stomach.

All right, so my feet were in agony, I was freezing cold, still drunk and absolutely ravenous, without a penny on my person, but at least I wasn't alone. If I'd been alone I could have added 'scared' to my list of problems. But we were together and there was safety in numbers. Cat even shared her coat with me. We passed it back and forth as we made our way through town and towards the big ASDA.

Once we were past the supermarket, however,

things got a little bit spooky. Away from the main road with its flow of cars and streetlights, we were left stumbling along in the dark. The side road by the canal was on the bus route but there weren't any cars going that way, towards the industrial estate. The lights were few and far between and every second one was broken or too dim to do any good.

On our right the canal oozed along invisibly, though the occasional splash or scuttling in the weeds made me worry about rats. Or worse. People camped by the canal, on the grassy verges and on the vacant remains of demolished buildings. There was a big homeless population and mostly I never had any trouble, they just wanted to keep themselves to themselves. But there were the odd few guys who could be a bit aggro, particularly to girls. Particularly this late at night.

'My feet hurt,' Cat whimpered for the fiftieth time. Mine did too, but I wasn't about to chance walking over the pavement in just my cheap tights. Not when I couldn't even see to check for broken glass and dog shit. That didn't stop Cat though. She stopped for a second, stood like a flamingo and within moments had taken off her boots and shoved them under her arm.

'You'll get stuff on your feet,' I pointed out.

'Better than getting it all up my back when I fall down.'

Maybe. But I wasn't taking the chance. Still, at least Cat seemed fairly with it, if pissed. Whatever she'd taken hadn't kicked in yet. I was praying it wouldn't hit her until we were safely home.

As for me, my buzz from the drinks was wearing off, leaving me in the clumsy stage of being drunk where you just want to pull a duvet over your head and sleep. At least in the fuzzy stage I'd not really noticed how much time was passing or how cold it actually was. The chill was inside my bones now like crystal-clear vodka. I shivered with my full body and even my scalp felt tight with cold. Without the stretchy time effect of being pissed I felt every minute of the trudge through town. Fuck, we weren't even halfway home yet. Cat had even further to go, but once we got to mine she could at least call an Uber, though I was probably going to insist she slept over. This late, or early, whatever the fucking time was, I didn't want her taking a chance with any kind of taxi. Especially not once that pill kicked in.

'God, I wish we had chips right now,' Cat said. Her voice bounced back at us from the darkness. This part of the canal backed onto old factories and warehouses. I couldn't see the massive buildings but they created a weird echo effect. Her voice seemed to get louder as it echoed, not softer. Until it was like a car alarm going off, drawing all attention towards us.

'Shhh.'

'I was only . . .'

'There might be someone out there.' I felt stupid as soon as I'd said it and Cat only made me feel worse by laughing. Her laugh bounced around until it sounded more like a shriek.

'Like who? A sewer clown? Ghosts? It's arse o'clock in the morning, Meg. No one around here is awake.'

'There's guys that camp out around here.'

'And they're asleep too,' Cat said, her eye roll clear in her voice, though I couldn't see it. 'Every sensible person is currently fast asleep. Especially the ones in freezing cold tents – trust me, they don't want to wake up until it's light out.'

'Well, then you should keep it down, or you'll wake them up and piss them off.'

That at least seemed to stump her. We carried on, almost to the end of the canal road now. Mist was crawling up from the water, threading between the scrubby bushes and flowing onto the road. The streetlights were blurry stars and my skin and hair felt damp. God, I wanted my bed. I was never drinking like this again. The last time I'd been this drunk was . . . no, I wasn't going to think about that. Not here, right now. But even as I tried to shake the thoughts off they grew stronger, like the hangover that was coming on. Barrelling towards me like a train out of a dark tunnel.

'Probably a good thing you didn't give me that pill after all,' I muttered, grateful that at least I wasn't high on top of everything else. I'd only really asked Cat for one because I felt like doing some damage to myself tonight. Well, I'd wanted risk and here it was. Just not the kind I'd bargained on.

'I know. Told you, it's not your thing and that's fine. Would have been wasted on only one club anyway. Kinda pissed I took mine tbh.'

I shuffled to a stop. 'What did you take anyway? How long've we got before I have to carry you?'

'Will you relax? It's fine. I don't even think it's up to much. I barely feel anything.'

I started walking again but stopping for just those few seconds had apparently caused both my feet to give up. They hurt twice as much as before, throbbing inside my pleather stilettos. The sweat between my toes had turned icy cold and my heels felt like someone was running a razor over them with every step. These shoes were going in the bin the second I got home. Maybe even before because I was not climbing the stairs to my flat in them.

We turned off the street and into the industrial estate, heading towards the railway line. This wasn't the bus route, which went around and then circled back to go over the bridge. On foot it was faster to cut through and take the underpass to the new development. I used to know people up that way and cut across fairly regularly before I met Cat. When Damian was looking to move us to this side of Bristol we'd looked at flats down there. Not on the new part, which was all coffee shops and offices, but the edge of the estate where a few old pubs had been converted into flats. But one look at the broken windows and the mattress dumped outside next door and Damian said he'd never stop worrying about me round there. It was worse than staying at Mum's. So we went to a chain pub for lunch instead of the viewing and he used their wifi to find somewhere else.

If he'd been waiting at home for me I could've had a proper little-sister go at him, told him that if we'd gone with that flat I'd almost be home by now. Then he'd call me a silly mare for not protecting my purse and not having an emergency tenner in my shoe. But he'd make me a tea after. He wasn't the sort of big brother who'd cancel your cards and sort out a new phone, but he would definitely have shown me some self-defence manoeuvre to use on bag snatchers. Or got his SAS book out to lecture me about survival kits and the importance of always being prepared.

I still had that book. It was in his room with all the rest of his stuff. I hadn't been able to let go of any of it. Not his army surplus gear, his action films, the games and comics. I'd just shut the door on it all and not opened it since. No matter how much the cat scratched at it when I let him in. Sometimes when I was half-awake I could kid myself that Damian was in there, playing a game or just chilling out. That he'd come out for dinner and everything would be like it used to be. It always hurt though, when the fuzziness left my brain and I had to remember that I was never going to see him again.

As soon as I was sober and my hangover was gone, I was going to go through his room. I told myself sternly that I'd only keep a few things. Honestly, I needed to move. The two-bed flat was sucking up all my money. I needed to get out of there. Move on. Maybe I could get Cat to help me out. She was good at all that decluttering stuff. As long as it was other people's stuff, not hers. She never found a bit of furniture on the street that she didn't cart home. I'd been roped into dragging a china cabinet on the bus with her once. It was still in her front room, now painted pink with leopard accents. Better than the armchair that gave her place bedbugs anyway.

I was just hoping Cat would have sobered up enough by the time we got in to make one of her fried egg sandwiches, because even the chippy would be shut by the time we got back. That was when I heard it. A sound that wasn't coming from us – footsteps echoing off the buildings on either side. Not skittery heels but the scuffing of heavy footfalls.

Cat didn't seem to notice; she was humming to herself. I glanced back over my shoulder. There was no one there. Or at least as far as I could see. It was still very dark and we'd left even the shitty streetlights behind now. The industrial estate was all walls and narrow railway arches, winding roads connecting old redbrick buildings to newer concrete ones. Maybe the footsteps were back past the last corner, or ahead of us? Maybe they were on another street entirely.

I threaded my arm through Cat's fluffy one and tugged her onwards, faster.

'Come on, we need to get moving.'

'Hey, careful – you'll pull me over. Meg! I'm gonna drop my—' Cat's silver boots clattered to the ground and she muttered a curse as she bent to pick them up. I still had my arm in hers and she yanked me down with her, making me wobble on my raw feet.

'Oh yuck, they're all wet now!' She exclaimed, so loudly that I winced. I couldn't hear the footsteps now, or anything else.

'Shhh!' I snapped, smothering the urge to shove her. We had to keep moving. I could feel panic rising up in me like vomit.

'You shhh,' Cat said, releasing my arm. 'Bossy bitch.'

I wasn't listening. I was looking behind us at the two men who'd just rounded the corner and stopped, watching us. I couldn't see much of them in the dark except for their trainers, which stood out, white on the ground. Everything else about them was dark – hooded jackets, trousers, faces in shadow. But I could tell they were looking at us. Looking right at us and not saying a word. Not moving but tensed and waiting.

You know those horror games where the monster can't chase you if you're watching it? Damian used to play one with a clown that scared me shitless. I used to see that thing in my sleep. You'd have to turn away to unlock a door and then honk-honk – there's a clown, right in your face. This felt like that. Like if I looked away or even blinked, they'd move forwards. Like we were safe unless I stopped looking at them.

But I was looking right at them when they came towards us.

Chapter Seven

I didn't think, didn't stop to question what the two men were doing or if they were just walking down the road behind us. I just grabbed Cat's arm and ran. She seemed to sense something in the way I did it, because she came with me without a word. She dropped her boots and kept pace with me.

That was when I knew I was right to be afraid. Because they weren't asking us if we were OK, or where we were trying to get to that late. They weren't even calling shit after us, giving it all that and being creeps. They didn't say anything. They just chased us.

I looked over my shoulder and saw them coming after us, jogging now. Not one word from them. I'd been catcalled before. God, who hasn't? I'd had a guy rub up against me on a bus and some dudes who followed me, jeering, when I cut through a park at night. But this was more than that. This was all the vile stuff behind those things and beyond them at the same time. This was what that stuff played at being.

If my heels hadn't been buckled on I'd have kicked them off. As it was I had to do my best in them. We ran up the street and around another corner, the road curving past a garage with rusted shutters. Was there nothing still in business around here? Around the bend the only doors I could see were those of a row of houses at the end of the road and they had metal screens over them. Fuck. I never should have brought us that way. What was I thinking?

'You have to run,' I panted to Cat. 'You've not got heels on, you can go faster without me.'

'I'm not leaving you, stupid cow,' Cat said, voice too high but decidedly more sober than she'd sounded minutes ago. She clamped her taloned hand around my arm. 'Come on. You'd better fucking move.'

I tried, like she was just pushing me for five more minutes on the cross trainer before we packed it in for a latte. But my lungs were burning with the icy air and I kept almost twisting my ankle.

We reached the houses at the end of the street. All of them dark, all of them silent. I turned round to look but couldn't see the guys. They were still just around the bend, right before the garage. I could hear them though. They were talking to each other, so low it was just a rumble of voices.

66

'In here.' Cat dragged me towards the last house, where the metal screen had been battered in and the door underneath was in bits. The gap was big enough for us though and I crawled in after her on my hands and knees.

Inside I felt carpet under my palms, covered in splinters of wood and crumbs of plaster. After struggling to my feet I rushed past Cat and towards the back of the house. There had to be a door there we could get out of. Maybe a garden from which we could reach an alley or climb over a wall.

I found myself in a kitchen, almost pitch-black. The windows had to be shuttered from the outside. The vinyl floor was sticky with old grease and I scuttled across it, praying for a back door. My scrambling hands found a handle, but when I tried it I realised it was locked. Not only that but through the textured glass window I could see more shutters bolted on to the frame. We weren't getting out that way.

Cat blundered into me from behind. I grabbed at her and got as close as I could so I only had to whisper.

'We need to hide. There's no other way out.'

'Hide where?'

That was the question, wasn't it? I felt around and found another door handle, this one to a tall cupboard with shelves in it. I pushed Cat down into the lowest section and swung the door to.

'Stay there until I come to get you.'

'What about you?' She sounded like a little kid, her voice cracked in the middle.

'I'll find somewhere else. Where I can keep watch.' I sounded braver and more in control than I felt. Inside I was quivering, praying the guys would pass the house by and keep going up the road.

'Meg . . . I'm scared.' Cat sounded like she was about to cry, or already crying. My own eyes started to blur as the reality of the situation we were in sunk home. If those guys came into the house, we'd be trapped.

'It's going to be fine,' I said, my voice slightly strangled despite my best effort to sound calm. 'Wait there, I'll come back when it's safe.'

Cat hissed my name but I ducked out of the kitchen. I'd hide somewhere near the door and listen, wait for the men to pass by or give up. Then we could make a dash for it, or wait until it was light out. With more people on the streets they'd probably give up, melting back into the shadows like the cowards they were. I tried to hold on to that, though my hands were shaking as I groped my way along the walls, looking for a hiding spot.

My fingers finally found something, a handle to the under-stairs cupboard. I pulled it open and the smell of hoover bags and damp wafted out. It didn't matter, so long as it was safe. As I crawled in, my bag snagged on a loose nail. I yanked hard, felt something give. I pulled the door in after me and tried to hear anything over my own pulse and shallow, raspy breathing.

Nothing. For long moments. There was just nothing. No sounds, no sense of anyone outside the door. My knees started to ache from crouching and I lowered myself to the gritty carpet. My hand bumped something cold and I flinched, but it was only a screwdriver someone had left behind. I grabbed it up and held it tightly to my chest. If the door opened I was going to start stabbing, biting, anything to get away.

That was when I heard it, scuffling and cracking. The sound of someone with a much larger frame than me cramming themselves through the hole in the door. I held my breath, trying to visualise what movements matched the noises. No more scuffling, they were inside. I heard the soft whoosh of trainers on carpet. A chunk of something brittle cracking underfoot. Were they heading my way or towards the kitchen, towards Cat? A light glinted in the cracks around the cupboard. They were using their phones to hunt for us.

Heavy thumps overhead made dust fall from the ceiling. They were going upstairs. I pinched my nose to hold in a sneeze. Please, please let them find nothing and assume we carried on up the street. Please, God, let them leave.

I listened as they went from room to room. Occasionally there was a bang or a scraping sound. It sounded like they were searching about, moving things, looking under beds and in wardrobes. Hunting for us like this was a party game.

The footsteps clomped back downstairs and I heard them muttering to each other indistinctly through the wall. Footsteps came towards my door, then away, like one of them was pacing. Then a moment of stillness.

I realised then that we'd just lost our chance to sneak out while they were upstairs. A deep hopelessness gripped my insides and I bit my lip in despair. The one shot we had at getting away and I hadn't even seen it as it passed me by.

'Come out,' a voice suddenly called, breaking the silence. 'We saw you come in here.'

'Yeah – come out now. Or it'll be worse when we find you . . . Megan Fellows.'

I crushed my hand against my face as a whimper built at the back of my throat. They knew my name. How did they . . .

My fingers snatched at my wrist. The bag was open. The keys were still there, my busted phone. But no driving licence. It must've fallen out. They knew for certain that we were in here. Trapped with them.

This was it. If we were lucky, we weren't going to die tonight. That was all I could hope for. But the house wasn't that big and it wasn't going to take them for ever to search every inch of it.

I remembered, then, watching one of those forensic shows with Damian. Back when we still lived with Mum, before that awful night. Before Damian got me out of there and moved us off the estate. We were both bunking off and watching whatever was on TV. I remembered it so clearly that for a second I was back there, watching the characters on screen talking about how lucky it was the dead woman between them 'got a piece' of her attacker. That her last act had been to scratch and bite and claw as if she knew it was all she could do to make sure he was caught.

My fingers clenched around the screwdriver. I was going to be that dead girl with blood and skin under her fingernails and bits of a stranger's hair all over her clothes. I felt weirdly cold and still thinking that. Like I was dead already. When they caught these guys, if they caught them, no one was going to get to say I wanted this. If they were leaving this house and I wasn't, they were going to leave with the marks to prove what happened in here.

I heard a clattering from the kitchen – the cupboard door being battered back against the wall? Something glass smashed on the floor and then the two men were snapping and snarling at Cat, at each other. Cat's scream cut through it all, high and loud and furiously terrified, as if she really was a wild animal, cornered and desperate for escape.

I didn't even think. I just threw myself out of the cupboard and ran to the kitchen, screwdriver in hand.

Chapter Eight

22:30

The blackout begins

I was woken by the end of the world.

For a moment I honestly thought the cottage had fallen off the cliff with me inside it. My second biggest fear. The crashing of the waves was deafening and the wind no longer moaned but screamed all around. From outside came a clattering which I'd heard before: roof tiles smashing on the ground. The cottage seemed to be breathing around me. The windows rattled and a strong draught sucked in and out under the doors and through the window frames.

I cried out when blinding white light flashed around me. I'd never been so close to a lightning strike before. It was brighter than daylight, stark and cold. Thunder followed closely after. The storm had to be right overhead.

It was only as the bright light faded that I noticed how dark the cottage was. My vision was still full of flashing dots from the lightning, but other than that, it was pitch-black. The fire had burned out, leaving me cold. Worse, the night light had gone dark. I'd just topped up the meter, so it couldn't be that. Had the bulb burned out?

I fumbled in the darkness and found the candles that had kept me going on my first night in the cottage. They were on the windowsill, caked in dust. I lit one and carried it with my hand cupped to the flame as I went through to the kitchen. Even then the flame swayed and dimmed in the draught. I tried the main lights and nothing happened. I desperately hoped the fuses had tripped.

The sight of the alarm panel without its blinking green lights made my skin tighten. I reached for the fuse box beside it and snapped a few up and down. Nothing happened, except that the candle went out with nothing to protect it from the gusts of icy air. It wasn't the fuses then. My last hope gone. There wasn't any power.

It wasn't my first power cut at the cottage but it was the first one to happen at night. The fact that it was the same night I'd seen those tyre tracks had me on high alert. Careful not to stumble over anything I crept from window to window, peering into the darkness. I couldn't see much, just the thrashing grasses and the sheets of rain falling. What worried me more was what I couldn't see; Churchcliffe ought to have been glowing in the distance but every single light was gone. It wasn't just the cottage, the power was out across the cliffs. A major cut then, not just a temporary glitch with mine.

There wasn't much I could do about it. Trying to remain calm I told myself that even if the alarm was dead the cottage was still secure. The doors were locked five times over and all the windows were stuck tight. Even if that wasn't the case I still had my backup plan in the bedroom. I had defences that didn't require electricity.

As my initial fear subsided the cold started to creep in. Although I was wearing a jumper and joggers as pyjamas and had fallen asleep in my slippers, the cottage wasn't insulated for shit and was already freezing. The stove was the only source of heat. I went to relight it and realised that I'd used the last of my wood. I'd meant to get more tomorrow, or today, depending what time it was now. I checked my watch. It was half-ten. I hadn't slept long.

I debated using my last couple of books but they wouldn't burn that long without wood to back them up. Instead I opted for a cup of tea made on the gas stove. Curled up in my sleeping bag again I cradled the hot mug against my chest. I wished Damian was with me, or Cat. Anyone braver than I was. Not that Cat would be any more resourceful in a full blackout, but she'd at least know how to take my mind off it. With her the whole thing would start to feel like a sleepover: candles, gossip, hot chocolate.

Damian was the one who'd be in control of things. Though he'd have probably set up a backup generator and God knows what else if he was in my shoes. I'd done my best but he was the one with survival skills. I was just cribbing from his books and favourite films.

The mug of tea was halfway to my lips when two beams of light sliced through the darkness and straight through the paper-thin curtains. Headlights outside, on the track no one ever used.

I didn't stop to think. I just put the mug down and ran for the bedroom. This was it. The moment I'd feared for the past year. The moment I'd prepared for and yet felt completely blindsided by, trapped as I was in the dark.

My lack of practice with the security measures immediately screwed me over. By the time I reached the built-in cupboard at the back of the bedroom I was bleeding from several cuts. The darkness hadn't helped but there was a time when I could navigate that room blindfolded. I was slipping, getting careless.

But it had been a year and that knowledge had loosened the rope around my neck. No amount of thinking I ought to practise was as good a motivator as real, chemical fear.

Once I'd carefully climbed inside I shut the cupboard door and reached up to lift the loft hatch. Or what passed for one. The actual hatch was in the hallway, but I'd shut it up tight with nails and adhesive. That thing wasn't budging. I'd cut this slightly wonky access panel inside the cupboard instead. There were chunks of wood nailed to the cupboard wall too and I used them as footholds to help me scramble up into the loft space. A sharp jab in my back told me I'd snagged one of the razor blades that studded the hatchway. Thankfully I'd missed the rest of them and not gripped the side of the hatch with my bare hands. Anyone who did that would be in for a nasty shock.

Although I'd created this safe space for exactly this situation, part of me never thought I'd have to use it. I hadn't even checked up there for months or restocked anything. So I was surprised and relieved to find that the torch by the hatch still worked. By its light I could see the small heap of supplies in the corner of the crawl space. I had food, water and everything else I needed to last several days up here, completely hidden. I just hoped it wouldn't come to that. The longest I'd spent in the crawl space was twenty-four hours. A test run. Even that had pushed me to my limit. The cramped, dark space was dusty and cold. The only thing that would force me to stay in it was a threat to my life.

A threat which had finally come.

I turned the torch off and as my eyes adjusted to the darkness I could see faint areas of lesser shadow. The peepholes I'd poked through the ceiling plaster by the light fittings. The soft light disappeared abruptly and I knew that outside, the headlights had gone out. The sound of a car door closing was muffled by the house but not completely silenced.

Was it really them? Now that I was up here in relative safety I wondered if I was overreacting. Perhaps it was Davy, coming to see if I was OK in the storm? He'd done that once before, after some strong winds sent Churchcliffe into chaos. That was the first time I lost roof tiles. He offered to try and replace them with ones I'd found in the shed. The shed which had blown off the cliff a few months later while I was at work.

God, what if it was Davy? He could've been woken by the storm, realised there was no power anywhere and thought of me, all alone on the cliffs. He'd probably driven up with a box of candles, matches, battery lights and blankets. He was just one of those guys that thought of everything. Overthought really. He reminded me of Damian in a weird way. Not that Davy was anything like my brother, but they both had that instinct for preparation and protection. Just in very different ways. Damian was a wolf with a pack, Davy was like his Labrador.

I listened hard for the sound of Davy's voice. He'd knock and call out and I'd have to slither out of the loft hatch and somehow get back across the bedroom. How was I going to explain the thin cut on my face and the slash across my hand? Just an accident in the dark?

Even if it was Davy out there though, the idea of being alone with him in the storm made me incredibly anxious. The weather was so bad I felt like I had to invite him in but I really didn't want to. This place was mine. Layers upon layers of protection. What good was all that if I was just going to make the same mistakes all over again? 'Trust no one', that was the rule. Right up there with 'tell no one what happened'. Damian had drummed that one into me at age fourteen. Not that I'd needed telling twice.

I didn't hear a knock, which was odd. It had been a while since the car door shut. It wasn't exactly the night to be lingering outside. I started to feel afraid again, deep down in my gut. Something was up. Davy would've knocked by now. Which meant it wasn't him. Reg Simmons maybe? Perhaps Sue had bullied him out of bed to go check on their one neighbour. Maybe he was out there, shining a torch around to check if I was awake, unwilling to chance meeting me. God forbid he have a conversation.

Straining my ears I held my breath and shut my eyes against the dark. Voices. Another car door shutting. More than one person was out there. At least two. Was it the two I was thinking of? The two people I wanted to see least in the world? The ones who'd driven me here, almost literally to the ends of the earth?

Lying there I tried to think rationally. Two questions presented themselves: how had they found me and why would they come after me now? It had been a year and I'd heard nothing. Not so much as a threatening postcard. I'd been checking the news, though not as religiously as I had to begin with, I had to admit. As far as I knew nothing had changed. There was no reason for this to be happening now.

I'd been so careful too; ditched my phone, my bank account, my name. All right, so I was staying in a cottage that was connected to Cat and her family but it was such a weak link. Besides, it was me they wanted. I'd seen them. I knew their faces, I knew what they'd done. If they were looking for me they had no reason to come here. Unless of course I'd let something slip to someone. Drawn attention to myself. I had to admit I'd been less security-conscious lately. Maybe I'd messed up somehow, recently. Or maybe I'd made a mistake back then. That was more than likely. I hadn't exactly been thinking clearly.

I remembered my phone, dead and useless in my coat pocket. I'd meant to charge it but had forgotten after the long journey home. Had they somehow found out that I was accessing Cat's playlist? The one connection I'd been too weak to sever. But how could they possibly track me with that? I had no idea if it was possible. Cat was the techie one and Damian was the one who watched all those spy films where people hack their hair off in a petrol station toilet and disappear. He'd have known what not to do. Then again, he'd never have ended up in this situation either. He'd have taken care of them that night, like I wished I had.

The sound of breaking glass was very loud to my straining ears. Not Reg then. He was too anti-social to even knock. No, someone was breaking in. Was that the back door? There was wire and wood over that window to keep people out. Even as I thought it I heard nails ripping and a man's voice swearing. There was a man down there, prising at my window, trying to get a hand in to undo the bolts on the door. I had meant to install a reinforced, windowless door with a heavy-duty bar across it, but by the time I had the cash for that I'd lost some of my paranoia. I'd let myself believe that some deadbolts were enough to save me.

Was it looters? The thought should not have sent a sudden surge of relief through me, but it did. There was a blackout after all – perhaps someone was trying to take advantage of the lack of security to break in? After all Clifftop looked like a holiday cottage, probably good for some TVs, consoles and fancy appliances. An empty house in a blackout made an easy target and there wasn't much to suggest anyone lived here. Not with the security lights out and no car parked outside.

If it was looters they'd quickly realise I had nothing worth stealing. Either they'd leave or stay long enough to trash the place. Whichever way they probably wouldn't find me and would be gone by morning. I just had to wait them out. Hell, if the power came back on it might just scare them off.

I strained my ears for the sounds of the bolts being drawn back, the Yale latch being twisted. I couldn't hear that, but I did hear the door open, disturbing the bell over it. Within seconds the bell was silenced, jingling metal yanked down and thrown out into the storm. Slowly I eased myself over the plywood ceiling. The insulation was a dense foam with foil backing, slippery and easy to move on despite the dust. Virtually silent, which was why I'd picked it. God knew it didn't really keep the place warm.

I reached the peephole over the kitchen and looked down on the intruder. He was a man from the size of him, though the deep voice had given that away already. He was wearing a dark cap and a bulky black coat. I saw a sliver of white skin as he turned his head – other than that it could have been anyone. If he spoke without the muffling of the storm and walls, I'd know if it was him at once. I'd never forget his voice. But he moved silently, looking around the kitchen on his way to the living room.

Outside, the rain thundered against the windows like a handful of stones. The wind was hysterical, shrieking into the darkness. Over it all the sea beat against the cliff, a full-throated roar that almost drowned out the thunder. Despite the noise outside I moved as quietly as possible, stopping at the living-room peephole.

Lightning flashed outside as I looked down and the man froze, mid-stride. He appeared to be looking at the pile of blankets and the sleeping bag. If he was an opportunistic burglar, he had to realise this place was occupied. As the lightning flash dissipated he moved quickly, raising a hand. I recognised the hatchet in it; it was the one I kept by the back door for log splitting and defence.

As he brought the small axe down on my bed I knew for certain that he was no looter. Apparently noticing that the bulky blankets didn't feel like a body, he ripped them aside angrily.

That was when I heard a second person at the door. A voice I'd heard often in my nightmares.

It was them. The pair of them had found me. My worst fear was here, in this house, looking for me.

'So, is she back yet or not?'

'Bed's empty. Maybe she did a runner again?'

'What are you doing with an axe? Jesus. Make it look like an accident, we said!' A sigh. 'I told you we shouldn't have come up here in the daytime. She probably saw us earlier and ran off again. We'll never find her now.'

'Saw us from where? You're the one who looked in the window and said no one was home. It's all fields and cliffs out here. Not exactly a lot of hiding places.'

'There's a panel for an alarm system here.'

'There's no electricity, idiot.'

'No, *idiot*. But it was probably working earlier and she might have cameras with phone alerts. If she saw us on those she wouldn't come back here. She'd just run.'

There was silence as he processed this. I hoped to God they'd decide that's what had happened and leave.

'Don't – call me – an idiot,' he finally ground out.

I wished I did have those cameras. Though that would have required internet access, an account and unlimited data. I didn't have anything that required a contract or ID. My phone was a second-hand one nicked out of a donation bin; it took credit, and even my electric was paid for on the old key that I'd found in the cottage. Who knew whose name that was in.

'She could be anywhere by now,' the figure by the door sighed. 'This was our one fucking chance and you blew it.'

'She must've left something here somewhere to say where she went. The bitch isn't exactly a genius. A bank statement, bill, something.'

Despite my fear I felt a flash of anger. I'd hidden from them for a year, hadn't I? Even though they'd had my home address I'd escaped Bristol and found myself a hiding place before they'd managed to hunt me down. If I wasn't a genius, what did that make them?

It seemed I wasn't the only one on that train of thought. A scornful voice came from the kitchen. 'Oh, yeah, she really made it easy last time. Face it – it was luck we even found this place. Luck and her friend's bloody social media.'

I bit my lip. Social media. They had looked into Cat after all. I'd dumped my phone, my ID, everything, but something on Cat's timeline must have tipped them off about her aunt's cottage. Probably a holiday picture on her Facebook page. I'd been so worried about legal documents about the cottage that I'd never considered Cat just tagging herself here way back when.

'What do we do then?' the guy in the living room said. 'We can't just let her go. Not now.'

'I know that . . . Search around a bit. Maybe she dropped her guard. Left a bank statement . . .'

'That's what I just said!'

'Jesus Christ, shut up! I'm just saying what we should look for – like a postcard or an address on a Post-it or a . . .'

'A what? Did you find something?'

There was a long, tense silence. Lying there in the loft cavity I held my breath, thoughts buzzing. What had they found? What had I overlooked? Was it something that would send them away from here, off on a wild goose chase? Or had I somehow doomed myself? As far as I could remember, though, there was nothing down there to suggest the existence of my hiding place. Even if they found the original loft hatch it didn't open.

Footsteps moved from the kitchen to the living room. Another cap and dark jacket passed me by but I didn't dare follow it back to the other peephole. Torchlight flashed around, before finally settling on something just outside my field of vision. When I heard voices again, they were barely more than whispers.

'There's a kettle in the kitchen. Still hot, and that' – the torch wiggled – 'is steam coming off that mug.'

'What does that have to do with . . . wait, so she's still here?'

'Yeah. She's still here.'

I closed my eyes and kissed any chance of escape goodbye.

Chapter Nine

23:00

Half an hour into the blackout

'Did you not check everywhere?'

He ducked away from the accusing beam of the torch. 'This place is a dump. I assumed the back room was empty. It's the middle of the night and that sofa looks like someone's been sleeping here. So if she's not in bed I figured she wasn't here.'

'Well, she might be hiding somewhere back there. Go and check.'

'Stop telling me what to do.'

'Why not, this is your fucking mess, remember? You're lucky I'm here at all.'

'My mess?' His voice rose indignantly. 'Our mess. This is both of our problem.'

'Yeah, yeah.'

They continued to bicker but I tuned them out, thinking instead of what my options were. There were no windows into the loft space, obviously. No other way out except the way I'd gotten in. Well, that and the chimney which went through the space. That was too narrow to be of any use though. I just had to stay put and pray they didn't find the way into my hiding place. Or that they stumbled into one of the less high-tech security measures and it convinced them to leave. Or rendered them less of a threat.

The rain was very loud this close to the roof. I had to concentrate to listen to their footsteps, trying to work out where they were in the house. It was a lot harder now that they weren't talking to one another as much, both of them absorbed by the hunt. Suddenly I heard a man's voice raised in pain.

'Ah! My fucking face – what the hell was that?'

It came from the bedroom. It was no mystery what he'd found. The entire bedroom was crisscrossed with fine filaments of piano wire. I'd spent days installing hooks in the walls and then biking out to a shop that sold the stuff. The only way to reach the cupboard that accessed the loft was to duck and weave through the web. Something that took patience and practice even in daylight, as my superficial wounds proved. Apparently the guy who'd tried to axe my empty bed had stumbled right into it. Face first.

I moved slowly to the bedroom peephole. The two of them were flashing their torches around, clearly looking at all the wires in the bedroom. They caught the light like spider silk, glittering dangerously.

'Who the hell does this?' the man with the cut face muttered.

'Someone hiding on the other side.'

My insides turned cold. Shit. I should have set some traps elsewhere as well. I'd been so focused on protecting my bolthole that I hadn't thought about a decoy. Thankfully, the guy with the bleeding face wasn't in the mood to let anyone else be right.

'Or she got out this way and expected anyone chasing her to get caught in this mess. Check the window.'

'Now who's bossing who?'

'Just do it,' he snapped.

I watched them navigate the wires, though they didn't see all of them in time. A few hissed curses filtered up to me. I'd strung them high and low, ready to catch the unwary. More than once I'd lain in bed and imagined one of them chasing me at full speed, hitting the wire hard enough to sever an artery. Or their head. Though the wires weren't meant to be lethal. Many of the traps in Damian's SAS books were, but those involved explosives, spike pits or sharpened logs rigged to fall on the enemy. Stuff I didn't have the means or stomach to do. Every time I'd thought of something a little more deadly, the image of Davy or the cat stumbling into it had stopped me.

'Ahhh!'

Well, it had stopped me using them outside the house anyway.

It was the other one this time, a high-pitched cry of pain and shock. They'd clearly reached the window. It was the only one not completely covered in wire, though it was still nailed shut. I'd done this on purpose so it would look like a good point of entry. It was four-paned and anyone trying to get in would have to break one of the bottom panes to get at the lock inside. Those were left clear of wire. Anyone reaching in through broken glass to unlock it, however, wouldn't notice the barbed fishhooks glued under the latch until they'd driven them into their hand.

'Fuck!' came a yell, followed by a cry of agony. 'My fucking hand, what is that?'

I knew from an accident while creating the trap that the hooks went in smoothly but were a bitch to remove. The barbs snagged on flesh on the way out, widening the puncture and causing more damage. I'd had to use pliers and had gone slowly. But if you just yanked your injured hand back, they'd rip your flesh apart. Non-lethal but unpleasant. The main idea was to hurt anyone trying to get at me. Make them cry out, alerting me. In the worst-case scenario, I'd thought as I rigged the trap, they'd leave blood evidence behind. Not that it would do me much good in this case.

'Right, get that cupboard open. I'm done with this bitch's games,' the one with the hooks in their hand snarled.

'Unless she's done something to that as well.'

'Check. It. Then.'

'You check it – that cheese wire shit could've had my eye.'

My stomach clenched. They were going to get to me. I'd thought I was being so clever, reading Damian's books and setting these traps up. It was only now that I saw it for what it was – childish games with no thought behind them. If I'd been more focused on escaping instead of trying to attack, I'd be away by now. But I'd felt so helpless the last time we met. Once I arrived at the cottage I knew I never wanted to feel that way again. Never wanted to have to run from them. I'd decided that standing my ground was the strong thing to do. But I'd gone about it all wrong. Out of the three of us, I was the one caught in a trap. One I needed to escape from.

I looked around, my lip between my teeth as I searched for a way out. No windows, no way into the too-small chimney. No chance at getting the old hatch open without tools and several hours' work. I shifted on the insulation and felt the plywood sheet under me bend. I couldn't stay where I was. I needed to get as far away from the entrance to the loft space as possible.

I edged my way back to the living-room peephole. I moved an inch at a time, trying to spread my weight evenly and stay quiet. The two of them were still navigating the wire maze between the window and the cupboard. I knew that as soon as they got inside they'd find the hatch. Even if they got cut up by the razors, they'd still see my supplies and know I was in here. My only option was getting across to the other end of the loft and hoping they gave up before they found me. As plans went it was the same as a child hiding under their bed. But it was all I had.

I reached the dividing wall between the bedroom and the hall and tried to orient myself towards the kitchen peephole. I had to be as close to the back door as possible, at the opposite end of the house to my pursuers.

As I moved I strained my ears for their voices. That would tell me how close they were to reaching the hatch. I was expecting more shouts of pain and anger when they reached for the handle and found the razor blade stuck on the back. But no cries of pain came.

They must've anticipated another trap and checked the handle. I heard the snick of the latch. They were in, just the hatch between them and my hiding place.

I still had the torch. It was heavy enough to do some damage. I thought of waiting until one of them popped their head through the hatch and trying to bash their skull in. But it was too late now. I'd never get back there in time. Besides, I didn't think I had it in me to kill anyone. Not on purpose. The idea of carrying another death on my conscience made me feel sick. Maybe that was why I'd put so much work into my traps, hoping to scare them off before things got that far.

'Ow, fuck!' The razors on the hatch had got them, as they'd gotten me on my way in. 'Watch out for the edge . . . there's stuff up here.' Their voices were clearer now that they'd opened the hatch. 'Sleeping bag, food . . .'

Torchlight flashed around and I stopped moving, praying they hadn't seen me.

'She must've planned to be up here a while. Probably thought we'd give up and go home. Like we drove all the way across the country for nothing.'

I bit my lip at the scorn in those words. They were right. I'd given them far too little credit. They'd come all the way from Bristol looking for me. They weren't going to turn around because of a few cuts and bruises. I'd been a fool to think they would.

Just like I'd been a fool back then, hiding in the dark, hoping for rescue. I should've known better this time. Rescue is for princesses in story books. It's not how the world works. In real life you save yourself, or you die trying.

'Any sign?'

'Can't see shit up here – battery's starting to go.'

'Typical.'

'What was that?'

'Nothing.'

'I thought so,' the guy in the loft grunted. 'I'm coming back down.'

'What do you mean, "coming back down"? Go and get her.'

'And get another faceful of wire? No thanks.' The voice became more muffled as he ducked out of the hatch. 'She's probably got even more traps up there. There's electrical wires and stuff – I'm not going to find out what she's done to those.'

'So what's your big plan then, eh? Stand here and wait for her to get bored and come down for a chat?'

'No,' he said softly, a new hardness in his voice. 'We burn the bitch out.'

Chapter Ten

23:30

One hour into the blackout

'That's insane.'

For once, I was in agreement. But now the idea was out there and I felt a deep dread that nothing would change his mind. There was something in his voice, an anger that was so deep it had become calm. The eye of a storm.

'Do you want her dead or not?' he said.

'Yes, obviously. But not like that. A massive fire on the cliff? They'll see it from all over and this place'll be crawling before the roof catches. Fire, police – the lot.'

'It's nearly midnight. Everyone's asleep. And even if they're not, the storm's knocked the power out.

Maybe the phone lines too. They won't get here in time to catch us.'

'You're willing to bet the rest of your life on that, are you? Because I'm not. What if the phones are working and we get cornered up here? We'd be fucked.'

'If we leave now, we're fucked anyway.'

Silence greeted his words. The sulky, charged silence of someone being talked round.

'Either we go down for this or she talks about what happened then and we go down anyway. Our only chance is to do this and get away before anyone knows we were here.'

I held my breath, desperately straining to hear their decision. At the same time my mind was clamouring, hunting for a way out. The same dead ends were thrown up again and again, faster and faster until it was like watching a demented slideshow. Hatch, chimney, cupboard. Hatch, chimney, cupboard. All of them useless. There was no way out.

'Fine . . . there's a bottle of vodka in the kitchen. A gas canister too.'

'Good,' he said. 'That's a good start. Do you hear that up there?' he called, raising his voice. 'This whole cottage is about to go up with you inside it. So why don't you come down here, while you still have the choice?'

Maybe they were bluffing? Perhaps they were betting on me being too afraid of burning to death to stay in the loft. It was a pretty good bet. The idea of being up here in a blaze, choking on black smoke and burning alive, was terrifying. Possibly more so than facing the pair of them again.

'Which is it then? You come down and we do it nice and quick – painless – or you stay up there and burn?'

Assaulted by memories of that night I clenched my teeth. Painless? Yeah, right. Was it better than burning? Probably. But up here I had a chance and a choice. Down there I wouldn't have either. Besides, it would only give them the satisfaction. I'd burn to keep that from them.

I could wait it out. They didn't know for certain I was here. Maybe doubt would start to creep in and they'd leave, determined to come back in daylight? Even if they decided to watch the house from the lane I could manage to slip away in the dark. I wouldn't be able to take anything with me but I'd be alive and they'd never find me again. I'd make sure of that.

I was thinking about it when a board in the loft space jolted, making a loud bang. I let out an involuntary squeal. One of them must've shoved something through the plaster, maybe the broom from the kitchen, or the hatchet.

'I heard you!' he called. Another jab at the ceiling made the plywood to my left jump. He was still in the bedroom but getting closer, though he had no way of knowing that. I looked around me in a panic. Underneath the plywood boarding there was only plasterboard, fragile and not at all load-bearing. With enough patience he could bring the entire ceiling down and me with it.

'Come down, now. Or this whole place is going up.'

I stayed still and held my breath.

'All right then . . . get the vodka.'

I heard them picking their way back towards the kitchen and started to crawl quickly. It no longer mattered how much noise I made. The web of sharp wires wouldn't keep them in the bedroom for long. There was only one way out of the loft and they'd found it. So I was going to have to make another. If they made it to the kitchen they'd be between me and the only exit. Like the windows, the front door was sealed shut.

They were hitting the plaster as they went. I could see the disturbance now, the dust motes spinning in the faint light from the peepholes as they shone their torches around. Chunks of plaster had to be falling below as well.

I reached the back door, well, what I guessed was the back door. I fumbled around for the edge of a sheet of insulation and pulled at it, exposing the plywood underneath. Once I had hold of the wood I pulled, trying to drag it to one side. It was difficult. I was on my belly and had no leverage, but the sheet of wood began to move, dragging over another piece and under the insulation. It kept snagging and I nearly cried out in frustration, but kept going. Inch by inch I was uncovering an area of plaster big enough to fit through.

My jumper and joggers were damp with sweat, partly from exertion but mostly from fear. If I did this I'd be down there with them, vulnerable. If I didn't do this exactly right they'd have me in an instant. There were two of them and I had no more traps up my sleeve. We were on a level playing field now; whatever advantage I'd had, I'd wasted it on traps and tricks. I hadn't been able to face attacking them directly and now all I had were my own two legs and the hope of outrunning my pursuers.

The sheet of wood shifted a final few inches and I felt around the space. Big enough. Were they still navigating the wires or were they in the hall? I had no idea and couldn't hear anything over my own rasping breath. There was no time to take it slow. Every second only brought them closer. I rolled over onto my back and shuffled my legs over the bare plaster. With my heart in my throat I bent my knees as much as possible in the narrow space and stamped down, once, twice. That was all it took. The plasterboard cracked like an eggshell and I pushed my feet through, followed by the rest of me in an uncontrolled rush.

I fell through the hole and hit the floor hard. In my head I'd seen myself landing in a crouch. It was more like a sprawl. I looked up, plaster dust billowing around me. He was in the doorway, swaying torchlight coming up behind him.

'She's out!' he roared, already dashing towards me.

I scrambled to my feet and threw myself at the back door, shoving it open. The wind snatched it away. I heard it slam against the back wall. I was already moving, plastic-soled slippers skidding over the wet ground. The rain was lashing down like ropes of lead weights, and thunder drummed across the sky. I could hardly see and within seconds I was soaked to the skin.

The only thought in my head was 'get away'. I had no more plans or preparations; it was just me and the pitch-black clifftop, with the two of them chasing after me.

'Get back here!'

Like that was going to happen.

I ran out the front gate and left, the way I'd come from work. It was pure muscle memory. I always ran that way in the mornings, when I bothered to run; off towards town, turned right down a trail towards the farm, across the footpath through their lower field and back down the Simmonses' drive to my front gate. The wind was cutting in from the sea on my left, making me stumble and veer right. The slippers were too loose to run in properly and soaking up water.

They were behind me. I could hear their heavy footfalls in puddles, the grunts and snorts of exertion. Aside from the rain and the rural setting, it could have been that night all over again. Fleeing into the dark in impractical shoes with nowhere to go and nowhere to hide. Only this time I was alone.

Where could I go? Town was so far away. I'd never make it all that way on foot, not without slowing down and being caught. On the road they'd easily follow me in the car. Who was going to help me there anyway? If any of them were even awake. Honestly I doubted even Davy would put himself on the line, not against these two. He was a white-knight sort of guy but I couldn't see him leaping into this grey area. Unlike my brother and his old mates, Davy didn't have a violent bone in his body. Like his Labrador he was a big, trusting softie.

Reg Simmons, though, he was another thing entirely. A grumpy bastard with about twenty 'no trespass' signs on his front gate and a gun cabinet in his house. I'd seen it the first time I went to return their egg boxes and was told, in no uncertain terms, to leave them at the gate next time. Even when using the public footpath I sensed his glare on me. He wouldn't welcome me banging on the door at midnight, but he'd look even less kindly on the people chasing me. I'd bet money that the only thing he hated more than new residents were strangers, and these two had more than just that against them.

The turn for the trail appeared out of the darkness and I darted towards it. Although I'd been neglecting my runs I was still in fairly good shape from all the cycling. Unlike last time I could outpace my pursuers, at least for a while. I wasn't stupid enough to believe I could keep this pace up for ever though. Sooner or later I was going to run out of energy. When that happened I'd be defenceless, unless I got my hands on a weapon first. Or found someone to help fight them off.

I could still hear them but they sounded further off now. Or maybe it was the blood pounding in my ears that made it sound that way. I wondered what they'd been doing for the past year. Why had they kept looking for me or started again after all this time? What had changed and why didn't I know about it? Had they been preparing, as I had, for this moment? Or had they convinced themselves that it would never come? Were they lagging behind, out of shape, or waiting for me to run myself ragged so they could take me down easier? The very idea made me quicken my pace, desperate to reach the farm before they could stop me.

That was when my slipper caught on a chunk of flint and I fell, tumbling over and over on the wet ground. Stunned and unable to draw breath, I heard them bearing down on me.

Chapter Eleven

2022

Cat's screams were almost lost under the burst of a police siren. I was halfway down the hallway of the abandoned house when two shadows bolted past me. It was the men fleeing the kitchen. I heard them struggling through the hole in the door as my outstretched hand found the kitchen doorway. Inside, Cat was just getting to her knees. From the looks of things they'd dragged her out of her hiding place by her coat. There hadn't been time for them to do much else before the sirens spooked them.

I stumbled over to where she was crouched on the floor and knelt down next to her. She was crying, but I guessed more from shock and fear than pain.

'They're gone,' I wheezed, my throat still furred with cupboard dust. 'You're safe, we're safe.'

She gripped my hand tightly, her whole body still

trembling with fear. The two of us were still sat there like that when a light pierced the darkness, sweeping over us. I flinched, but the voice that came wasn't one of them. Though it was a man. It was someone else, someone new, who sounded shocked but in control. I dipped my head out of the light, my hair falling over my face. It was damp with sweat.

'Scarlett!' he called out. 'Get in here – it's not kids messing about.'

A second light joined the first, both aimed at the floor so as not to dazzle us. I heard the fragmented chatter of a radio, then a woman's voice.

'Oh, shit. Are they OK? What did those guys do?'

'Did you see where they went?'

'They were right down the road. Running.'

'I'll go look.' The man and his torch disappeared and I heard the heavy clump of his shoes as he left the house and ran off up the road.

'Hey, are you all right, love?' The woman put down her torch and crouched beside us. She reached out hesitantly and touched my shoulder, her other hand motioning to Cat as if to calm a scared animal. 'We're police – someone over the back called in a disturbance. Do you know who did this to you?'

Cat broke into fresh sobs. I shook my head. 'They were . . . they were following us. They tried . . .' I couldn't finish the sentence but the policewoman must have understood.

'Do either of you need to go to hospital?' she asked softly, so kindly I felt my eyes start to well up.

'No. I don't think so. We're just . . . we were out and we had to walk home. It was my idea. I was so stupid . . .' My voice cracked and tears began to trickle down my face.

'Hey – it's not stupid,' the policewoman told me, firmly but gently. 'I'm sorry this happened but it's not your fault. At least you stayed together.'

'Cat wouldn't leave me behind.' I found Cat's hand and squeezed, and she gripped back, tightly. 'She could've but she didn't.'

'We've got to look out for each other,' the policewoman said. Through my hair I saw her outline nodding in approval. 'I'm going to do my best to find those two but for now, let's get you home safe. Are you sure you don't need to go to hospital? It's OK if you've been drinking but I don't want to leave you if there's a chance of alcohol poisoning.'

I shook my head. 'It was just some shots, cocktails. We're good. We can handle it.'

'Any drugs?'

I felt my face flame. I wasn't about to dob Cat in to the police. 'No! Look – we just got attacked. It's not our fault.'

'I know and I'm sorry – but I have to ask,' she soothed. 'I just want to know if there's any danger of either of you getting into difficulty. We've seen our fair share of overdoses. This isn't about getting you in trouble, or undermining your statements, I promise. If you're sure you're OK, we can give you a lift home.'

A creaking sound preceded the male officer reappearing in the kitchen doorway. His torch bobbed about as he struggled to catch his breath.

'No luck. They're long gone,' he huffed.

The female officer sighed. 'Did they say anything to you, or indicate where they were from?'

'No.' I felt my insides clench up. The pair of them were going to get away with this. 'I saw them as they ran out though. I think I'd know if I saw them again.' It was just a flash but I'd seen them, one tall, one a little shorter. One had a beard, reddish brown.

'Me too,' Cat said, taking a shuddery breath. 'Two white guys, um . . . they sounded local. One of them had one of those eyebrow piercings, the kind that looks like a dragon?' She sniffed. 'It was infected. Crusty-ass moron.'

I managed a weak laugh. At least Cat sounded like herself again, if a little brittle and scared. The policewoman patted her shoulder.

'That's good. That's really good. Don't worry about the details right now though. There'll be plenty of time for that once we're out of here and you've had a chance to get yourself together.'

'They need to make a statement, Scarlett,' the male police officer said. 'They'll probably forget anything they saw when they sober up.' He lowered his voice, though not enough to keep me from hearing what he was saying. 'If what they're saying even happened.'

I wanted to hit him. Police or not, I'd give him something he wouldn't forget about. Bloody shaming us when Cat was in the state she was in. Of course it happened, or nearly did – he could see it all over her face. Hear it in how she was still struggling not to cry.

'Later,' the woman – Scarlett – said, in a tone that quickly shut him up. 'When you're up to it,' she said to us, in a much kinder voice.

Between the two of us we got Cat upright. She was hiccupping now, wiping her face with the fuzzy sleeves of her coat. Her silver dress was torn across the front, showing part of her stick-on bra and the tattoo along her collarbone. I wasn't sure how that had happened – maybe as she was pulled out of the cupboard? The thought of one of those guys getting even that far with her made me feel sick. I helped her do the coat up to cover herself. Unfortunately it looked like whatever she'd taken was kicking in. It was probably helping to calm her down but she lolled against me like a sack of spuds when we got her standing. It took all three of us to manoeuvre her through the hole in the door and out into the street where the police car was parked at an angle. I could tell she was starting to space out and hoped the cops thought it was just shock and alcohol.

Inside the car it was blissfully warm, the internal lights welcome after the darkness. I took Cat's hand and she leaned against the window, eyes peering around but not taking much in. Definitely the pill. Fuck. I hoped the police didn't notice and ask to search her. God only knew what else she had on her.

But I needn't have worried.

'Bit of a wild one, was it? God, it's been ages since I had a proper night out,' the male officer said as he got into the driver's seat. He found my eye in the mirror and winked. I couldn't tell if he was trying to be cute or just being an asshole.

It was my first time getting a proper look at them in the light. Both of them were younger than I'd thought. The guy was maybe a few years older than me. Scarlett was older still but not by as much as I'd imagined. She'd just sounded so sweet and practical that I'd assumed she was my mum's age. Or the age Mum was when I last saw her.

She twisted around in her seat and looked surprised at the sight of me. I guess maybe we weren't what she was expecting either. She probably thought we were students or teenagers. I felt suddenly ashamed. What was I doing still making these mistakes in my mid-twenties? I knew enough to know better, had done since I was fourteen. She turned around to face the front without comment.

'Seatbelt,' her colleague prompted her, when she didn't move to put it on.

'What? Right . . . just a minute.' Scarlett got out of the car and walked around behind it. I turned to watch her but it was too dark to see. Moments later she was back, cheeks pink from the cold.

'Sorry – forgot to note down the house number. For the report.'

The man snorted. 'Gotta dot those t's, huh?'

'Shut up,' she sighed. 'Whereabouts do you live?' she asked briskly, not turning to look at me. Maybe she felt less sympathy for us now that she knew we weren't teens out late.

I reeled off my address. It was then that I remembered. Panic raced through me. 'My licence. They had my driving licence – that means they know where I live.'

There was a pause as the pair of them digested this.

'One of us can stay in case they turn up,' she said, finally.

'We can't just—'

'Just drive, Craig,' she snapped, and that was the end of that. The car began to move. After a few moments she chipped in, pointing at some sign or another in the dark.

'Take a right here.'

'You sure?'

'Trust me, it's faster.'

109

Craig didn't argue and the car turned. We carried on until Scarlett spoke again.

'You two had a pretty lucky escape there.'

I glanced at Cat, who was leaning against the window with her eyes shut. 'I know . . . thank you, I don't know what would've happened if you hadn't come along. When I think about what might have happened if you'd arrived a few minutes later . . .'

'Well . . . you can't change what happened and thankfully you're both OK now.'

She'd opened her window a little and the smell of the river crept into the car. The metallic stink of slow-moving, murky water. A familiar smell to anyone who's lived in Bristol, but coupled with the smell of vodka on my skin and the darkness outside . . . this was why I didn't get this drunk often. It took me back to before we moved. To the smell of waste water and vodka, bonfires and wet leaves. To the night of the worst thing I'd ever done.

I met Scarlett's eyes in the mirror and I saw how tired she looked. Even though she was younger than I'd thought, there were lines around her eyes. How many times had she found girls like Cat and me too late? Both of us had seen shit I bet we wished we could forget.

'I'm never going to do anything like this again,' I promised those tired eyes. 'Neither of us will.'

She didn't say anything, just turned the regular

radio on. I suppose she'd heard it all before but was too nice to say so. A sad love song started playing and I shut my eyes. Soon I'd be home, in bed. Cat would be curled up on the sofa and all of this would be a story we told until it was just one of those things that happened. Maybe those guys had dropped my licence, or were too stupid or scared to try and track me down. Maybe it was all going to be OK.

I squinted through the window, tried to work out where we were, but I couldn't see much, just the odd streetlight passing by and my own exhausted reflection in the glass. It reminded me of night-time car rides as a kid. You don't know where you are but you know you're safe and sound with Mum and Dad in the front seat. Or your friend's mum and dad at least. Mine had never had a car and it was Damian who'd taken me everywhere on the bus. The first time my mate's parents had picked us up from the cinema I'd felt downright posh.

I could hear Craig and Scarlett talking but not the individual words. It was all just a soothing babble, the radio just slightly too loud over the top. Maybe I was already getting a hangover.

'Does your friend need something to drink?' Scarlett asked.

Probably a good idea. Depending on what Cat'd taken she was likely going to be dehydrated. After nothing but alcohol all night I was parched too. My mouth felt coated in dust from crawling around in the house. Scarlett passed a water bottle back to me.

'It's got squash in it – sorry,' she said.

'That's fine, thank you.' I had a sip but blackcurrant squash always reminded me of cough sweets. So I handed the bottle to Cat, who took it in a limp hand and obediently chugged most of it.

'Hey, slow down, you'll be sick,' I muttered, but she didn't seem to hear. I took the empty bottle back and passed it through to the front, then I leant back and shut my eyes. I was starting to feel a bit car-sick but I was also too tired to do much about it. Besides, it wasn't like I could open a window. It was probably the fear and adrenaline leaving my system. I felt boneless.

I wasn't sure how long I'd been dozing when the car stopped. When I peeled my eyes open and looked at Cat she was passed out against the door. The window behind her was dark. I twisted around and looked out my side. Darkness there too, except for the shimmering lights of town, which seemed to end a little way away. I frowned.

'Hey, I don't think this is right . . .' I said, before realising that the front of the car was empty. Both officers were gone.

Struggling upright I peered through the front seats. Where had they gone? Had they spotted something else they needed to deal with and just left us locked in the car? I was feeling more and more nauseous by now. If I threw up in the back of the cop car they weren't going to take it well. Last thing I needed tonight was more trouble.

After a few minutes though, I realised that being sick was the least of my worries. The more I looked around the more certain I was that we weren't anywhere near my street. We didn't seem to be near anything at all. There were no lights around, nothing even lighter coloured to show up in all that darkness. It was just pitch-black outside. In the distance I thought I could make out the illuminated roof of the train station. Nowhere near my flat.

I was leaning so hard against the door that when it was suddenly opened I pitched out onto the ground. My scrabbling hands and feet met cold, wet grass. I could smell damp growing things and the metallic sewer reek of the river. Much stronger than it had been before. I could hear the river too, or thought I could – there was water anyway, the rush of it as it plunged down an unseen drain or over a drop.

Dazed, confused by the out-of-place sounds and smells, I felt hands grip my arms. Twisting around I saw the female officer, her face set in a stony expression as she hauled me upright, nails digging into my skin.

'Where are we?' My voice came out funny, like it was coming from somewhere far away instead of my own lips.

She didn't answer but shifted her hands under my armpits and dragged me backwards around the car. I tried to flail out of her grasp but I couldn't make my body do what I wanted. I felt untethered, like all my joints had been dismantled. When the policewoman dropped me on the ground I cried out but couldn't otherwise react, only move my head to try and catch a glimpse of what was going on.

The male officer was leaning against the bonnet of the car, watching me. I could only just make out the shape of him in the dark. The orange pinprick of a cigarette, which flared, making his face glow red. I turned and saw the woman opening the passenger door on the near side of the car. Cat fell out onto the ground. Unlike me she was completely unconscious. She landed only a few inches away from me, sending up a splash of muddy water. She was going to be so pissed about her coat, I thought, the words floating around inside my skull.

I felt unreal, like I was watching everything from five hundred yards away with binoculars. Like this was all a nightmare that I was trying to remember. Somewhere in the distance a bird screeched. It was the only sound anywhere nearby, aside from the river. I couldn't even hear any other cars. It was late, very late. No one else around, not even a horn honking in the distance.

'You're sure about this?' the man, Craig, said.

'Definitely,' Scarlett snapped.

'But this one isn't . . . I mean, she didn't do anything, right? What if something happens to her out here?'

'She hasn't done anything that we know of. You know what they say – birds of a feather do bad shit together. Look at her, for Christ's sake. Besides, like you said, she's not going to remember us tomorrow. We're the only ones that're gonna know this even happened.'

'Well . . . if that's the case . . .' Craig left his perch and stood over Cat, chewing his lip. Then he crouched down and started to ease her tight dress up her thighs.

'What the fuck are you doing?' Scarlett hissed.

'Shut up,' he retorted, without looking up. 'You're having your fun. My turn.'

'Fun?' she said. 'None of this is "fun" for me . . . Stop it!'

'Shut. Up. Scar.'

For a moment I felt a thread of fear connecting the two of us. Me and Scarlett. I held my breath and prayed she'd do something, anything to stop this. Whatever she'd brought us up here for, this was not it. This was all him.

Then the moment passed and Scarlett came around by me, facing away from Craig and whatever he was doing but standing between us. She wasn't looking at me but staring fixedly into the dark, her face set and hardened.

The horror of it all nearly reached me, like the beam from a lighthouse cutting through the fog. My head was so muddled. I tried to grab at Scarlett's trouser leg to make her look at me. To make her do something. I wanted to crawl over and push Craig off Cat's limp body. But I couldn't do more than bat the air in front of me.

'Stop it,' I managed. 'Leave . . . leave her alone.'

But he didn't listen. Neither of them did. She just kept staring into the dark, like she was willing herself to stay still. Like she was as barely there as I was.

The last thing I was really conscious of, before Cat became the only thing that mattered and I blocked out everything else, was Scarlett's voice. Her words were soft, her lips barely moving. If her breath hadn't come out as fog I wouldn't have known they came from her. But what she said mirrored the terrible sickness in the pit of my stomach, coated in anger and fear.

'This is all your fault.'

And as my memories blurred together, water and wet leaves and the dead, cold night, I couldn't say she was wrong. This was punishment for back then, it had to be. But Cat, poor Cat. She didn't even know me then. She was just another casualty of my awful mistake.

Chapter Twelve

I don't know how long the four of us were trapped in that awful moment together. Scarlett looking away, Craig holding Cat down. But eventually he got to his feet and I was left staring at my friend, unconscious and limp on the wet ground. At first I'd been glad she was out of it, as if that made any of this more bearable. Now I was starting to worry there was something very wrong with her. She wasn't moving, not even her chest or her eyes twitched.

'Her turn.'

Craig's voice brought my thoughts around to myself. This wasn't over. Clearly the universe thought I hadn't paid for what I'd done yet. I looked up and found that Scarlett wasn't looking at him or off to the side anymore; she was watching me. There was some light now. Not sunrise but a pre-dawn gloom that made everything look flat and grey. Her eyes shone as she watched me, unblinking. There were tears drying on her cheeks, but she didn't say a word. In that moment I was almost more afraid of her than him. Why was she doing this to us?

Who the hell were these people? Not police, they couldn't be. Though they had the uniforms, the car. That didn't mean much though. You could probably buy that shit online. A mate of Damian's bought an ambulance once, kitted it out as a camper. You could get anything online.

Were they a couple who got off on patrolling the streets looking for vulnerable girls to drug? Because I was certain now that we had been drugged. Something in the squash that had knocked Cat out and made my body feel like it belonged to someone else. Though it was wearing off now. I felt horribly present as Craig stood over me, looking at me like I was a dessert he wasn't sure he had room for.

Without warning, Scarlett moved, making me twitch in panic.

'It's getting light out. We should . . .'

'There's time yet,' Craig said, cutting her off.

'This isn't a good idea.'

'There's no one around for miles – you said so yourself.'

'But what if we miss a call or—' Whatever she was about to say was cut off by a horrible heaving noise.

A guttural sawing of air that made all the hair stand up on my body.

I rolled my head over, still feeling my way back into my limbs. What I saw made my skin turn to ice. Cat was still completely out of it, but there was foam around her mouth and she was jerking around as if being shaken, her skin turning greyish.

'Fuck!' Craig grabbed at Cat's wet coat and threw her onto her side. Froth leaked from her mouth onto the ground, but she didn't stop spasming.

'You said she wasn't on anything,' Scarlett snapped at me. Her eyes were so wide I could see the whites all the way around. She looked as terrified as I felt. I tried to crawl over to Cat but Scarlett pushed me back down and went to help Craig.

With both of them over her I couldn't see Cat properly, just her thin legs shaking and jerking. One sock had rolled down and her bare leg was almost purple with cold.

'Help her,' I croaked, but I don't think either of them heard. 'Please.'

'We should call an ambulance.'

'Are you mad?' Craig nearly yelled. 'We're not calling anyone.'

'She's ODing!'

'I know that! Shut up and let me think!'

Then Cat's legs stopped moving, and everything went very quiet.

It was Scarlett who broke the pre-dawn silence. Her voice so soft that it might have been coming from inside my own head.

'Oh . . . shit . . .'

Craig moved away then, stalked off a few feet and stood with his back to me, to us. I could see Cat now. Her dress was torn down at the front and I desperately wanted to crawl over and put it right. Cat wouldn't want to be humiliated like that. She was going to be so upset that her beautiful coat was ruined too. When she woke up. Only of course she wasn't going to, and that thought slapped me in the face. She didn't look like she was sleeping. She looked like someone had tried to carve her out of wax from memory and it had gone really wrong. I didn't need to see her still chest to know that she was gone. But still there was a tiny part of me that thought if I could just reach her, just warm her up or hold her hand, she'd be OK. I tried to say her name, but no sound would come out. I felt like I was about to cry, or be sick. Both.

I was about to try and crawl to her when Craig spoke again. He was still looking at the distant lights of the city, which were winking out, one by one. Morning was coming.

'We need to get rid of her.'

I heard Scarlett's sharp intake of breath. Somewhere inside me, a sliver of survival instinct took hold and

I closed my eyes, letting my body slump against the ground. It wasn't until after I'd done it that I realised how much danger I was in now, even more so than only minutes ago. I was the only witness to what had happened here tonight. The only person who'd watched them kill my best friend.

'We . . . uh . . .' I heard him pacing around, the grass squelching. 'We make it look like an accident. Pissed party girl ODs, not really a hard sell.'

'And what's she meant to be doing out here, genius?' Scarlett said, suddenly flying into anger after so long spent in stunned silence. 'With our tyre treads right there and your fingerprints, your . . . all over her?'

'Fuck!' I heard what sounded like a kick at the car door. 'What do we do with her then? Scrub her off, bury her?'

In the few seconds of silence that followed I felt the balance between them shift again. He was the scared one and she was the one in control.

'The canal. We dump her in the canal and it all gets washed away. They won't find her for days, maybe weeks. It's high right now with all the rain. She could go a long way.'

'Right, yeah, OK.' Craig sniffed, pacing again. 'Stupid bitch, falls in on her way home with a skinful. Clean out the car, it's like it never happened.'

'. . . except for her.'

'Yeah . . . we need to deal with her,' Craig said. 'Do you reckon she'll remember? How much did you give her?'

'I don't know. It was all in the bottle but I didn't see her drink much. Can we even take the chance?'

I had to fight to keep my face slack and my body limp. Every cell in me wanted me to run for it, but I knew I'd only get a few steps before they caught me. I'd absorbed the shock of everything that had happened, or let it wash over me. Now I was thinking again and I knew the only chance I had was if they thought I was already dead.

'Looks like she's out of it now too. She probably had some of whatever her mate was on as well – just took a while to kick in,' Craig said.

'All right, so . . . we chuck her in as well. She overdoses or she drowns. Either way, problem solved.'

'Why'd you have to go and get me involved?' Craig muttered, but I heard him straining to lift something heavy, footsteps squelching off into the distance. Cat. He was carrying Cat. I felt my chest tighten. I wanted to scream at him to leave her be, but I held it in.

'Why'd you have to go and be such a fucking prick,' Scarlett hissed to herself.

Unexpectedly a foot connected with my shin. I only just managed to contain a cry of pain, glad that my face was mostly against the ground.

'You deserved it,' I heard Scarlett say, and prayed she was talking to herself. That she hadn't noticed that I was wide awake and listening to every word.

My blurry brain tried to make sense of her words. For the second time she'd blamed me for this. I knew what I'd done to deserve it, but what was she thinking about? Maybe she was just one of those kinds of women, the sort who hate other women only slightly less than they hate themselves. The kind who always seem to have sons and husbands who are absolute creeps. The pair of us, short dresses and high heels, drunk and unaccompanied. She probably thought we had it coming.

She had no way of knowing that she was half right.

I heard Craig coming back, felt him bend over me. His breath was sour with coffee and his touch came with a waft of Paco Rabanne that hit me as he hauled me up over his shoulder, my head dangling towards the ground.

I felt sick as he carried me, swaying, across the scrub ground towards the canal. His hand rested on a hole in my cheap tights. His skin on my bare legs made me want to vomit. I kept thinking of Cat, who was already in the freezing water. Cat who only a few hours ago had been smiling and laughing, telling me my legs looked sexy. Cat who was never going to smile again. Because of me. Because I'd chosen to walk this way, right into the path of these two psychos.

He threw me without warning. One moment I was being jolted about over his shoulder, the next I was falling with a crash into water so cold it was like fire. I couldn't help the shriek that burst out of me. Below the brown water's surface a strong current snagged my legs and started to drag me. I dipped under, swallowed water and emerged choking on it.

For a moment I was facing up and saw Craig's pasty, horrified face. Then I was snatched away under the water. I flailed as I went down, feeling weed and trash bump against me. I surfaced, gasping for air. Looking up, Craig was already several metres back along the bank, with Scarlett just appearing behind him. I went under again.

In the dark, freezing water, I knocked against something large and soft. My fingers caught on waterlogged strands of fluff. As the thing moved, my hand trailed along, finally meeting another icy hand in the water. Cat's fingers brushed against mine for a moment, then she was gone – swept away by the water.

Choking and sobbing, I surfaced again. There were trees overhead now, no sign of either of the people who'd done this to us. I couldn't hear anything over the roar of my waterlogged ears and the thumping of my heart. Barely able to breathe, I was sucked under by the current again, thrashing and clawing for light and air.

Then I stopped.

I thought of Cat, her empty body carried off by the canal, and I thought of Damian, drowning in his own blood as surgeons worked to fix his internal injuries. The only two people I'd ever loved were gone. I thought of another night, a fading bonfire. The dark trees all melting together. I let the current drag me down. Why was I fighting? What was I fighting for?

The water tossed me up again like a cork and my body gasped for air. Inside, though, I was still grappling with the impulse to let it take me down. The idea of having to live with all of this but without both of them made me want to shut my eyes and stop fighting.

But then – who was going to search for Cat? No one else knew what had happened to her. To us. They'd never find her in the canal without my help. She'd just stay there for ever. Until she was bones. Lost in the river with no one to care.

Shivering to my core, I started to kick against the current. With great effort I managed to get onto my back, floating on the surface, where I could breathe. I couldn't fight the current, but it had to let go of me somewhere. Eventually I would get out of this and find someone, anyone, who could help put this right.

I wasn't going to let Cat rot in the river. One way or another, those two were going to pay for what they'd done to her.

Chapter Thirteen

It didn't take me long to wash up out of the canal. The current dragged me along until I hit a floating raft of rubbish caught on a shopping trolley. The steep walls along the edges of the canal had given way to a towpath low enough for me to drag myself onto. I threw up then, the river water and bile coating my mouth. Then I lay there like a landed fish, shivering so intensely that the world around me seemed to be rippling.

It was still barely sunrise. Wisps of mist were rising from the brown water and somewhere close by I could hear the crashing of lorries being unloaded. There were a few people shouting to one another as early morning deliveries were brought in. Bristol was waking up. Yet the thought of calling out to anyone, asking for help, made me feel immediately afraid.

How could I trust that those shouting voices belonged to people who wouldn't try and hurt me? The idea of accepting a lift home, or even a hot drink, from anyone right now made me feel sick. My heart pounded at the very thought of even speaking to another person. People were dangerous. All of them, any of them.

I unbuckled my heels and got to my feet. There were leaves caught on my ripped tights and my dress was stuck to me, waterlogged. Where was I anyway? The pavement was bordered by bushes and trees. Through them I could see a road, a Lidl and the sign for one of the commercial estates I'd been to, for the cinema there. I was actually closer to home than I had been before. Not by much, but I at least knew how to get there from here. The towpath went under the overpass and from there you only had to cross the council estate to reach my flat.

With my arms wrapped around my waterlogged dress I stated to walk. My feet were so numb from the cold water and my uncomfortable shoes that the pavement didn't bother me. I'd left the heels by the edge of the canal.

I didn't see anyone on the path, by some miracle. No joggers, dog walkers or parents taking kids to school the scenic way. It was quiet and still. Which was just as well. The way I felt I might have run from anyone I saw. If I could find the energy. Really

I felt like a zombie, plodding my way home. It wasn't just my skin that had gone numb. My insides felt cold and dead, hollowed out like the rotting pumpkin I passed on a front doorstep.

In the estate I saw people from a distance, mostly in cars. A horn honked and I winced. It was too loud and the sun was too bright. I needed darkness and silence. As I turned a corner towards another underpass someone called out, 'Walk of shame!' I flinched and scuttled into the shadowy tunnel.

Finally I reached my street and the mossy sandstone steps to the rundown Victorian house. My keys were thankfully safe in my beaded bag, which was attached to my wrist by a bangle. Though both it and my broken phone were waterlogged, my keys and Cat's were still inside. I unlocked the door and shut it behind me. Finally I was safe.

'The absolute state of you.'

I shut my eyes to hold back tears. Mrs Clarke came down the stairs, shuffling in her slippers. Her horrible little dog glared at me from under her arm.

'You look like you slept under a bridge. You girls these days – no self-respect, no notion of what's proper and decent. Out all night with God knows who. No wonder the police were after you.'

That had my eyes flying open. I stared at her and she nodded, pleased by my shock and fear.

'That's right. Two of them came by this morning,

asking about you. Where you worked, how they could get hold of you. Whatever you've done this time, I hope the council chucks you out. Excuse me!' she shouted as I shouldered past her and ran upstairs. 'Learn some respect!'

I locked the door of my flat behind me and looked around. No sign that anyone had been inside. The door was undisturbed as well. They hadn't been in. I was sure of it. With my back to the door I sank down onto the carpet and felt my breathing slowly return to normal. Mrs Clarke was still chuntering away in the stairwell, but even that brought me a tiny bit of peace. It was so . . . normal. And normal was what I desperately wanted after last night.

But even as I sat there on the floor, I knew I wasn't safe. I'd told them where I lived. They'd been here, trying to find me. Whoever those people were, they weren't about to let me go after what I'd seen. After I'd watched them rape and murder my best friend.

I thought of Cat, dancing at Tea Party, mixing drinks in my flat, huddling me into her coat. Cold and dead, floating in the river, her fingers brushing mine. I convulsed and landed on my hands and knees, retching onto the carpet. I tasted passion fruit, bile and river water. My eyes burned and my nose ran, but still my head was full of Cat. I sat back, covering my face, and sobbed.

The sound of a siren whipping past outside jolted

me into a ball. I whimpered, tears still streaming over my cheeks. It wasn't coming this way, it was just another sound in the morning chorus, but that didn't bring me any comfort. What if the next siren was coming for me?

Had those two really been the police? The car, their uniforms, the chatter on the radio. It had all felt real enough and they'd said they were cops when they came looking for me. Would they do that in the broad light of day if it was all just an act?

I wasn't naïve enough to think real police never broke the law. Mum used to say to me when I was younger, 'A man in uniform is still a man – you should always look for a lady.' It was the only bit of advice she ever really gave me. That and that the TV licensing people can't legally come in unless you invite them. She was big on avoiding them, and bailiffs, landlords, anyone who wanted money really.

But I'd done what she said. I'd trusted a woman, one in uniform no less, and she'd fed Cat and me straight to the wolves. So what now? Who could I trust?

If Damian was still alive he'd tell me what to do. Actually, there'd probably be no 'telling'. He'd just get some of his mates around and find those people. Only he was gone and all his old friends were either away with the army, in prison, abroad or living normal lives they were unlikely to fuck up by going after a cop. If they were really the police I was completely on my own.

A buzzing noise from the direction of the sofa drew me over. It was Cat's phone on the coffee table, slowly turning in a semi-circle. I flipped it over. The screen had a picture of the two of us dressed in souvenir T-shirts from Weston-super-Mare and Union Jack boxers. My twentieth birthday, when we'd gone to get trashed on the beach and play arcade games. Both of us fell in the thick, gloopy mud at low tide and had to buy new clothes. In the background I could see Damian, buried in the sand with tits and a mermaid tail sculpted around him. His friend Jake raising a pink spade above his head like a sword. Last I heard, Jake was hiding out up north after pissing off the wrong people round our way. The kind of people who repay mistakes with missing fingers.

That was really the sort of help I could use. Unless those two were just psychos in fake uniforms? I needed to find out the truth before I did anything else.

I unlocked the phone and brought up the browser, then copied the number for my local station. I had to know if those two were really police. If not, I could go to the cops and tell them what happened, though I was reluctant to talk to the cops generally, given my history. But if those two *were* really police . . . I didn't want to think about it. I had no idea what I'd do. I held my breath as the phone rang, rehearsing what I was about to say so it'd come out more normal than I felt capable of.

'Hi, I'm calling about two people who I think work with you there?' I said, once the voice recording dumped me off with a real person. 'Or maybe at another station around Bristol. They were working last night?'

'Right . . . Is this about a specific incident? Do you need to make a complaint?'

'No! I . . . well, I think . . .' I cast about for inspiration. 'I was a bit shitfaced and they took me home, but I think I left my phone in their car. I'm just not sure which station to go to and pick it up.'

The woman on the other end of the line sighed. 'Names?'

'I only got their first names – Craig and Scarlett.'

'Well, there's a lot of Craigs but only one Scarlett I know of. Dark hair, quite tall?'

My stomach sank. 'That's . . . that's her. Yes. So she does work there?'

'She's a police officer. I'm not sure I can tell you where she works. It might be against confidentiality, I'll have to speak to my manager—'

She was still talking when I hung up. A moment later the phone rang and I declined the call, then blocked the number.

Scarlett was really in the police, which meant Craig was too. That everything Cat and I had been through was at the hands of real cops. Cops who weren't going to listen to someone like me making accusations about people like them. Not only that, but they knew where I lived. By now they probably knew my full name and had found out all sorts about me. They'd know I lived alone, my job, my arrest record (two lots of shoplifting at fourteen and the one time I got picked up with Damian for selling knock-off trainers). What about the stuff I'd never been charged with? Was there a record of that night somewhere? A case that could be reopened and used against me?

I had to do something – tell someone. Cat was still out there in the river, drifting. Someone had to find her. I had to . . . but who was there? I couldn't go to the police. All right, so not all of them would be on Scarlett and Craig's side, but how could I tell the good from the bad? Even the good ones might not believe me. Especially if they looked into me a bit, started dredging up any mention of me from before we moved off the estate. Besides, as soon as those two got wind of it I might find myself getting a visit in the night. It wouldn't be the first time someone disappeared or died in custody.

The police were out. I had no one else. Unless I could report it anonymously? Call in and tell them what I saw, then vanish before anyone could come and get rid of me. But vanish to where? These people could look at my whole life on a computer somewhere. They could find me in a million different ways and all they needed was one.

Cat's phone buzzed in my hand. I panicked, thinking it was another call from the police station. It was just an email from some beauty company, but it brought up a bunch of other unread messages. I read the subject of one, then clicked it open. An idea was forming, my one and only option.

The email was about Cat's inheritance. Well, her pending inheritance. It was still tied up in probate or whatever. Her Aunt Claire's holiday cottage in Norfolk. I'd been excited when Cat first told me about it, only as it turned out, it was a bit of a death-trap. An uninsurable wreck on the edge of a cliff that crumbled into the sea more and more with every storm. Not the kind of place you'd ever be glad to inherit. More like a total mess you'd pay money to avoid dealing with.

But it was, I realised, the perfect place to hide.

Chapter Fourteen

What do you pack when you're starting your life over again?

Standing in my flat on the worst day of my life, I was frozen with indecision. I couldn't imagine the next half hour, let alone the weeks and months to come. What would I need, where would I end up when I finally felt able to stop running? On top of all that was the image of Cat in the water, the fear of a knock on the door, of dozens of heavy footsteps on the stairs. I didn't have much time to pack, but I'd have a long while to regret what I chose to take with me and what I left behind.

For most of the bulky, expensive stuff, the decision was unfortunately made for me. I didn't have a car. Given a day or so I could get my hands on one but that was time I didn't have. Besides, I couldn't chance being pulled over in some marketplace banger with dodgy plates or broken brake lights. I didn't have a licence anymore and I couldn't risk ending up where those two could get at me.

I'd have to carry everything with me and that limited my choices. I had no idea how I was even going to get to Norfolk. Train was probably the best bet but even that would take hours. I'd have to chop and change my way through London too, hauling my things with me. But at least I'd be just another anonymous face there. Someone going to or from uni or a festival. Or off on a cheap holiday. Nothing to see here.

Where to begin? I found myself at the door to Damian's room. Months I'd kept out of there, but now it was the only place in the flat where I thought I might feel safe. I turned the doorknob and let myself in.

The carpet was dusty, the blinds drawn. It was dark and smelled of musty washing and the unmade bed. I hadn't changed anything. It was easier to just ignore the room altogether.

I picked my way across the carpet, stepping over books, shoes and puddles of discarded clothes. Damian had a big canvas duffle in the wardrobe and a thick coat that would do me better than my pleather jacket. I'd been to the Norfolk coast once before, with the school. It was a trip for Geography, in February. The wind had cut through every layer of clothing on my body and my fingers had been red raw after only minutes of grading pebbles by size. Before that day I'd never seen snow on a beach before. Never knew that ice could form on seaweed.

At the bottom of the wardrobe was a box of Damian's stuff. SAS books, several types of folding knife, sleeping bag, all kinds of survival kit he'd found at boot sales or online. It seemed a good idea to pack some of it. The only thing I really knew about the cottage was how remote it was, how run down. Hadn't Cat said something about the electric being shut off? Or was it the gas? Something to do with stuff underground being disturbed in a landslip? Pipes or cables. Yeah, taking a camping stove sounded like a good move.

I packed some of Damian's clothes too: thick jumpers and hiking socks. In my room I added some of my clothes and any jewellery that I could sell. There wasn't much that was valuable, but I had a gold necklace of Damian's and some thick silver hoops from Auntie Faye. They'd get me some money, once I found somewhere to sell them. Though the thought of parting with Damian's most valuable treasure made me feel bitterly ashamed, it couldn't be helped.

I realised when I saw my charger that the police could probably track my phone, so it was kind of a good thing it was broken. I'd have to bin Cat's as well, eventually, but for now I needed it. I grabbed it off the coffee table and then packed the few photos of Cat and Damian that I had in my room. They were all I'd have where I was going, though looking at the tiny images of Cat's smiling face made me want to curl up and sob, or punch a wall.

The bag was already filling up and quite heavy. There was still so much in the flat. Stuff that I never would have left behind on any other day – stuff that I could really do with the money from, like the games console, my laptop, the TV. Could I take some of it to trade in on my way to the station? Something told me there wasn't time. Already my skin was prickling, ears straining for a heavy knock on the door. I had to go, now.

I'd changed out of my wet dress into jeans and a T-shirt. My hair was still damp and I reeked of river water, so I shoved the wet tangles into a woolly hat. Between that and Damian's coat I didn't look like me. I hoped it would be enough to help me blend in if those two drove past, looking for me. They might still be on the estate, circling like vultures.

Mrs Clarke wasn't still hovering about, thankfully. At the bottom of the stairwell I found Mr Barrett's fat cat pawing at the glass, begging to come in. When I opened the door he hurried inside, butting his wide, clueless head against my legs and making a noise like a cement mixer.

'I've gotta go out, Pud – I'll see you . . . later.'

I was almost in tears saying goodbye to a sodding cat that wasn't even mine. But I hadn't been able to say goodbye to my brother, or my best friend. That cat was the only thing that'd miss me. Except maybe his owner. The cat's confused mew chased me down the street as I hurried towards the town centre.

I snivelled all the way there, unable to keep the low-level crying at bay. My insides were twisted with guilt and fear. I kept thinking I saw Cat, heard her – a bright pink miniskirt in a crowd, a cry of delight as someone spotted their mates, a flash of sequins or the clatter of heels. I'd been here with her less than ten hours ago and it was already so different. I was so different. I passed by the locked-up front of Tea Party with a shiver, my throat thick with suppressed tears. Cat's lipstick-printed glass was probably still in there, beside mine, waiting to be washed. Our fingerprints were still smudged on the bar, the scent of her perfume lingering with a thousand others. It had all happened so fast and now she was gone. Gone for ever.

I stopped at a payphone near the bus station. I was hoping that if they ever traced the call, they'd think I'd taken a bus instead of the train. I couldn't stay and put my name to a complaint, but I could try and report what happened. Even if I had to run right after.

It was rank inside the phone box, because who even used payphones anymore except drunks looking for a place to piss? I rang the police station again, trying and failing to clear my throat. My eyes were stinging, the tear tracks whipped raw by the wind outside. The same automated menu came on the line and then the same receptionist.

'How can I help?'

'Last night, Catherine Walker was . . . she was . . .' I stuttered, then remembered the look on that woman Scarlett's face and realised I couldn't do it. Even in that anonymous little cubicle I was too afraid to say their names. To tell anyone what they'd done. What was the point in even trying? It wasn't like anyone was going to listen to someone like me. I smacked my hand on the broken window in front of me, hating myself.

'She was what . . .?' prompted the receptionist, sounding annoyed.

I had to say something. They had to find her.

'Cat Walker, she . . . They put her in the canal. The canal upstream of the Lidl underpass, in back of the train station – the industrial area. I think she went in somewhere with grass. Like a field. A park.' It came out all at once in a rush as I desperately tried to get across everything I knew, while realising how little that was.

'OK, calm down,' the voice soothed. 'I need to

put you through to someone who can take a report. Can you tell me who you are? Then you can talk to someone about who might have done this and what happened.'

'I can't, I'm sorry.' My voice caught in my throat, betraying me. 'They'll get me. I know they will. I have to go.'

'Don't hang up – please, just stay on the line.'

I put the phone back in its metal cradle, suffocated by shame and the reek of stale piss. I couldn't do it. I couldn't say who did it. But it had to be enough. They'd find her now. Someone would find her.

'I'm sorry,' I whispered, watching people pass by outside. 'I'm sorry, Cat . . . I should've done more. I never should've . . .' I covered my face with my hands to keep people from staring and sobbed in the tiny cubicle.

When I was finally able to control myself I stepped out and hurried to a cash point. Most of my cards were sitting in my purse in someone else's pocket, but the emergency credit card had still been at home. Damian's idea, that, to be prepared in case of a sudden massive bill. It was exactly where he'd left it, gathering dust behind an old family picture. I took out as much cash as it'd let me. It wasn't like I was going to have to pay it back. Then I threw the card in a bin. It felt surreal. I was doing the kind of things people did in Damian's spy films.

It was the only blueprint I had for what I was trying to do – disappear entirely.

At the station I paid for an open ticket and got on the first train headed in the right direction. I wasn't about to waste time hanging around waiting to be caught. As it was, my heart was beating way too fast as I went through the station, glancing sideways at transport police and staff in case one of them suddenly shouted, 'There she is!' and ran at me.

When the train started to move I sat back and let out a sigh. Safe. Or, at least, getting there. With every second, Bristol was disappearing into the distance behind me. My whole life was back there, every memory I had with the people I loved, but by sacrificing them I was going to be safe. No one could find me all the way across the country.

Sitting there I wondered what the receptionist would do with the information I'd spewed at her. Was she relaying it to someone now? Were they calling in divers and boats to search the canal? Or had she decided I was a timewaster? Maybe they'd send a solitary cop to poke the bushes around the canal. As soon as I got where I was going I'd have to get online or find a newspaper, keep checking to see if they'd found Cat. To see if they were investigating what happened to her. If not . . . well, I'd have to call again. Maybe this time I'd have the courage to tell them everything.

How to get online was another matter. I had wifi on the train but what about when I reached the cottage? It wasn't like I could just toddle off to a café. It was in the middle of nowhere and if it probably had no electric, that meant no wifi. Not that there was likely to be any installed anyway. Or phone signal, come to think of it. Besides which, if I wanted a phone, electric or internet I'd need money to pay for it, a name to put on the bill and some kind of ID that couldn't be traced back to me or where I was.

Slowly the enormity of what I'd just done started to hit me. Running away had been my goal but it wasn't the end of anything. It was the start. I'd have to give myself a new name, find a way to get money, plan where to go from the holiday cottage. I couldn't stay there for ever. Eventually I'd have to move on and for that I'd need money and official documents which didn't have my real name on them.

I told myself I'd get to it when I had to. I would cope. Sitting there, I remembered a stupid poster Damian used to have in his room. Some US Marines thing. God knows why, but then he was into anything that involved camo and a gun. He loved to parrot the motto on it and I could see it in my head now, in glaring yellow letters: improvise, adapt, overcome.

Well, I'd had to improvise. As for the rest, I'd have to see.

Chapter Fifteen

It had long since got dark by the time I reached the cottage. The train had taken hours and then I'd had to take a bus to the town closest to the house – a nowhere place with one shop and maybe four roads. The woman in the post office called it a town. This place was like a toy version of what a town could be.

After buying some bits at the post office shop and shrugging off the cashier's questions, I began the walk to the cottage. That part of the journey took even longer, along lanes and up steep hills. I'd never thought of myself before as being out of shape. I'd become downright skinny after Damian died and I just didn't want to eat at all. But on those hills I felt like I was about to have a heart attack. My breath came in horrible gasps and I felt like I was sweating every last drop of liquid out of my body. Though most of that was probably the hangover from last night and maybe a chill from being churned about in the river.

The lanes trailed off into a gravel track which passed by a farm gate. A sign zip-tied to the metal gate said 'Simmons Farm' in thick black letters. It was surrounded by about eight 'no trespass' and 'no solicitation' signs. According to the map I'd screenshotted on Cat's phone at the station, this was the only neighbour the cottage had. Clearly not a friendly bloke, but at least I was getting close.

The gravel track continued, getting more and more uneven and narrow as it went, surrounded by scruffy grass and hedges full of thorns. A chill wind was cutting in off the sea and I could hear the crash and roar of waves far below. It was pitch-black and the phone's torch only helped a little. I was so worried about plunging over the edge of the cliff that I nearly missed the house.

The stone wall around the edge of the postage-stamp garden was so covered in grasses that it looked like just another verge. Only the sign peeping through the clumps of plants told me that there was something back there. Clifftop Cottage, a cruelly ironic name. Cliff Edge Cottage would have been a better one.

Once I stepped past the wall and found the building I looked beyond it and the only thing out there was darkness and distance. I dumped my bag on the ground and eased my aching shoulders. The front door was solid wood, and someone had left a thick, rusted chain wrapped around its handle and through a metal bike rack screwed tightly to the wall. I'd need bolt-cutters to get through that.

Feeling more anxious than ever that I'd have to spend the night outside, I went around the back looking for an easy point of entry. There was a back door all right, and two big steps down from it the ground just ended, sucked away into blackness. The wind pushed me back from the edge, worrying away at the cottage behind me like it was a loose tooth.

When I picked up a stone to smash the window in the back door I found a rusty key underneath. Whoever chained up the front door must've either not known about it or forgotten the key in the moment. That, or they didn't fancy going too close to the cliff edge. The lock was stiff but I eventually got the door open. A scent of musty dampness crept out to meet me. I grabbed my bag, stepped in and shut the door behind me. Finally, I felt safe.

The first thing I did was flip the light switch. Nothing happened, which figured. Too tired to explore, but desperate for a wee, I passed through the tiny kitchen and into a smallish living room. It was crammed with two big sofas, both sagging from use. The rest of the space was taken up by a pine coffee table and an old-fashioned wood stove. I could see the front door in the hallway beyond. Across from the living room was the bedroom, empty of furniture except an antique-looking wash basin. At the very back a built-in cupboard took up a square metre of space, floor to ceiling. Maybe Cat's aunt had decided the bed was the only thing worth saving from the cottage. Or it'd been too gross to keep – after all, this place had been a holiday let. God only knew what had gone on in these four walls.

At the end of the hall I finally found the bathroom. It was tacked on to the back of the house, close to the cliff edge. I could actually hear the sea through the wall. The door practically opened into the shower. My knees touched the bowl of the sink when I sat on the loo. It was only then that I realised there was probably no water. I got up and tried the flush, which, surprisingly, worked. I did the necessary and retraced my steps to the living room.

Using the phone's torch, I discovered some candles in a niche by the stove. I moved them to the coffee table and lit them. In their jagged light I saw the patches of black mould on the whitewashed walls, the holes chewed in the sofas by unknown teeth. This place hadn't been used for a long time. I hoped. Outside, the wind moaned softly, like it was in pain. I opened the back door to it and threw Cat's phone, as hard as I could, over the cliff. Hopefully the sea would take it somewhere far far away, or destroy it entirely.

I'd bought some food at the post office, along with matches and the local paper. But right then I didn't feel the least bit hungry. Thinking about it, I hadn't eaten since instant noodles the night before. Waiting for Cat to turn up for our big night out, dressed like a popstar and ready to lift my awful mood. My best friend.

A fist clenched around my stomach and I bowed over on the ratty sofa. The sobs took my breath away, as convulsive as vomiting. I moaned and howled with the wind, thoughts of Cat in that brown, stinking canal blotting out everything else. Even the faces of the people who'd done this to her. To us. I was safe from them now, but Cat was still dead. Dead and floating in the water, waiting to be found.

That woman might have been pure evil, just like her colleague, but she'd been right about one thing. This was my fault and I was a terrible friend. I'd been the one to drop my phone, lose my purse. I'd chosen the path we took through town, thinking it would be OK. That the chances of something happening to us were too low to worry about. I should have known better. I should have protected Cat.

The worst part was the memories last night had dredged up. Another night, just as dark and endless. Me with a skinful, miles from anywhere. How long had it been since I'd let myself go back there? Since I'd dared let that memory in?

It didn't happen often, but it was always there at every major turn my life took. When I left school a part of me was thinking about Chrissy. Two years behind me, she'd have been fourteen then. The same age I was when we met that night. She'd have been picking her GCSEs as I got pissed in the park with my mates, celebrating the end of school. Weeks to go until the start of college. I had no doubt her grades would've been better than mine.

When I hit eighteen I couldn't really celebrate my birthday. Not when she should've been having her sixteenth that year. Not that she'd be leaving school at that age. Chrissy was one of the ones that'd go straight to A levels, on to university. Probably pick a wholesome career too, like a teacher or a vet.

At twenty I thought of how she'd never get dropped off at uni by her family. The same family I thought about every Christmas. Every New Year's Eve and summer holiday. A family without her in it, because of me.

All those thoughts came crashing on me like a wave. Chrissy and Cat. My fault, both of them. I cried until I thought I'd pass out, but I stayed wide awake. I felt like a zombie; no matter how exhausted I became, there was no end to it. I couldn't just lie down and be still. If I stopped moving I'd have to think about it all again. There was no escape. No relief.

In need of a distraction, I found some wood in a basket by the stove and lit a fire. It smoked, but the chimney was clear enough to vent most of it. By fire- and candlelight I searched around until I found cleaning products in a bucket under the sink. Very old products but still, bleach was bleach. I cleaned the walls and scoured the kitchen and bathroom. Finally I got down on my hands and knees, scrubbing the floor from end to end. With each bucket of black water I tossed off the cliff, I felt, if not better, at least more in control. Pushing those memories down where they belonged.

While checking the kitchen cupboards for nests of mice I found a faded ring binder. On the front was a peeling label that read 'Guest Information'. The pages inside were stippled with mildew but still readable. Inside that binder was everything a guest needed to know: that the electric was metered and the post office was the nearest top-up point, the water was a private supply and the drainage went to a septic tank buried nearby. No mention of wifi, or much in the way of mod cons. Not that it mattered. I felt like I deserved the horrible dampness and the lack of anything modern. Like this was the prison cell I'd been dodging for years. It was where I deserved to be, waiting to fall off the cliff. Waiting for my worthless life to end.

Part of me knew I wasn't entirely to blame, for Cat at least. But it was a very small part. The guilt was just too strong. It pulled at me like the current in the canal, dragging me under. That guilt had a voice that sounded a lot like Scarlett. It hissed out of the darkness, telling me that I deserved this. All of it. Living in a cold, damp little cottage would be like serving a sentence for what I'd allowed to happen to Cat. To Chrissy. Punishment for everything that I'd done wrong and tried to block out.

Thinking of Scarlett filled me with dread. I kept racking my brain, trying to think of any way she might find me. I'd run away with practically nothing, left nothing behind that might lead her here. I'd only told them my address, not Cat's, and they didn't know her full name. Well, until I phoned the police and told them. What if they found Cat's flat and went through her emails as I'd done? I'd deleted the one I knew about but what if there were more? Would they put it together? Or would they be satisfied with my disappearance, with my silence?

I knew deep down that if I would never feel safe from them, they'd never feel safe from me. As long as they knew I was out there, somewhere, they'd want me dealt with. I had to make sure that I was ready, if it ever came to it.

For the train down I'd taken one of Damian's books to stop people talking to me or noticing the tears I couldn't hold back. But I'd ended up reading it anyway. I'd already had some ideas for keeping myself safe. I couldn't be sure after all that those two bastards wouldn't search Cat's history and find out about the cottage, though I hoped to be gone by then. More than that, I knew first-hand how dangerous the world was for a girl alone, like me. I never wanted to feel that way again.

This cottage was a prison, but it was also going to be my fortress for the time being. A clifftop castle locked up tight against the outside world. Not just with spotlights and an alarm system, the best my limited cash could buy, but with the traps and fortifications in Damian's books.

As dawn light began to creep in through the dirty windows I stood back and looked over the place I was going to call home. Every inch of it was bare but clean; only the muck on the outside of the window panes remained. My sleeping bag was unrolled on one of the faded sofas and the tins and packets I'd bought at the shop were lined up on the kitchen counter. Beside them I'd set up the tiny gas stove and the two cooking pots I'd found in a cupboard.

I cast about for something else to keep me occupied but there was nothing. Only the watery dawn and a deep ache of exhaustion that not even guilt and fear could stave off. I collapsed onto the sleeping bag fully clothed.

Lying there I felt my body shut down, limb by limb going limp. Staring at the ceiling I made myself a promise. If those people came looking for me, to cover their asses by making me disappear, they'd be in for a hell of a surprise. I was not going to hold back. If I had to, I would do whatever it took to defend myself. To end the people who'd taken Cat from me.

As if by giving them justice I could somehow escape it myself.

Chapter Sixteen

Midnight

One and a half hours into the blackout

Facedown in the muck I heard footsteps running towards me. My bones were still jangling from the fall, my lungs seized up and winded. There was no time to shake it off and get back to my feet. No chance of outrunning them when they had momentum and I was barely able to breathe. For a moment pure panic seized hold of me. I couldn't think, couldn't move. I might as well have been back there, that night, drugged and limp.

Then, sense returned. My brain screamed at me to move, so I did, in the only way I could. I sank my fingers into the dense black mud and dragged myself off the path. Slithering on my belly into the ferns I pressed my face to the ground and prayed to become invisible. I held my breath and forced myself to stay as still as possible.

In the first piece of good luck I'd had since arriving home, the footsteps passed me. Heavy, practised steps, used to chasing people down. I was out of my league. It was probably too dark for them to see my footprints in the mud – that, or there were so many from my runs that they were next to useless. I waited for the sound of their running to fade. My constricted lungs were easing and I managed to get to my feet.

Following them was out of the question. At any point they might decide they'd missed me and come back. I had to get to the Simmonses' house. They were the only people around for miles; the one chance I had of outnumbering and, hopefully, outgunning my pursuers. Reg hated strangers but, more than that, he hated any and all officials. I'd seen him chase a council enforcement officer out of the gate before with a rusty farm tool that looked like a machete. Even Davy didn't dare go up to the house and he was just a postie. Two police out of their area on a midnight mission, trespassing on his land? He'd probably dreamed of something like that. All his conspiracy theories were coming home to roost tonight.

I struggled out of the ditch and climbed the two-rail fence into one of Reg's fields. The ground was humped with thick tufts of grass and I didn't dare run full tilt, but I could jog. At least my steps were virtually silent on the springy turf. Looking around I couldn't see any lights at the farmhouse; obviously they were blacked out too. But I knew by memory which way to go.

Inside I was still reeling from seeing the two of them again, from being at their mercy. I'd had nightmares about them, heard Scarlett's voice in my worst moments telling me it was all my fault. I'd felt Craig's hands on me as I wrenched myself awake in a cold sweat. Now they were here in the flesh and I was completely helpless. At least, until I got to the Simmonses' house and found backup. There was no doubt in my mind that the pair of them had come all the way from Bristol to kill me. It was just my luck that they'd come when half my defences were useless in a blackout.

The lack of lights at the house started to bother me as I did my best to jog through the boggy field. I'd always assumed the Simmonses to be quite self-sufficient, maybe with an emergency generator or solar battery. But then again, a man who fixed his fences with bits of old furniture and sold eggs in the same cartons every week wasn't the kind to splash out on that kind of thing.

Looking up as I rounded a metal feed container I saw the house, standing out as a black hulk against the night sky. I was going the right way. No sound of the others; they were probably still on the way round via the path.

The rain was still hammering down on me, making it hard to keep my head up. Eyes glued to the ground and one hand shielding my face, I nearly blundered into an open-fronted shed. Startled bleating greeted me and a great mass of sheep shivered into action, drawing back from me.

'Shhh,' I said, stupidly, afraid the noise would bring my pursuers running.

The sheep did actually quieten, though they continued to huff out clouds of foggy breath. I could feel them watching me, trying to work out if I was meant to be there or not. It was oddly warm in the shed, despite the open side. Heat rose off the packed bodies of the animals. Even that trace of warmth made me shiver. My jumper and trackie bottoms were soaked through and rain was running off my hair and down my back.

For a second I considered hiding in there with the sheep, out of the weather. No one was going to come looking for me out here, surely? I could hide and stay warm until morning. Maybe it was the best option. I sighed, annoyed with myself. That was just exhaustion and fear talking. The urge to cram myself into a hiding place and stay there. Well, that hadn't worked out for me before, had it? In the end they'd come to the cottage and I knew they wouldn't give up now. I had to find help.

I left the sheep to their shelter and crept towards the farmyard. As I approached I bent low and moved slowly, listening for any sign of my pursuers. There was nothing. At least, nothing I could hear over the gale and the waves of rain. I couldn't see their torches either. Cutting across the field meant I'd arrived first while they were on the longer path. Falling might have actually helped me. I was both relieved and annoyed with myself. I should have realised cutting across country was the only way to beat them here. Dumb luck wasn't a survival strategy. It would eventually run out. I had to be smarter, better. What had all my time at the cottage been for, if I was still just as unprepared as I'd been then?

Even with no sign of them my heart was in my throat as I climbed the fence and crossed the open yard. I felt too exposed on the concrete forecourt, between the sheds and the house. I finally exhaled when I reached the shadow of the porch, only to suck in another breath as I knocked loudly on the door, praying Reg would hear and the others wouldn't.

Waiting for an answer I pressed my face to the glass panels in the front door. Not a single light inside, which wasn't odd given the power cut. Reg and Sue were probably still asleep. I knocked again, harder this time. Surely they had a candle handy in case of emergency? How long would it take to light it and come downstairs?

Peering through the glass I almost jumped out of my skin to see a pair of yellow eyes looking back. Duzzy was sitting on the stairs inside, tail waving. What the hell was he doing in there? He was a barn cat and that's where the Simmonses kept him, along with his brothers and sisters. Unlike their pair of prized sheepdogs, he wasn't allowed in the house. That was why he came around the cottage, wailing for treats and attention.

I felt a chill in the pit of my stomach. Something was wrong here. Duzzy wasn't allowed in the house, Sue would've put him out if she saw him, and no one was coming to the door. Where was everyone?

Looking down I could see the door handle but no keys in it. No release handle either. Breaking the glass wouldn't do much more than make noise. I'd have to check the back of the house, or the windows. I looked behind me for torches in the dark. In the distance I saw a flash, and that was enough for me. There wasn't much time. If I wasn't armed or inside by the time they got here, I'd be going up against the two of them empty-handed and alone. A fight I couldn't win.

The back of the house faced a cliff, though at a greater distance than the cottage did. It was also where they apparently stored anything and everything

162

that they hadn't found a use for yet. I had to navigate piles of broken furniture, bits of plumbing, rusty tools and empty paint tins – all half consumed by brambles – to reach the back door. I kept hitting stuff and making a noise, and more than once I heard something scampering away into the darkness. Rats, or rabbits? Either way Duzzy and friends weren't doing their job.

I finally battled my way through the weed-choked rubbish to the back door. There I saw how Duzzy had got inside: a dog flap leading from a wire-fenced run to the kitchen. The other end of the run was attached to a shed further back from the house. Probably for the dogs themselves. The cat must have clawed his way up the fence and over the top. Fortunately there was a human-sized way into the dog run. I unlatched the gate and crawled into the house through the dog flap.

Inside, the house was very still and felt weirdly normal after everything I'd gone through to reach it. A faint smell of toast, washing powder and wet dog food surrounded me. Duzzy raced across the lino and twined himself around my legs, mewing for attention. I shushed him and tried to get my bearings. I'd never been this far into the house before. I'd only really seen the front room from the door. The kitchen was big and, from what I could see, packed with yet more junk. By the dim moonlight I could see boxes and sacks of bulk feed and human food stacked together. An enormous bale of toilet rolls was wedged into a kitchen chair like it was waiting to be served. On the counter, though, I noticed two bags of pet food and a piece of paper in a clear spot. I took it to the back door to read by the window.

> *Mary,*
> ~~*Dogs – 1 red cup each 2x per day plus half a can of*~~
> *Change of plan, Sue said dogs should be boarded if we're away for 2 weeks. Just see to the cats (and make sure the flap is locked or they'll come in).*
> *Cats – 2 blue cups per day, bowls in barn.*

They were away.

I scrunched the note in my hand, overwhelmed by fear and frustration. Reg and Sue were off on holiday or whatever and I was all alone. Not even the dogs were here to scare the police off. Fuck. No one to rescue me, no one to tell me what to do. It was all up to me, again.

I dropped the ball of paper and hurried out of the kitchen, bashing my leg on a chair as I did so. I limped towards the front room. A large bay window let in the chilly moonlight, though with all the cloud cover it was blotchy and fleeting. Sue and Reg were gone. I needed help. I needed a phone.

Duzzy leapt up on a spindly hall table, startling me. He knocked over something fragile-sounding and I jumped, then spotted the phone beside him. He looked down at it with fatheaded confusion, then bolted when I leapt on the handset. Landlines worked in a power cut. I knew that from all the times the meter had gone dead at home. As long as the phone lines weren't down in the storm, I could call the local police for help. They didn't have any loyalty to two invaders from Bristol. I didn't even need to tell them who was chasing me. Screw worrying about my past. I just wanted to survive the night.

I brought the handset to my ear, then frantically jabbed buttons. It was dead. Stupid cordless phone! It had probably been left out of the base unit for too long. I looked around but couldn't see any glowing lights amongst the decorations. If the unit was in here it was also dead. Why couldn't they have a normal, old-fashioned landline?

No neighbours and now no phone. That just left the gun cabinet in the front room. I wasn't too sure what the law was but the little diamonds of glass in the front seemed like a security risk. It wasn't really a cabinet for guns at all, just one that Reg had clearly repurposed. That was how I'd noticed

165

the guns to begin with, through the glass. I fumbled for the handle and found a padlock drilled into it, with no key attached. Great. One look around the cluttered room told me that searching for it was no use. Every surface was covered in stuff. I could just make out the shadowy shapes of dozens of china dogs, sitting or lying on piles of papers. No time to check under everything for one tiny key.

Grabbing the sturdiest-looking dog ornament, I swung it at the glass. It spider-webbed and the dog's leg chipped off. I swung again. The glass broke and I tossed the trinket aside, reaching in to grab the cold barrel of Reg's shotgun. It was an awkward angle and the glass still in the frame cut into my hand. It didn't matter, I just needed the gun. I finally got a good grip and lifted, inching it out through the hole, only to have the end get stuck. I jiggled and yanked as hard as I could but it wasn't coming out. The gun was too big for the tiny windows. I dropped it and it smacked back down, very loud in the still house.

There had to be a way to widen the hole. I pulled hard on the wooden frame that held the glass. It didn't budge, so I stepped back and tried kicking it a few times. The whole cabinet wobbled on its feet but nothing gave. Frustrated I whirled around, looking for something to prise at it with.

In the corner of the room, surrounded by a whole pack of china dogs, was a fireplace. A poker set stood out against the pale tiles. Perfect. I knocked the lot over when I grabbed a poker and hissed at the sudden noise. Not that it mattered; I was about to make more noise than the storm outside.

I wedged the tip of the poker into the lattice on the cabinet and leant my weight against it. There was a promising creak but then nothing more. Where had he found this thing? It was built like a safe. I tried the other way. This time something cracked. Unfortunately I also heard voices from outside. They were nearby, almost here.

In one final attempt at getting my hands on a gun, I smashed at the padlock with the poker, then, when that didn't work, I pulled the whole cabinet over to break the front. The voices outside became louder and closer as I hauled the cabinet over to have a look. Some of the wood lattice was fractured, splintering away from the sides, but when I tugged on it, there wasn't much movement.

I wasn't getting anything out of there in a hurry and I was out of time. At least I had the poker. Maybe I could get back to the kitchen and grab a knife? That was when I heard them, right outside. So close I could hear Craig panting from the run.

I instinctively dropped to my knees, only moments before a torch beam danced across the living room through the window. On my hands and knees I shuffled behind the sofa and glanced around quickly, looking for an escape. In my hurry to duck and crawl I'd dropped the poker. It was all the way across the room, out of reach.

'Think she stopped here?' Craig whispered.

'Not sure . . .' Footsteps crunched over the mucky concrete. 'She might've come here to get help.'

Craig swore. 'We should leave. Before anyone else gets involved.'

'Bit quiet though,' Scarlett said, ignoring him. 'You'd think a soaking wet, hysterical neighbour would send the house into a spin. I can't hear a thing.'

Slowly I inched towards the hallway, crawling beside a very confused Duzzy. When I reached the kitchen I started opening drawers as quickly and quietly as possible. In the dark my fingers searched for anything sharp but found only scraps of paper, batteries, piping bags and cookie cutters. At last I found a drawer full of jangling cutlery. I grabbed a large carving knife and held onto it as if it was the last ticket out of hell.

Pages from one of Damian's books flashed before my eyes: jugular vein, heart, kidneys, lungs. Cut a man's throat and he drowns silently in his own blood. I'd never practised that stuff. No real way to, was there, until it came down to it. Until you were creeping up behind a person with a knife in your fist. Could I do that to someone? Take a weapon and end their life on purpose? Would I even get the chance to face that question? It wasn't like I didn't have deaths on my conscience already, but this would be something else entirely.

Where could I go now? Back out into the storm? Aside from the Simmonses' the only place to go was the lighthouse. No one worked up there anymore. It was all computer operated. Probably monitored from somewhere hundreds of miles away by another computer. But, I realised, it had to have some kind of backup power for emergencies like this. Perhaps there was a way to call for help too? Or something I could unplug to get some emergency assistance? At the very least, a solid door to put between me and my pursuers.

My eyes fell on a Barbour jacket draped over a chair. It was obviously Reg's, big enough for his grizzly bear proportions. I dropped the knife and grabbed the coat, pulling it on over my soaking wet jumper. If I was going back out into the storm, I needed all the protection from the cold and wet that I could get.

As I tucked my drenched hair into the hood of the coat I heard the front door crash open. It rebounded off the wall with the force of the kick that had splintered it from the frame. I immediately grabbed the knife up off the table and whirled towards the back door, just in time to be blinded by torchlight.

Chapter Seventeen

01:00

Two and a half hours into the blackout

As the back door crashed inwards I realised that they'd caught me in a simple manoeuvre. One I should have expected. Stupid, stupid Megan. They were the police, they knew how to box someone in. How many times had I seen them do it? On the estate and on those weekday morning TV shows. Two cops at the front door, two waiting to grab you by the jacket if you bolted out the back. I hadn't thought, hadn't planned. Now I was cornered.

I'd only taken two steps towards the hallway when I saw Craig coming through the front door, blocking the only other way out. He came running down the hall at me. I darted to the side, circled the kitchen island and looked back at Scarlett, who was blocking the back door.

'Time to give up now, Megan,' she said. 'No more games.'

She moved towards me and I brought the knife up, swiping it through the air.

'Stay back!'

It had the desired effect – she stopped moving – but I saw her gaze dart sideways. I only just turned in time to raise the knife at Craig, who was trying to creep up on me.

'I said, back off!' My own voice sounded strange to me, high and panicked.

Craig raised his hands and took a half step backwards. 'Don't do anything stupid now.'

I laughed, though it came out all choked up and wrong. 'I suppose they train you for stuff like this, do they? Go on, what does the rule book say about confronting women you tried to kill?'

I turned and waved the knife at Scarlett, who'd inched slightly closer. Or was it my imagination? I shuffled my wet slippers on the floor like a boxer, pivoting between them. It was like something out of a horror film. Every time I looked away they crept just a little bit closer.

'It says deal with her before she opens her mouth,' Craig said shortly. I turned back to him.

'Who said I was going to do that, eh? It's been

a year. A year since you killed my best friend, and God help me but I haven't said a thing. Nothing. So why the fuck are you here? Why don't you just leave me alone? I haven't done anything to you!'

Scarlett laughed, short and sharp. Her words from that night came back to me. She'd said I deserved it. I thought she just hated me because I was out late, drunk. Maybe it was more. Maybe this wasn't just about where I'd been and what I was doing, but about me. A chill ran over me. Maybe she knew something.

Craig looked past me at Scarlett and slowly shook his head. 'Things've changed.'

'What. Things?' I ground out.

Scarlett clicked her tongue. 'Craig messed up again.'

'Shut it, Scar,' he snapped.

'Why? We're going to kill her anyway – does it really matter? It'd be kind of nice to tell someone the truth, for once. Even if it is her.'

I glanced over at her. She'd crossed her arms and was leaning against the counter furthest from me. Her body language was casual, but her eyes glittered with the same fury I'd seen by the canal that night. Even in the semi-darkness of the kitchen, it was clear she loathed me. Maybe even more than he did. I just couldn't understand why. If she did know about what I'd done and this was some kind of vigilante thing, how the hell had she managed to find me that night, out of hundreds of other drunk girls? And if she was only out for justice, why let Craig hurt Cat? She'd been a partier, sure, but Cat was the sweetest person ever. She'd never even shoplifted as a kid.

'We don't have time for messing about,' Craig said, but she cut him off acidly.

'Craig here got a taste for it after what happened to your friend. Or he always did and he just used what happened to get me to go along with it.'

'I told you to shut up!' Craig spat.

'You shut up!' she roared, shining her torch on him. 'I've had it with dealing with your mess and your sick little mind.' She jabbed a finger hard at her temple. She'd lost her cap at some point and pushed the hood back. Her dark hair stuck up all over, half wet and all windswept. She looked deranged.

'This is your mess,' Craig snarled.

'Yeah, well, I think I've more than paid for it.'

'It was her idea, you know,' Craig said, pulling me back to him with his sudden pleading tone. 'She told me to do it that night, in the car. Said it was to teach you a lesson. That we ought to drop you and your mate off in the middle of nowhere, scare you a little. Leave you for whatever creeps came around. It never would've happened if it wasn't for her.'

'Scare them, that's all I said,' Scarlett shot back. 'Leave it to chance. Not what you did.'

'You didn't stop me though – I saw you. You

174

thought she deserved it. You didn't say it but I knew what you wanted me to do to them.'

For the first time, Scarlett was silent, breathing heavily. My head was spinning. The two of them were ripping into one another and I was just stuck between them, struggling to keep up. Scarlett had planned that night? How, when we hadn't even known we'd end up in that house, that the police would be called? I was certain I'd never met her before, but maybe she knew about my past. Maybe she was one of those cops like in Damian's films. The ones that don't play by the rules and get justice without paperwork and courtrooms.

The ceasefire didn't last for long. Scarlett piped up, changing the subject.

'You didn't say anything, but one of the others did,' she said. 'One girl cries rape, not that hard to gloss over, but if you turn up talking about rape and murder, well . . . that's another crime entirely. One they might actually take seriously.'

Her voice was so bitter I could almost feel the heat of her words in the air. Like sparks flying up from a collapsing bonfire. I flinched at the thought. The memory of that place, of that night, didn't belong here with these two, in this room. Yet I felt like I was right and this was about what I'd done. She sounded so furious at the lack of justice, though it seemed that need for it didn't apply to her.

'I'm not going to say anything,' I said, thinking maybe that would help get rid of them. Craig wasn't some kind of warrior for justice. That was obvious. I could maybe sway him. Though hearing that someone else out there had spoken out, that I wouldn't be alone, was a powerful thing. I just wanted to get away from them. Later, perhaps, I could tell someone what happened and finally, finally, feel safe. But something must've shown in my voice or on my face, because when I looked back at Craig, his own face was set.

'Nice try. But I'm not going to prison and you can put me there so . . . you're not leaving this house.'

He lunged at me but I was ready. As he'd spoken I'd tensed up, sensing what was coming. As soon as he moved I threw myself at the island counter, rolled over it and ran past him, through the unguarded door, further in to the house. Unfortunately the fear in my chest got the better of me. Instead of heading for the front door and the raging storm outside, I scrambled up the stairs towards the first floor. It was impulse, the urge to stay inside and get behind a door. No matter that they could just kick it in. My instincts drove me to find a hiding spot like a child would – under the bed or in the wardrobe, where the monsters couldn't get me.

I'd just put one foot on the landing when someone grabbed my other leg. I twisted, kicking out, and

176

was pulled to the floor. I lost my grip on the knife as I went down, clawing for purchase. It was Craig, pulling me downstairs by my ankle. Although carpeted, the steps still bruised me and my head hit the top one, making my vision swim.

'Got her!' he shouted, breathing heavily. He let go of my ankle and made a grab for the waistband of my joggers. I heard Scarlett call instructions but my own pulse was too loud to make out the words. I had to get away.

I kicked out with my free foot. In my head I could see the words, black type on yellowing paper, 'crush the larynx'. I aimed my slipper at his Adam's apple but he ducked at the last minute and I missed. My kick landed on the side of his nose. I felt a crunch through the thin sole of the soaked shoe. Craig roared and clapped a hand to his face, the other one still reaching for me as he rose to his full height.

I kicked out again. This time it wasn't some SAS guide that directed me, but personal experience. My foot hit his crotch with all the strength I could muster and he curled in on himself, dropping onto the stairs and clutching at the carpet for purchase. I clawed my way up the stairs and ran for the first door I laid eyes on.

'You let her go?' Scarlett shouted.

'Get after her!' Craig wheezed.

After slamming the door shut I searched for a lock but found nothing by the handle. Peering around in the dark I realised I was in a spare bedroom, possibly a child's old room. Everything was half-sized. There was a small chair in the corner and I grabbed it and shoved it under the door handle. Not a moment too soon. The door shook as someone tried to open it, then I heard Scarlett's muttered curse.

Without the knife, I was once again empty-handed, defenceless. Looking around I tried to spot a potential weapon but there was nothing. Tiny books on a mini-chest of drawers, dusty toys piled in a corner, a mobile clogged with cobwebs. Nothing I could turn into a weapon. But there was a window. A way out.

I rushed across the room and unscrewed the fastening, hoisting the sash window up. The wind flew in, stirring up decades of dust and pushing me away from the ledge. I gripped the frame and climbed onto the sill, one leg out and dangling down the side of the house as I looked down. And down.

There was no annexe roof, no garden wall to jump to. Just a straight fall down into long grass studded with rusted scrap metal, rubbish bags and bits of rotting wood. I'd never thought of a first floor as being high up before. But now that I was halfway over the sill, it seemed a long drop. Deadly even. What if I hit my head? Split it open like a jar of jam on the rusty washing machine below? What if I broke my leg and they got me anyway? Even if I made it, where was I going to go? There was nothing out there to help me, nowhere to hide. The lighthouse was up a rocky incline from this side of the clifftop – a mini cliff in itself. I looked out of the window as Scarlett pounded on the door. Beyond the drop, the edge of the cliff was a clear line against the starry sky. Not close enough that I was worried about falling, but offering me an escape route if I chose to take it. A permanent one, but at least one on my terms. One that would deny Craig the pleasure of ending my life.

Behind me, someone thrust their body against the door, making it shudder in its frame. Scarlett, or maybe Craig if he'd recovered. The two of them would get through in no time. The little chair shifted on the dusty carpet, old wood groaning. I heard a crack like a gunshot, then Scarlett burst through the door, skidding on bits of smashed chair as she ran towards me. When she looked up and saw where I was, she came to a standstill, arms up.

'Wait!'

I was out of time and out of chances. I swung my leg over, and dropped.

Chapter Eighteen

01:30

Three hours into the blackout

If it hadn't been raining so hard, for so long, I'd probably have broken my legs. Or my back. Instead, when I hit the ground and tried to roll, all the wind was knocked out of me. A second later I hit my head on something hard and angular. Searing pain shot through my skull and was joined by a burst of pure agony in my shoulder. Clutching at it I felt something hard against my fingers and moaned in pain. My legs and back were fine, but I'd been stabbed.

A jagged piece of wood had gone right through the coat and into my arm. My fingertips found the slippery wound and I gagged, rolling onto my front. The splinter was several inches long and felt about the width of an index finger. I had no idea how much of it had gone in, but it felt like it was in danger of poking out the other side. I jostled it by accident and another wave of white-hot pain went through me. I screamed.

From above me I heard Scarlett shouting and Craig's answering yell. In a few moments they'd be on me and a spear through the arm would be the least of my problems. Dizzy and sick, I managed to get to my feet, though the ground lurched underneath me. Rain ran off my scalp and into my eyes, blinding me with watered-down blood from a cut on my forehead.

I tried to move but taking a step made my whole body shift, muscles contracting. My shoulder burned. I wouldn't get far with that thing stuck in me. With trembling hands I gripped the chunk of wood, shallow, uneven breaths making me shudder. With a sudden wrench I pulled it out. My scream bounced off the house and out over the cliff.

Clutching my shoulder I set off at a lurching run. Behind the Simmonses' house the cliff sloped steeply up towards the lighthouse. As I dragged myself up the first rise I could see it – the only light for miles. It might as well have been the moon for how far away it was. But I had to try. I had to get there. It was my only chance.

Looking behind me I saw Scarlett leave the back door and peer into the storm. A moment later she spotted me and came running up the slope. I turned and hurriedly began to climb, gritting my teeth against the pain in my shoulder. I had nothing left. No fight in me. If they caught me again, it was all over. All I could do was climb.

The turf and mud quickly gave way to rocks and tufts of razor-sharp seagrass. The strands slid through my wet hands like the piano wire strung across the cottage. Each new cut stung feeling back into my numb hands. The rain seemed like it was coming from the lighthouse itself, thrown down on me to keep me away. I could feel hot blood dripping down my chest from the wound in my shoulder. It soaked into my sodden clothes and turned cold as I climbed.

Every time my slippers lost purchase on the rocks and I dropped, my heart leaped into my throat. It wrenched my shoulder and made me feel nauseous, the pain blooming red behind my eyes. If I fell, I would keep falling, unable to stop myself, and this time I would not survive the landing.

A scream from below had me peering back into the darkness. Was that Scarlett or the wind? Had she fallen a few feet, or was she rolling towards the cliff edge? I couldn't see her, or Craig, but that wasn't any guarantee. Visibility was incredibly poor. Below me the rain struck the rocks and threw up mist. It was as if I'd climbed higher than the clouds. I could hardly even see ahead of me.

I held tight to the rocks and kept going, pulling myself up and up, towards the lighthouse. I'd only gone a few more feet when a fork of lightning hit the cliff only yards above me, to be overlapped immediately by a deafening roar of thunder.

The lightning was so close, it had a sound. A sound like nothing I'd ever heard before. The cliff lit up in fluorescent white, the lighthouse a black pillar that remained even when I closed my eyes. For a few seconds it sounded like the cliff itself was coming apart, cracking and ripping open underneath me. My heart was in my throat, beating hard enough to choke me. Then the light was gone and the hissing barrage of the rain was audible again.

Terrified that I'd be the next thing struck by lightning, I climbed as fast as I could. Rocks grazed my hands and caught my clothes, rivers of water gushed between the boulders and threatened to wash me away, but finally I reached out and grabbed turf. I'd reached the highest point of the cliff, and the lighthouse.

With the last of my strength I pulled myself up, crawling on the drenched ground. With limbs like overstretched rubber bands I could only lie there a moment, struggling to breathe. Then a threatening rumble overhead had me scrambling to my feet. I wasn't safe yet – from the storm or my pursuers.

I had to find some way inside. Even an automated

lighthouse needed a door, and this one had a crew at some point. The keeper whose family had once lived in my cottage. I ran for the shadowy bulk of the building, desperate for a way out of the rain and into the safety of the lighthouse.

I'd come up on the wrong side of the building. I had to circle it to find a door. As I did so I looked for any sign of sunrise but it was still a long way off. Hours to go probably. Even then it'd have to fight its way through the storm. Although it made it easier for me to hide, I was craving the safety of daylight like an animal. As if the sun had the power to end this nightmare. The only thing that could save me now was outside help and I knew it. I had to find a way to raise the alarm and get someone to respond. Anyone.

At the front of the lighthouse an overgrown patch of gravel led to the door. I looked for an emergency phone, like the ones near beaches, but there was nothing. Any kind of help was clearly locked up inside. Locked being the operative word.

The lighthouse door was dense and mostly metal, with a tiny window of wired glass at the top. The sight of a card reader made my heart leap, as I hoped that, like most magnetic locks, it had released during the blackout. Like the ones back at college, which popped open every time there was a fire drill. But the door wouldn't budge. Either the same emergency power that kept the light going was also wired to the door, or there was another lock somewhere.

I searched frantically, looking for a release or a hidden key, but found nothing. The lighthouse was locked up tightly and there was nothing I could do to get it open. What the hell was I going to do now?

Looking down the slope towards the lane I briefly considered trying to make it back to the cottage on foot. The two of them had turned up in a car – perhaps they'd left the keys inside? Probably not the kind of thing police were prone to do, but they'd certainly made mistakes before. Or else I could get inside the cottage and get a knife, maybe hide somewhere and catch one or both of them by surprise? Not a terrible plan, but I wasn't sure I could bring myself to use any of the moves from Damian's books. Maybe with enough of a head start I could try and make it back to Churchcliffe across country where they couldn't catch up with me in the car. Though in the state I was in, I'd struggle to make it. It was so far it'd be hours before I reached the town. If I didn't get lost in the dark and freeze or fall off the cliff.

It was no use. I was spent and there was no way I could get all the way back to the cottage before one or both of them caught up to me. For all I knew one of them had already gone back there to head me off. They'd caught me in a pincer movement at the house before, after all.

Turning back to the door I looked helplessly for an alarm that I could trigger. Surely this place had some kind of security system? After banging my fists against the door and shaking the card reader as hard as I could, I had to admit defeat. If there was an alarm I couldn't trigger it. Unless I found a way to break the window?

Searching the ground for a rock that was big enough, I cast frequent looks towards the cliff edge. No sign yet of Scarlett or Craig. Perhaps they were struggling with the climb or one of them really had fallen and the other was trying to help them. Either way, I'd take it.

Finally, near the end of the lane, I found a large piece of flint. If the window glass was wired to an alarm, this would set it off all right. It had to. If it didn't I had no idea what I'd do. I was out of options and probably almost out of time.

I turned back to the lighthouse, rock in hand. I nearly dropped it when I saw Scarlett standing there, soaked to the skin and blocking the door. Her hair was like seaweed plastered to her face. For a moment she looked like a vengeful ghost belched up by the sea.

Unsure what to do, my body made the choice for me, jerking back towards the lane. The rock slipped out of my hand as I went. My one chance at escape. Before I'd even registered the shape of a person in front of me, Craig had me by the shoulders. Within seconds he'd turned me round and wrapped an arm around my throat.

I bucked and clawed but there was no getting away from him. His feet were too firmly planted for me to pull him over and he soon had my wrists pinned to the small of my back. With two quick kicks he had my legs out from under me. I crashed to my knees in the wet mud and he dropped to a crouch to keep me there.

Though watering eyes I watched Scarlett come closer. When she was only a few feet away she stopped and let out a sigh. Not of disappointment but of satisfaction. She knew as well as I did that the chase was over. They had me and I wasn't getting away again. Not with Craig's ham-like arm crushing my windpipe and his other hand restraining my wrists.

'I'm thinking we chuck her off the cliff,' he panted, hot breath against my neck. 'Make it look like she jumped? Looking at that cottage, anyone'd think she had a reason to.'

'And the house?' Scarlett said.

'Burglars. Unrelated. That place was seriously old-school. No surveillance. If they bother to check and find her prints, they'll probably think she was trying to rip them off in the blackout. She's got previous.'

188

'Yeah . . . she does.' Scarlett settled a hard glare on me, one that contained an emotion I couldn't quite read. Something like rage but more bitter, more complex. Uncertainty pulsed in my gut. What was this about? Who was she really?

'He'll get you too,' I managed to get out around the forearm wrapped round my neck.

'Shut up.' Craig shook me.

'You know what he did.'

'I said, shut it! Come on, Scar, are we doing this or not? No more time to waste if we want to get home before they find her.' He leaned in close to my ear. '*If* they find her – you might end up like your friend, all bloated and blue, swallowed up with the rest of the trash.'

I snarled through clenched teeth, felt hot spittle run down my chin as I thrashed in his arms. The thought of Cat, kind, funny Cat, rotting in the river, had been in my nightmares for a year. I couldn't stand it. He only laughed and choked me back like I was a rabid dog. When he pressed a wet kiss behind my ear I lost my mind, struggling without reason or thought of escape. I wasn't trying to get away, I was trying to get at him. I wanted to claw his eyes out.

'We don't have time for you to get nasty with her,' Scarlett spat. 'Jesus Christ, Craig. You really don't know when to pack it in, do you? The whole reason we're here is because of you.'

'Bullshit. You started this when you directed me out there that night. Slipped that GHB to them. The whole vial! You should've known what was going to happen.'

'I never meant for her to die,' she said, softly now, but dangerously, like she was daring him to go on.

'You meant something,' he said.

'You both killed her,' I choked out. 'She never hurt anyone in her whole life. You killed my best friend, for nothing.'

Scarlett moved too fast for me to brace myself. She crossed the space between us and grabbed me by the hair, pulling so hard I felt it tear at the roots.

'You killed your "best friend" by being an evil little cow. If it wasn't for you, she'd have been fine. You're the one who got her killed by getting her drunk and high and off in the back end of nowhere.'

She slapped me across the face with an ice-cold hand, then dragged me back by the hair so I had to look her in the eye.

'But she wasn't the first – was she?' Scarlett said.

My mouth moved but I couldn't dredge up the words. Couldn't think of a thing to defend myself with. I wanted to deny it, to tell her she was crazy, but I couldn't. I knew who she was talking about. But how could she know? It was impossible. No one knew the full extent of what I'd done. Even Damian only ever had half the story. But I could

190

see it in her face. She knew that I was to blame for it all. That I had another death besides Cat's on my conscience. And this one was my fault and only mine.

The dying bonfire flashed before me. The smell of sticky sweet booze and skunky weed, dead leaves and wet earth. The sound of running feet, screaming, retching. The sudden quiet.

'Starting to sink in now, is it?' she hissed. 'This isn't about your friend, about that night. This is about what you did to Chrissy.'

Suddenly the year in hiding didn't matter, and the time before that was washed away. With just the sound of that name, I was fourteen again. I wasn't remembering those sights, those sounds, I was trapped with them. Trapped and alone with what I'd done.

Chapter Nineteen

2013

'Come back here!'

Sam and I made it around the corner and up the bank towards the railway tunnel before he was even out of the shop. He was never going to follow us up there. You could get jumped under the bridge. For all he knew we had a gang of lads waiting for him to puff his way up to us in his saggy trackies. Sad old git.

'You bloody bitches!' I heard him yell after us. Followed by a loud car horn and some swearing. He'd probably stopped right in the road.

I collapsed against the wet brick wall under the arch and laughed myself breathless. Sam, her bag weighed down with a bottle of cider the size of a toddler, wheezed along with me.

'Did you see his face?' she choked, trying to do

an impression of huffy confusion but crumpling back into giggles. 'You know he loves it, don't you? Having an excuse to chase after a pair of girls. Probably gone back to rub one out behind the counter.'

'Gross, Sam!'

'Me? He's the one doing it.' She made a filthy gesture and my imagination did the rest. I choked on a laugh and felt snot bubble out of my nose.

'Gross, Meg!' Sam mimicked, ending with a wet snort.

'Stop it! I'm gonna die,' I shrieked, holding my side where a stitch still had a grip on me.

'I'll get you next time, you bloody bitches!' Sam gasped, in a near perfect impression of the cashier. 'Just as soon as I get my slippers on!'

My laughter turned into a high-pitched whistle. Finally, Sam jumped at me, twirling us round. My own bag, stuffed with WKD and Smirnoff Ice, jangled like wind chimes.

'Get off! You'll break them!' I giggled, shoving her.

Calmer now, we headed through the tunnel and back towards the flats. Sam lived in one of the houses clustered around the bottom of my block. We mostly hung out at hers because there was more room and her parents worked shifts. The only time they were at home was when they were in bed with earplugs in. They also had more money than us and only one kid. So they had better snacks and a PlayStation 3. If it wasn't for Damian I'd have never been at home.

Tonight, though, we were going to have a party and that meant going back to mine for supplies. Sam's house had Mini Rolls and Monster Munch, but mine had the hottest clothes and cartons of foreign cigarettes.

'We're back!' I called from the front door.

'Keep it down!' Damian's mate Gary roared back.

I found them in the lounge with two guys I didn't know and another one of Damian's pub friends, Billy. The air was blue with smoke and smelled like stale lager – the familiar smell their weed left behind. Not that they weren't also drinking lager. Damian wasn't really a 'who wants a cuppa' kind of guy. Come to it, none of us were really. Mum had diet cola with her breakfast.

Damian and one of the new guys were showing each other pictures on their phones – either cars or tits, it was hard to tell from their faces. Billy was on our old PS2, running around shooting enemy soldiers, and the other two were exchanging cash. For what I didn't know. Could've been anything.

'Got any more of that stuff? We're having a party tonight,' Sam piped up, miming a bong. Though neither of us had ever actually seen one in real life. Everyone we knew smoked joints.

'Where's the party?' one of the new guys asked, looking up from his phone.

Sam went all flirty. 'Down by the cycle path, in the woods. Want to come?'

195

He exchanged looks with his friend and they sniggered. 'Jelly and ice-cream, is it? We gonna play pass the parcel?'

'Fuck off,' Sam said sweetly, landing on the sofa in a puff of dust and helping herself to a can.

'You want a drink too, sexy?' the guy dealing with Gary asked.

'Hey, that's my sister,' Damian said.

He held up his hands. 'No worries. But maybe she might be interested in some of what I've got on hand – for the party, eh?'

'She don't touch that stuff, mate,' Damian said, bristling. The easy atmosphere was turning thick around me and I wondered what the fuck he'd been thinking, bringing these guys into the flat. At least Mum and her boyfriend were both away. Though I had no idea when they were due back from Calais. Her latest was always on at Damian to get a proper job and 'contribute'. Like he could talk.

'Too right,' the guy agreed. 'I'd never let my sister near it. But she don't have to do it to move it. She's what, fifteen?'

'Fourteen,' Damian said, pointedly.

'Even better. No one's going to charge her. If anyone catches her – which they won't – she'll just get a warning.'

Damian just looked at him, but I could see him thinking. Considering. Obviously they were talking about dealing. Not weed, because I'd done that with Damian, but something else. I wondered if that meant I could take some to the party. Forget the cider, that'd show Nicole and her mates right up.

Besides, we could use the money. Mum emptied her account to go on this trip to France with Jason. God forbid he ever pay for anything. All right, so they were bringing back fags to sell, but until they did we were stuck. The landline was already cut off, and if we didn't feed the meter we'd be sitting in the dark by Saturday night.

'What is it?' Sam piped up. 'I'll do it if she won't.' This set off some sniggers and Sam blushed bright pink. 'Shove off!'

'She'll do it,' Damian said, talking over her. He shook hands with the guy, who took out a plastic baggy of pills and handed it over.

'Same cut as your boy,' he said. 'She sells the lot, I can get more by next week.'

Damian handed the bag to me. 'MDMA – you want fifteen quid per pill, OK?'

I turned the bag over. I'd not seen pills like this before. I'd blagged my way into a few clubs with Sam and some others and seen people with them before. But those pills were white, or capsules. These were kind of cute actually, pale blue and stamped with a heart.

'I could sell some too,' Sam pouted.

Damian's new friend laughed. 'See how she does. Could be a whole new market.'

'Come on, let's go get ready.' I snagged Sam's hand. There was something off about these two guys and I knew Damian felt it too. To them he probably looked relaxed but I knew him too well to be fooled. My older brother was definitely on edge and not happy with the way this meet-up had gone. I could tell he didn't want me around those guys, but they hadn't given him much of a choice. I had no idea who they even were.

I wondered if they were some of the people we owed money to. Well, not us, but Jason. Odd people came around sometimes looking for Mum's boyfriends and Jason was the worst by far. People were always knocking and demanding cash or to know where he was. Most of the time he bunged them some money and they left, but if he wasn't around, like now, they sometimes got nasty or took stuff. A week or so ago someone had taken Mum's stereo and the microwave. Something to do with dog racing. We were both getting pretty sick of Jason. I hoped Mum would too, before someone nicked the PS2 or the TV.

In my room Sam upended a bin-liner of clothes I'd just had from Auntie Faye, my dad's sister. He might've pissed off but she stayed in touch. She had two girls a few years older than me and sent us all their old stuff. She had two cars and a hot tub at her house and was probably the richest person I knew in real life, mostly because she'd married a travel agent. It annoyed Mum that she sent stuff, like we were a charity, but we both loved going through it.

'Ooh, yes please.' Sam held a red halter top up and checked herself out in my bedroom mirror. 'How would I look in this?'

'Like someone who hasn't got boobs yet.'

'Bitch.' She threw the top at me and picked up a crop top with long princess sleeves instead. 'How do they get through so much stuff?'

'No idea. Mum says it's just throwing money away. Some of the stuff still has tags on it. She returned some jeans the other month and got enough for a full week of shopping.'

Sam whistled. 'Wish I had posh cousins.'

'You are the posh cousin.'

She stuck her tongue out and picked a pair of jeans from the tangled heap of clothes. I dug around looking for something that wouldn't make me look like someone's chubby little sister. Both of Faye's daughters were taller and thinner than me and wore some very skimpy stuff. Sometimes it was like getting a bag of clothes from outer space, the kind of things they sent. Tops with weird ties, trousers with diagonal zips or made of shiny, cold fabric. Skirts you tied shut through metal loops, jumpers with

199

high necks and no sleeves, and jackets made of bright-coloured fur. It didn't matter how skinny you were, if you wore some of that shit around here, you'd have the piss ripped out of you.

In the end I settled on a long black skirt with a slit in it. For a top I went with a purple strappy vest under a sort of poncho made of black glittery threads with lots of holes in it. I also stole Mum's black boots. She was going to kill me when I ended up getting mud all over them. It was worth it though, I was looking quite witchy, especially once Sam did my eyes and lips in shades of dark purple.

Sam herself went with the crop top and a teeny, tiny skirt almost thinner than the belt she wore with it. Though she did wear tights, which was a good thing because it got cold and wet out in those woods.

'Jesus, you look like you've got two black eyes,' Billy laughed, when I passed the living room.

'So will you if you don't shut it,' I said.

A chorus of sarcastic 'ooooohs' followed me to the front door, broken only by whistling as Sam strutted down the hall. I rolled my eyes and tucked the pills into a little Chinese silk pouch that hung around my neck, normally reserved for my lighter and cash. It gave me a thrill to have them there. Tonight I was the one who'd be making money for the family. Not Damian. Tonight I wasn't anyone's little sister – I was all grown up.

Chapter Twenty

Our usual meet-up spot was well off the road and hard to find unless you knew it was there already. I had no idea who'd found it first. Maybe no one knew anymore. It was a great place to hang out – no nosy people passing by or houses to overlook us. No one to call the police if you lit a bonfire or got a bit loud. It was as close to the middle of nowhere as you could get without actually leaving town.

Sam and I left the flats and headed straight for the cycle path. It wound its way under and around the railway tracks and we followed. Eventually, at an overpass, we climbed up the steep bank and made it to a sports field. I had to practically drag Sam up behind me. She was wearing spike heels and they kept getting stuck in the mud.

'Don't laugh!'

'You're walking like a duck. I'm gonna laugh.'

Across the field there was a hole in the fence and a steep narrow track probably made by rabbits or foxes at some point. Now it was ours. At the bottom we picked our way over a metal grate and hopped a greyish stream flowing out of a drainpipe. It splashed its way around piles of old cans and bottles, throwing up yellow foam. Finally, under the cover of trees, I saw the glint of a bonfire. We weren't the first ones to arrive.

There were about fifteen people gathered around the fire on logs and plastic crates. From the sounds of it there were others off in the darkened woods, hooking up or dealing. Someone was playing music on their phone. I dumped my bag of alcopops by a huge tyre and took a seat beside them. Sam gave me a nudge and went over to Sean on the edge of the fire's circle. Under his arm she practically disappeared. I knew she wouldn't come out again until it was time to leave. I didn't really get what she saw in Sean. Catch me squatting under some boy's stinking armpit. You could smell the fumes of Lynx from all the way across the clearing.

Speaking of bad smells, it wasn't long before Nicole saw me and came over, towing two girls with her. One of them I knew – Kim, from a few floors up from us. One of Nicole's tough mates. The other wasn't even trying to hide her age like the rest of us. She looked like she'd taken a wrong turn on her way home from school – jeans, pink top and an Alice band, for fuck sake. Even Nicole didn't dress that cutesy. She had on some ripped jeans and real Converse. Though she still had the same hairstyle as her mum. Right down to the fringe. Embarrassing.

'You came then,' She said, then eyed my bag of drinks. 'You're not seriously going to try and get drunk off them, are you? Like you need the calories.'

I clenched my teeth. Nicole was like Sam – she lived in one of the houses on the edge of the estate and she liked to think she was all that. Problem was, it was hard to contradict her. Her parents bought her a jumbo trampoline, Sky TV and anything else she wanted. Even when we were little kids she had all the Barbies and the dolls you saw in adverts on TV, not the no-name knock-offs from the market. She was IT. Had been ever since we were like six and her family was the only one that could afford to go to Disney. The American one.

Her mum taught aerobics at the leisure centre and Nicole was always talking about slimming, toning and trimming. She brought a can of diet shake to school in her handbag every day, while I had a bread bag with salad cream sandwiches in it. The only difference between her and Sam was that Sam knew what she had and shared it around. Nicole held it over everyone so she could watch them beg like starving puppies.

'I don't drink them – but I thought you kids might like it,' I said, trying to match her sneer with one of my own. 'Like your little friend there. Is she not late for her bedtime?'

Alice Band blushed and looked away. Nicole grabbed her hand and yanked her forward.

'Chrissy is from the riding club. We're going to the new girls' school together when I transfer next year.' The end of each sentence rose like a question, just missing a 'like, duh' to really cap it off.

I felt a weird mixture of envy and satisfaction. If Nicole was moving to the new school I wouldn't have to deal with her anymore. But it also meant she'd be guaranteed a place in their college and be going to a school with its own pool, gymnastics equipment and computer room. I'd been to a jumble sale there with Mum once and it was insane in there.

'Where's your little friend anyway – getting off with Sean Weaver?'

I prayed she wouldn't spot Sam huddled under his puffer jacket. Nicole was even worse when she knew she was right.

'Anyway, I promised I'd show Chrissy a fun party, not stand around talking to chavs all night, so . . .' Nicole snapped her fingers and turned away.

'You want a fun party?' I heard myself say. I wasn't really thinking, I just wanted to get her, once and for all. Show her I could be IT too. 'How about an E?'

Nicole turned back to me. My heart was thumping with nerves but I took the pills out and showed them off to her.

'How did you get those?' Kim said, sounding just slightly impressed.

'They're probably sweets,' Nicole sneered.

'No, they're from one of Damian's contacts. Genuine MDMA – fifteen quid.'

'Fifteen quid?' Nicole said. 'All that proves is you're a con artist, just like your brother.'

I felt my face go hot. 'He's never conned anyone. You're just scared to try it. Or you can't afford it. Which is a shame,' I said, brain finally firing, 'because on one of these you'd dance all night and not have to worry about the calories in a Bacardi Breezer.'

I watched Nicole lick her lips and knew I had her. It was a matter of record that she'd been making herself sick for months now. I got it from someone who actually heard her do it. Not that I hadn't suspected it. Nicole's mum was an aerobic stick with perfect everything. Nicole had to be perfect too. Sometimes I almost felt sorry for her, before I remembered how she treated me and everyone else and that she had two weeks abroad every year as well as a pet chinchilla.

Still, she wasn't stupid.

'Give it to Chrissy,' she said, gesturing at her friend, who looked like she wanted to melt into the

205

shadows and disappear. 'She gets a freebie and if it works I'll pay double for hers and get one for me as well.'

'Oi, and me,' Kim said, folding her arms. Nicole rolled her eyes but nodded.

I wasn't so sure all of a sudden. Damian had said to get fifteen quid per pill. He hadn't said anything about free samples. Still, if that free pill got me sixty quid back . . .

I weighed my options. Nicole was a bitch but she had money. There was no doubt in my mind that she'd want to rub that in my face more than she wanted to skip out without paying.

'Sure – horse girl gets first try.' I dug my fingers into the bag and pulled out a single pale blue pill. It felt slightly crumbly, like it wasn't pressed together tight enough. I wondered who Damian's mate had making these things. I could probably do a better job.

Nicole shoved Chrissy forward. 'Come on, it'll be fun.'

Chrissy looked at me with wide brown eyes, but she held her hand out like an obedient puppet.

'Tongue,' I said. 'So I know you took it – no saying, "It doesn't work" and bagging it for later.'

'She's not a cheat,' Nicole said. Then, to Chrissy, 'Do it.'

She poked out her tongue and I dropped the pill

onto it, then watched her swallow. She showed me her tongue again, her brow already creased with worry.

'How long is it going to take to kick in?' Nicole demanded.

Fuck. I didn't know. 'Like, half an hour?'

Nicole's eyes narrowed but she jerked her head for them to come over to the fire. 'We'll be back. If it doesn't do anything, you'll be sorry.'

Kim shot me a look that promised a beat-down and I swallowed. Kim might not have liked Nicole – even Nicole knew that – but she did like going round her house and watching her big TV and eating fancy ice-cream all summer. So if Nicole told her to smack me senseless, she'd do it, no questions asked. There was a rumour that Kim had once put a boy's head through a window because he touched her arse. Out in the woods she'd have to get more creative.

I watched them help themselves to drinks and then move off to another part of the clearing. My insides squirmed with worry. What was I going to do if the pills were duds? Or if they didn't work that fast? If they didn't come back to pay for it I'd owe Damian's friend fifteen pounds. Meaning my first chance at making money for the family would have cost me more than it made. Then I'd have my arse handed to me by Kim and her footballer muscles. Fantastic.

I decided to calm down with a drink and helped myself to an alcopop. Screw Nicole and her stupid comments. I chugged about half then topped it up with someone else's vodka.

With Sam busy with Sean there wasn't anyone I really wanted to talk to. Everyone had come partnered up and the few girls who also had best mates that were off sucking face hadn't turned up tonight. It was just me being a sad loner. I also kept worrying about the pills, trying to think of a way out of the mess I'd made for myself.

I must've gotten up at some point because I realised I was on the opposite side of the fire to where I'd started. I was also on the ground, with my back against a log. The wet mud had soaked into the back of my skirt. I'd drunk more than I usually did, out of boredom, and I was pretty wasted, nodding off on the spot. That was probably why it took me so long to realise that something was wrong.

At first I thought someone had fallen down, or that there was a fight. Nothing special. There was a tide of people moving towards the trees and there were raised voices, shrieks of alarm. Then Sam was dragging me up by my arm.

'Come on, you fucking moron, we've got to go – now!'

Tripping over my feet I let Sam haul me across the clearing and back towards the stream. I was confused, wondering if someone had called the police. But there were no adult voices, no lights and sirens. It had actually gone a bit quiet. Very quiet. I twisted around and looked back.

Most of the others had legged it into the woods. Which explained the sudden lack of noise. But there was still someone there, bending over someone on the ground. The fire behind them made both figures look too big, shifting with the shadows.

'Wha's happ'nin'?' I managed, my throat burning with bile as my stomach sloshed around inside me.

I wasn't prepared for the slap. Sam absolutely belted me across the face. It was sharp and stinging, but also sobering. I clutched my cheek and looked at her. For the first time I realised how scared she was; her eyes were really wide and her skin was dead white.

'What happened?' I said, clearer now. 'Did Sean do something, because I swear—'

'He didn't do anything. It's Nicole and her new mate.'

I knew then, before she even said it. I felt a deep cold take me over, realising what those words meant. What the figures by the fire were all about. Sam said it anyway.

'She won't wake up. They've probably called 999, we need to get out of here.'

I looked back again. I knew it was Chrissy on the ground and I swear to God I felt it when Nicole, hunched over her, looked up at me. I felt it all the way through me.

'Megan!' she howled, though Sam was already dragging me across the stream and up the dark slope. 'This is all your fault!'

Chapter Twenty-One

We fell a lot in the dark on the slippery mud and
leaf mulch. I was too numb to care about it. Sam
was clearly too afraid to slow down. At one point
when we rejoined the cycle track we heard sirens
on the overpass and she pushed me into the long
grass to hide. But the car blazed off on the road
and we carried on, back towards the flats.

'Keys,' Sam said, snapping her fingers in front of
my face. I was leaning on the doorframe, swaying.
I reached for the silk purse around my neck but it
was gone. No keys, no pills.

Sam swore, then hammered on the door with the
heel of her hand.

Damian was still up, watching a war film on TV.
I could hear the gunfire through the front door. It
was so loud it took ages for him to answer Sam's
panicked knocking.

'Jesus, what happened to the pair of you?' he asked, then frowned. 'Give me his name – I swear I'll kill him.'

I looked down and realised that my clothes were smeared with mud. The split in my skirt had ripped and there were bits of leaf and twig in the poncho. Even to my booze-soaked brain it was clear what Damian thought had happened. He ushered us both inside to have a look at me under the light. I felt for the wall to lean on it but somehow missed and stumbled. Damian grabbed me and parked me against the hall table.

'She's blackout drunk. Christ, Sam – you're meant to be her friend! What happened to her? You fucking tell me his name, right now, or I swear—'

'Nothing happened to her!' Sam said, jerking the door shut behind us. 'It's not some bloke you need to be worried about. It's the cops.'

'What happened?' Damian asked again, a deeper panic creeping into his voice.

'Those pills from your new mate? They're dodgy. Probably cut with drain cleaner or something.'

'Shit. Shit.' Damian grabbed her by the shoulders. 'Who took 'em – what happened?'

Sam struggled. 'I don't know who had them. But I turned around and there's some girl on the ground, with Nicole throwing up next to her, and she points at me and says "Megan". Just that. Megan. So I got her out of there. Everyone was freaking out, running, talking about calling 999 . . .'

Damian punched the wall, leaving a fat hole in the plasterboard. Sam barely flinched.

'Where are the rest of the pills?' he demanded, rounding on me.

I shook my head helplessly. I felt like I was about to pass out, or be sick. Maybe both. I felt all cold and somehow sweaty. The hallway was rolling around me.

'She lost them,' Sam said. 'Her neck thingy's gone. Someone must've taken them while she was out of it.'

'Did they call the police?' Damian asked.

'I don't know. Like I said, I just got her out of there. You're welcome, by the way,' Sam snapped.

Damian looked ready to punch her.

'You said . . .' I managed. 'You said they called 999.'

'I didn't want to stick around for that.'

'But someone did? Someone was coming to help?' I asked.

Sam and Damian looked at me, then at each other. Damian went grey. Sam didn't look much better.

'They're probably fine,' Sam said eventually. 'Nicole was throwing up. Probably didn't have time to kick in.'

'What about the other girl?' I winced at the shrill sound of my own voice.

'Don't worry about them right now. Worry about you.' Damian caught hold of me and started pushing me towards the bathroom. 'Get cleaned up and into bed – anyone asks, you were here all night.'

'Right,' Sam said. 'I'll talk to Sean, get our stories straight.'

'No texts. No phone,' Damian ordered. 'Go to his and tell him, then get home and stay there.'

'But Nicole saw us there, her and Kim and this new girl. Plus everyone else,' Sam said.

'Did anyone else see Megan with the pills?'

'No . . . maybe . . . Look, I don't know!' Sam yelled. 'But what if someone did? Anyone could've.'

'And if they're not totally stupid, they'll keep it to themselves. Trust me. This kind of thing, no one saw it happen, and even if they were there, they weren't.' He rubbed a hand over his face. 'As long as everyone keeps quiet, no one gets in trouble.'

Sam nodded and disappeared up the hall. A moment later I heard the front door. Damian sighed and gestured to the bathroom. Unable to think of anything else to do, I went inside and managed to turn on the shower. Too unstable to undress standing up, I collapsed on the toilet lid and pulled at Mum's boots, prising them off and getting mud all over my hands.

Damian came in while I was behind the curtain, staring stupidly into the running water. I heard him gathering up my clothes and the rustle of a rubbish bag. Then a few seconds of silence.

'It's gonna be OK, Meg,' he said quietly. 'I'm not going to let anything happen to you. Never should've involved you in this.'

My brain was still working too slowly to say anything back. I heard him leave and stepped under the shower, letting water fill my ears. Resting my forehead on the tiled wall I listened to the drone of the shower unit and tried to get the image of the fire and those two figures out of my head.

Damian ordered me out of the shower a while later. I had no idea how long I'd been in there. But I tripped out and got into a towel, made it to bed. He'd put a mug of instant coffee on the bedside table.

'Drink that – it's got six spoons in it. Gotta sober you up a bit in case the police come round.'

After making me drain the whole thing and dosing me with painkillers he finally left me alone. Despite the coffee I fell asleep quite quickly, though the bitter black liquid warred with the vodka in my stomach. But it wasn't really anything like sleep. I was aware for quite a lot of it but unable to move, ever so often slipping into something deeper than sleep.

When I finally snapped out of it and dragged my heavy body upright I felt like death. My head was banging and there was a big mark on the carpet like it had been scrubbed raw. The room smelled like vodka, coffee and rancid sick. Damian must've cleaned it up but I couldn't hear him moving around.

It took a while for me to get out of bed and shuffle to the lounge. He was in there, staring at the blank TV. The ashtray on the coffee table was full and there were rings all over it from many, many mugs of coffee.

'Damian?'

He turned slowly, like we were in one of my nightmares and he was going to have Dad's face when he turned round. But it was just Damian, looking exhausted and pale, his eyes ringed in red.

'What's happened?' I asked, though, like the sick churning in my gut, I could feel it there. The truth, hanging over us.

'She's missing, one of the girls. Christine Seaton.'

Chrissy. 'Missing? But I thought she and Nicole would be home by now, or in hospital . . .'

Damian acted like he hadn't heard me. 'Her parents said she wasn't in her room this morning – it was on the news already. Sweet little twelve-year-old goes missing.'

'Twelve?' I felt my skin go cold and tight. 'She was with Nicole. I thought she was our age. But . . .' I was scrambling, seizing at hope. 'If someone did call the police, an ambulance, then they must've found her by now? They'll tell her parents what hospital she's in.'

'Or,' Damian said, 'everyone left, even her mates, and she's still where they left her.'

He didn't say 'dead'. Neither of us did. But I felt both of us think it. Like even letting the word circle our minds changed the pressure in the room until it was suffocating. As if it'd crush us both.

I was shaking, but I couldn't move to one of the chairs. I just stood there on the spot, shivering with something more than cold. Clutching at my dressing gown and feeling very, very small.

'But . . .' I finally managed. 'Someone had to have called. They wouldn't just . . .'

Even as I thought the thought, I knew what had happened. I'd known Nicole and Kim for years. Since primary school. When trouble occurred they were the furthest from it, even if it was all their idea. For Kim it wasn't so bad – her mum cared less than mine did – but Nicole would do anything to avoid being told off in case it got back to her parents. Trouble meant no designer clothes, no phone, no end-of-year party at her place. I'd only seen a fully grounded Nicole once. We were like ten and she got caught scribbling over some girl's denim jacket with marker pens. Her dad took her new bike away and donated it that afternoon.

Nicole wasn't going to say anything and that meant Kim wasn't going to either. They were the only people who knew for sure where the pills had come from. Unless someone had seen me with them, but if they had, it wasn't like anyone down by the stream was keen on going to the police for anything.

'So,' Damian continued, in a weirdly mechanical voice. 'It looks like Nicole, and whoever else was there, isn't going to say anything. Hasn't yet, anyway. She was the one who took a fucking kid out there, she might've even taken the pills off you – shared them round. She'll cover her own arse.' He looked at me. 'You ought to be all right. By the time anyone finds her, no one'll be looking for you.'

'But . . .' I choked on silence for a moment. 'I have to tell someone. She's just out there, in the woods. Her parents are looking for her! I can't just keep quiet about what I did, how will they find her? I—'

Damian was in my face before I could finish, gripping my shoulders.

'You will say nothing,' he hissed. 'Christ, Meg. It's not just your arse on the line here – it's mine and Mum's for letting this happen and it's Jay Fucking West's pills in the mix.'

'That was one of the Wests?' I felt my heart clench tight, like Damian just announced I'd met the Devil in person. I'd never seen any of them in real life, only heard stories. None that I wanted to find myself in. The Wests did business all over our estate and the surrounding ones. For a while a few years ago they'd had a flat in the same building as us. One that had visitors at all hours and usually had girls in dressing gowns or pyjamas outside, smoking. I was too young to know what that was all about back then, but Damian never let me out of his sight until that flat was suddenly empty, taped off by the cops.

'If you talk, that brings them into it and that would be very bad for us. You wouldn't make it to court – they'd make you disappear. Make all of us disappear.'

'What do we do then?' I asked. 'We can't just leave her there. Can't just pretend this never happened.'

'That is exactly what we've got to do! Block it out, pretend nothing's wrong and get out of here as soon as we can. I can get us a flat over the other side of town and I'm going to see about finally joining the army.' I swallowed and he set his face, suddenly looking so much older than the Damian I knew. 'It's my job to take care of you. No one else is going to.'

I don't think I knew what fear was until that morning, with the numbing effect of the alcohol well and truly gone. That was when I saw what was hanging over us, the threat of prison, of losing our flat, of being on the wrong side of the Wests. The idea that I'd have to live the rest of my life knowing what I'd done, with that girl's death on my conscience.

The worst part was looking at my big brother and seeing how out of his depth he was. I'd always thought Damian was tough enough to protect me from anything. That he knew everything. But in that moment I realised he was just a teenager, like I was. He was only four years older than me and he was scared out of his mind.

'I'll never tell anyone,' I promised.

And I kept that promise. Even when I started to remember, to fill in the blanks of that night. Even once I knew that there had been no mistake but a clear choice. One I'd made all by myself, that had ended the life of a twelve-year-old girl. I wasn't sure if I kept it a secret to protect Damian or to protect me from losing his love, his care. Because if he'd known what I'd done he never could've forgiven me. Family or not, some things were just too much to come back from.

I kept it all to myself and never told a soul. Until the truth kicked my door in and cornered me on a dark clifftop, demanding answers.

Chapter Twenty-Two

02:00

Three and a half hours into the blackout

I stared at Scarlett in horror and she glared back, unflinching. She was tensed like a wire, sharp and dangerous. She was waiting, I realised. Waiting for me to speak first and damn myself. Waiting for any justification I could offer or just allowing me time to beg. To confess. None of it would help me, I knew that. Nothing I did could get the stain out of my conscience and it certainly wouldn't give Scarlett second thoughts. She had me and she wasn't letting me leave this clifftop alive. That much was obvious.

Why and how she knew, I had no idea. Perhaps there was something about it on record somewhere. Not enough to charge me with, but a suspicion.

Something she'd grabbed hold of to excuse what the pair of them had done to me and Cat.

Damian had been right that no one at the bonfire that night was going to talk. If any of them knew who'd given Chrissy the drugs they'd never said. I guessed it was only the four of us, plus Damian, who knew what happened.

Nicole transferred to the new girls' school and I never saw her again. After our move I stayed in the same school and gossip reached me when she got pregnant. I've no idea who by, but rumour was she had to marry the guy and her dad bought them a flat outside of town. Which figured – she fucked up and still ended up better off than me, than my whole family.

Without Nicole to keep sweet, Kim rarely came to school and last I heard she was locked up for helping her cousin out with a ram-raid on an off-licence. The last thing she needed was to confess she'd bullied a kid into taking drugs. Drugs that had caused her death.

I had no idea where Sam was now. If Sean ever knew what we got up to that night he never said. They broke up almost straightaway and her family moved up to Scotland for her dad's job. That was all I saw before she unfriended me everywhere online. I understood; after that night I couldn't see our friendship lasting. Better to cut ties than to have a reminder of it all every time we spoke.

Still, there was no way Sam would've told anyone about that night. It was a secret we both had to keep, for our own reasons. Though most of the blame was mine, she wasn't completely innocent either. She'd run like all the rest, leaving Chrissy to die.

None of them would have talked, certainly not to the police. So how did Scarlett know about that night? Why was she looking at me like she knew it all, even the parts I'd never spoken about to anyone?

Still she watched me, waiting. I wondered what she'd do to me if I dared say anything. Was she going to torture me? Interrogate me? Make me write it all down like a suicide note, to leave behind? That would keep the blame off them all right. Maybe it would even make me feel just a little better as I faded out of consciousness for the last time. Maybe then I'd finally be able to escape from the awful weight in my chest, the one I'd carried since I was fourteen years old.

It was weird but after all the fear of that night, the frenzied chase and my pathetic attempts to defend myself, I felt almost relieved. Not only because now the waiting was over, the awful paranoia and watchful fear. The pair of them had caught me, but also someone had finally come to punish me for what I'd done to Chrissy.

And Cat, part of me whispered. Pointlessly, because I'd never forget how badly I'd let my friend down by leading her off into the night. I'd led her right to these psychopaths and I'd never forgive myself for that.

'Nothing to say?' Scarlett asked, as I stood there, feeling the weight of my guilt threaten to crush me.

'Let's do this and get it over with,' Craig grunted, arm still tight around my throat. 'Toss her off the cliff, make it look like an accident, suicide, I don't give a shit.'

'Not until she admits what she did,' Scarlett said sharply. 'I never got the chance that night, not with what you did and the state the pair of them were in. But I still want my answers.'

'It was years ago,' Craig complained.

'She was my sister!' Scarlett cried out. 'You will never understand what that was like. How it felt to be so fucking helpless, to not know! So shut up, and let me talk to her.'

Sister? Oh God. Sickness swelled in my stomach. I knew nothing about Chrissy. Had only met her for a second about a decade ago. I hadn't known anything about her family. If Scarlett was her sister, that made the age gap between them at least ten years, maybe more. She looked about thirty-five now. Back then, when Chrissy died – when I killed her – Scarlett must've been my age now: mid-twenties. I couldn't imagine it. I'd been enough of a mess after Damian was hit by that cyclist, and that was just an accident. Plus he was an adult, not a kid. I'd known where he was and what happened. I looked at Scarlett and saw what the pain of not knowing had done to her. The deep and bitter fury in her was more powerful than any storm.

I'd never seen such an expression of hatred and rage on someone's face before. Despite feeling those things myself about her and what she'd allowed to happen to Cat, my hatred was tempered by shame and guilt. Maybe Scarlett felt the same about her little sister, who'd snuck off to a party and never come home. Maybe she wasn't just mourning her loss and blaming me, but blaming herself too, for not being there. For not knowing what there was no possible way she could have known.

'I was just starting out back then, new to the force,' she said, as if reading my mind. The wind shrieked around us, tossing her hair across her face, but she never broke eye contact. It was like she wanted to watch each word make its home in my very soul.

'It took three days for them to find her body. Can you even imagine what a city full of rats and foxes did to her in that time? Can you?' Her face twitched, caught between tears and fury, disgust and violence. 'When the investigator told me about the pills I knew they weren't hers. That someone had left them behind after they drugged my little sister. Chrissy would never have touched that stuff on her own. Wouldn't have taken anything from a strange man, because I always told her not to trust anyone like that. I knew it had to be someone around her age. A girl. But no one else cared what I thought. They saw those blue pills and it went straight to gangs – to the Wests. They wanted to get them at any cost. They only cared about using her picture to bring down the Wests. They wouldn't look anywhere else. She was just a . . . useful tool to them.'

Damian had nearly said as much when Chrissy was on the news the day after the party. A young, cute white girl from a nice family, gone missing from her bed? Of course it was straight into the local news. Then the national. Before we moved I used to see posters of Chrissy all over the estate. Big black letters on red paper: 'If you know what happened, you owe it to her. Speak out!' The police came and did an assembly at our school. I remembered white-knuckling my way through it, my belly sour and swirling with sick. Sam was across the hall from me. Getting as far from me as she could. But I felt her eyes on me.

I hadn't checked up on our old estate after Damian moved us away. Hadn't wanted to look back. To do that would be to let thoughts of that night in and I couldn't let that happen. If I let myself remember, I'd feel the guilt cut through me all over again. Fresh. Sharp. That would only lead to me talking, turning myself in. Putting myself and my family in danger and wasting all of Damian's effort in keeping me safe.

If my brother kept tabs on the Wests after we left, he never let on. After that night Damian was secretive, focused. He cut off a lot of his old friends, gave up old habits. The flat he found us wasn't full of guys hanging out and smoking, playing games; it was just the two of us. But now I wondered if all those posters had worked, before the rain battered them off telephone poles and fences. Maybe people had spoken out against the Wests. Maybe we'd run for no reason and I could've gone to the police with what happened when I could still bring myself to. Maybe I hadn't had to carry it with me all this time. No matter the consequences, I'd have been out from under the guilt. In prison, perhaps, or young offenders, but without it stuck in my mind like a shard of glass.

Maybe. Or maybe I'd still feel this guilt, this awful weight, even locked up by myself. Maybe there was just no escaping it.

'I found one of the girls she'd been friendly with,' Scarlett said. 'On my own. Out of uniform. It took some persuading but I got the truth out of her. Or enough of it to guess the rest. I had your name, and I found you online.'

Nicole, it had to be. Kim was tough, no way she'd crack. Fucking hell. I'd been so sure Nicole wouldn't talk. That she'd bury every hint of wrongdoing like she always had before. But maybe becoming a mum had softened her up, made her think twice about what she'd brought little Chrissy into. Or maybe things in her new flat weren't all rosy and she'd been so pissed off at the state of her life, she figured I needed tearing down too. What had she told Scarlett? That she'd taken Chrissy with her that night for a fun little party, a bit of harmless rebellion? Only then some nasty kids from the estate rocked up and ruined it all? What had she been thinking, dropping my name? She had to know I'd point the finger at her if I got caught. Perhaps she was counting on her reputation to defend her, that or she had convinced herself that she'd done nothing wrong.

Scarlett's jaw was tight and she shook her head. 'It was just her word. But I was going to get you for what you did – for giving my baby sister that shit . . . I was going to . . . but then I thought about my job, my parents. They'd been through enough, were barely hanging on. I wasn't going to put them through a trial – my trial. You weren't worth it. I figured you'd be dead soon anyway, keeping company with the Wests, pushing drugs. It was only a matter of time. So I left it and I let myself forget about

228

you, bit by bit, just carrying it around inside until I only searched for you every few months. Just to see. See what you were doing with the life Chrissy deserved to have. And every time you were just wasting it. Stealing, selling knock-offs, failing your exams and fucking posting about it like it was funny. Just a waste of life.'

I wanted to be angry, to defend myself. But she was right and I knew it. I hadn't done anything special, anything important. Despite avoiding prison or whatever would have happened to me if I told the truth. I hadn't done anything worthwhile with my stolen time. Just pissed it away like I did with everything back then: money, friendships, boyfriends. Let it all slip through my fingers as I wandered on, directionless. Even Damian had more of a purpose than me.

What had it all looked like to her? Like I was laughing at her, at all the pain I'd caused. Like I'd forgotten about Chrissy. To her it must've seemed like I hadn't learned anything, like I didn't care about what happened. She didn't know the half of it. All the stuff that had come back to me, more and more every time I peered into the dark parts of my memory. I wasn't partying. I was running. Every time I made a friend, got a boyfriend or a goodish job, I'd remember that I didn't deserve any of it. Then it was just a matter of time before I let it all fall apart.

Cat was the exception. She didn't let me ghost her or push her away. She kept turning up, kept inviting herself along. Like a stray that ran to greet me every time I set foot outside. Even when I tried to shut her out she found a way in. That's who she was – full of light, of energy. She wanted to cheer everyone up, make sure everyone was having a good time, and she could see that I wasn't. Cat followed me around relentlessly, trying to fix me, to get me to open up. She was always there with a bottle, a make-over or a movie. Always determined to make me feel good. Eventually it worked, mostly. I couldn't bring myself to tell her what I really was. What I'd done. But I hid that last bit of darkness really far down, never letting her even suspect it was there.

'Then that night happened. I think sometimes that I did as many weekend nights as possible, on the off-chance that I'd find you. But when it happened . . . I was just in shock. I never really thought I'd meet you, face to face.' Judging by the look in Scarlett's eyes, she wasn't with me on that cliff anymore. She was back there, in the police car, seeing me in the light for the first time. She looked like she'd been visited by a ghost. Perhaps that's how it had felt to see me. In the flesh, after so long looking at my life through a screen. I felt a shiver go through me. I'd been completely clueless as to who I was putting my trust in – a woman who'd practically stalked me, with plans to end my life.

'All that time later and you were still just the same piece of shit,' Scarlett ground out. 'Stumbling around with another drugged-up girl, endangering her life. I got back in that car and my mind was a mess. Then I thought, this is it, I'm going to have to kill her. It's the only way to make it stop. To stop you.' She was breathing fast, her eyes practically black in the shadows. 'I was trying to think, to plan, to get it straight in my head, then it all came back, the shame and the fear. If I got caught it would destroy my parents, all the work I'd done. The drug awareness days, the charity runs, all the people I'd managed to help. If they found out what I did, it'd all be for nothing. So I thought, fine, I can't kill her. But I can let her kill herself. You were already out of it, I guessed you were high like your friend, and no one was going to question some extra GHB in your system. We'd confiscated some and I gave you the lot. Thought I could dose you up, drop you in the middle of nowhere, wait for some other scumbag to take advantage. Maybe you'd fall in the canal, freeze or overdose. Maybe it'd be your eyes the foxes ate.'

She blinked and a fat tear slid down her cheek, shining on her chin in the torchlight.

'The more I thought about it on that drive, the

more I realised that girl with you was probably just the same as you are. Selfish, a waste of space. Only out for herself, for a good time. If she got lost out there with you, she probably deserved it. You both deserved to die, I just couldn't do it myself. I thought if I left it up to fate it would be like – judgement. What you deserved.' She sniffed, looking unsure of herself for the first time since confronting me. 'But what happened then . . . I never intended that.'

'Don't act like you didn't see it coming,' Craig said. 'The two of them out of it, dressed like that, in the middle of nowhere? You wanted it to go down like that, you're just too self-righteous to admit it. You wanted it to happen, you just didn't want to see it.'

'At least I can admit it was my choice to do it! That I decided to leave them there,' Scarlett snarled. 'She might be a piece of shit, but I can admit I chose to punish her. It was my decision. You just act like it's nothing to do with you. Like it's natural, or it's their fault! Every time! "They know the risk, what men are like"? Well, fuck you, Craig – it's bullshit and you know it. You're a rapist. A sick little man who doesn't want it when it's on offer, but'll batter someone to get it when it's not.'

I felt Craig's chest heaving at my back, furious hot breath on my neck.

'Fuck you, Scarlett.'

'Not even if you knocked me out first.'

There was a long, strained silence, filled only by the screeching of the wind and the lashing rain. Thunder rippled from further away but the storm around me wasn't just the weather. It was those two and their hatred for one another. Their shared guilt and me, the last thing that kept them trapped together. The last bit of evidence to destroy.

'Are you going to say anything?' Scarlett finally asked, grasping my chin and lifting my head. 'Anything at all – after what you did?'

There was a lot I wanted to say, but it wasn't Scarlett I wanted to say it to. Maybe if she hadn't killed Cat it would have been different. But she had. She'd snuffed out the one good person I'd ever called a friend. Someone who was everything I wished I was: smart, kind, generous. Cat might've liked short skirts, high heels and partying, but she wasn't a waste like me. Aside from Damian she was the best person I'd ever known. I wasn't about to apologise to her killer. No, the only person I wanted to plead my case to was Chrissy. I wanted to tell her that I was sorry, that if I could've changed places with her I would have. That even though I had killed her, I hadn't been trying to. That every nightmare I had would bring her face into my head. That I would never, ever forget what I'd done. What I'd had every chance not to do, but had anyway, for my own selfish needs.

But none of that would change anything. I'd made the worst choice of my life when I was fourteen and nothing could undo that. I knew that Scarlett didn't want my apologies or my guilty conscience. She wanted her sister back and nothing else mattered.

I wasn't just facing the sister of the girl I'd killed. I was face to face with the person who'd drugged Cat and let her get raped and dumped in the canal. I could never make things right with Chrissy. Scarlett could never make things right with Cat. Both of us were guilty as hell and neither of us were ever going to wash that stain off, no matter what.

I wasn't going to go to my death on the rocks below having apologised to Cat's killer. Scarlett would have her revenge when I hit the sea. I was going to get some for Cat before I left the ground, even if it was only a small, hollow hurt that I could inflict on her. I'd do it for Cat, and for the other poor girls Scarlett had turned a blind eye to.

'Yeah, I'll say something,' I managed, though Craig's arm was still pressing too hard on my windpipe. 'I deserve this . . . and I hope one day soon you get what's coming to you too. For letting this animal loose on my friend. Cat never hurt anyone, she was a good person, just like your sist—'

The punch hurt like a bitch. I was thrown back against Craig, who gripped me so tight I thought I'd suffocate. His fingers felt like they would meet around the bones in my wrists. A searing pain travelled through my nose and throbbed around my eyes. I wasn't going to live long enough to bruise, but if I was, I'd have two black eyes by noon.

'Careful!' Craig snapped. 'It's gonna look suspicious if they find her beaten up.'

'It's not going to matter after she hits the rocks,' Scarlett pointed out. 'Besides' – she looked me in the eye, her mouth twisting in grim satisfaction – 'with that storm out there I don't think anyone'll find her body. She'll be picked clean before her bones wash up somewhere far, far away.'

'Are we doing this then?' Craig said.

'Yeah . . . take her to the cliff.'

As Craig manhandled me away from the lighthouse, back towards the cliff edge, I felt weirdly calm. For several moments I could only think that it would finally be over. I wouldn't have to live with the guilt and the memories. Wouldn't have to spend every day missing my brother and carrying all that regret. Finally I'd have answered for what I'd done and could escape another few decades of a life spent in limbo.

Then I saw the cliff edge.

It stood out against the night sky like a patch of spilled ink. Above there were stars, and below nothingness. The black edge of the cliff blended with the dark air. Only far, far below could I see the shining white crests of waves against the pitch darkness. The very edge of the sea clawing at the rocks in great swells of water.

That was when fear took me over. The part of my brain that dealt with finer human emotions like guilt and regret was overwhelmed by the animal instinct to survive. I kicked and struggled, trying to unbalance my captor. I twisted and jerked and tried to bite the arm he had around my throat. Nothing I did made any difference. We moved forwards as one, with Scarlett trailing alongside.

Finally we reached the edge, where a broken wire fence was just visible in the grass. The wind threw itself against me and the pounding of the waves was almost deafening. I could feel it in my blood, stronger than my heartbeat. Pebbles of rain struck my face and I screwed my eyes shut, not only to protect them but so I wouldn't have to see the yawning terror below.

I don't know what I expected. For Scarlett to demand my last words or offer some final judgement. Something to mark the moment of her revenge. But no. One moment I was being crushed within Craig's grip. The next he'd let go of me and shoved me, hard, over the cliff.

A scream ripped loose from my bruised jaw. It bounced around, half swallowed by the wind and rain. Only cutting off when I landed, far below.

Chapter Twenty-Three

02:30

Four hours into the blackout

'Well, that's that handled,' Craig said, raising his voice against the wind. 'If we can beat the rush we'll get back to Bristol before anyone knows we're gone.'

'Hmmm. We should probably torch the house, just in case. We both left DNA behind. Not to mention she might have written something down about what happened. Something someone might find if they go looking for her.'

'If we have to. One last loose end to tie up, then it'll be over,' Craig agreed.

'I'm starting to think it'll never be over. I mean, I thought that was it, that night. That I'd finally get past all this, but . . . it just made it worse. What if doing this, coming here, only brings more shit down on me later?'

The pair of them were silent for a moment. The wind stirred the grasses and far below the sea crashed through crests of rock, foaming over the debris on the shore.

'It's not what you thought, is it? Revenge?' Craig said finally. 'You thought this would be a whole big moment and now it's just another thing you did. Another nobody dead. But hey, at least you got to kill her – that's what you wanted, right?'

'I don't know that killing her once is enough,' Scarlett said in a voice heavy as clay. 'What she did to my sister, my family . . . there's nothing that's enough for that. Nothing I could do anyway, and live with it afterwards. Christ, if I can even live with all this. Days like this, you really hope there's a hell. But I guess if she's there, I'd have to see her again one day.'

Craig sniffed. 'You're so bloody Catholic sometimes. All that doom and guilt business. I'm not too bothered. No offence, but as long as she can't spill her guts I couldn't give two shits if she rots in hell or the sea. Either keeps me out of trouble.'

'And if you end up facing the Devil someday?'

'Oh, he'd have to catch me first. And I don't intend to get caught. Besides, he's the Devil, right? He probably doesn't see the issue with it. I'm just doing what's natural. Following my urges. He'd be into that, right?'

'I meant it, you know – I think you're vile,' Scarlett said sharply, cutting into his light words. 'And I am never covering for you again – do you understand that? I am out. I'm going to put in for transfer as soon as we get back. Say I need to get away from Bristol, from what happened to Chrissy. That I can't take it anymore.'

For a long moment only the wind disturbed the silence.

'No, I don't think that'll happen,' Craig said eventually, as if to himself.

Scarlett clearly wasn't expecting that. Probably thought there was an explosion coming, rage and accusations. She stammered, 'What?'

'You're not going anywhere, Scar. We're a team. I like having you around.'

'You . . .' She floundered in obvious disbelief. 'You "like having me around" because I cover for you. Because you have something on me.'

'That's what makes this work so well. You know me and I know you and we both rub along together.'

'By "this" you mean the fact that I can't tell anyone about what you get up to? That I have to help you get the drunk girls home after you've got what you wanted out of them? That I help clean up your mess?' Her voice rose, getting louder and higher like

239

a kettle reaching its boiling point. 'I'm not doing it anymore.'

'Yeah, you are – unless you want me to dob you in for this. And for your part in that night. Drugging two girls, trying to dump them off by the canal. Killing one. Trying to kill the other.'

'You'd be damning yourself.'

'And so will you if you open your mouth.'

Scarlett was silent.

'You can't tell anyone about what I've done without letting on that you allowed it to happen. That you were part of it too,' Craig continued. 'And if you stop helping me and I get caught – which you insist I will because you are so much smarter than me – you're screwed. If I go down, I take you with me. So you can't end this. Because it'd end you.'

Still Scarlett said nothing. Maybe she had nothing to say. There was a ring of truth in Craig's assessment of things. That each of them could only hope to survive if the other kept their secrets. Just like the cliff and the sea below, they'd struck an uneasy balance. Neither one quite willing or able to let the other win. Until, inevitably, something had to give.

'Maybe I deserve to get caught.'

'What the fuck are you talking about?' Craig snapped, but he was afraid now. It was obvious. He'd outlined a future with only one possible outcome but this was not what he'd expected. He'd

240

brought out his nuclear option and Scarlett wasn't scared but reaching for the launch button.

'You heard me.' Suddenly Scarlett's voice was stronger than the wind and driving rain. Sharp and bright as lightning.

'Don't talk crap. You'd never do it. That'd be your career over, your face in all the papers. Your parents with the press outside their door. Their hero daughter carted off to prison and the whole community turning on them. Blaming them. Snatching back all the pity they've smothered on them over the years.'

'Maybe I think that's worth it? Maybe if it gets you out of my life and off the force, I'd do it.' The words were definite but her voice was desperate. It was obvious she wanted to believe them, but Craig's harsh image of what was to come was getting to her. It's easy, after all, to say you want to do the right thing. Doing it is something else entirely. Especially when you stand to lose everything, even your freedom.

Craig's voice became a shrill parody of hers. 'What about the "drug awareness days, the charity runs", all that shit you spouted about why you couldn't just do that bitch in yourself, ages ago? If you can't sacrifice your reputation to get revenge for your dead sister, you can't do it to get at me.'

'But I did kill her – didn't I?' Scarlett said quickly. 'I came up here with you, I chased her down and now she's at the bottom of the cliff. Dead.'

241

Craig was silent, not shocked but watchful. Waiting.

'You think I don't hate you as much as I hated her?' Scarlett seethed. 'That I don't think you're just as much of a piece of shit? She gave drugs to my twelve-year-old sister and you're a vile little rapist. Is there some kind of moral distinction there that I'm missing, where you're any better than her?'

He said nothing.

'You see, recently I've had to think a lot about what would happen if I got found out,' she continued, rallying now that he was speechless. 'About how it would look to my family, the world. Thinking about it, which is better? To be the policewoman who let her partner assault women and got caught? Or to be the policewoman who turned her partner in? I don't think there's much in it. But I'd rather be the evil woman who grew a conscience than the one that didn't. Don't you think?'

'I think,' Craig said, slowly, 'that you've missed a pretty big part of the equation here.'

'Oh yeah? Enlighten me.'

'You said it yourself. Police*woman*. Who do you think is going to get the worst of it if you bring all this out into the open? Hmm? You think what I did is even unusual? That it's not just white noise to the world now? You're the unnatural one, Scar. You're the one people are going to hate. A woman that lets other women get assaulted, that helped to do it?

That's newsworthy. That's incendiary. That's what they'll focus on, and all I'll have to do is let them tear you apart. A less than two percent conviction rate? – I'll take those odds. What do you think yours are with the CPS? With a jury? You're the one they'll make an example of. I'll be a footnote in your scandal. The murderer who let her partner get away with being a "vile rapist".'

'You . . .' she spluttered, unable to find a comeback, a counter to his version of their shared future. 'You . . . complete arsehole.'

'Takes one to know one, eh? You want to talk about who's better than who? Well, if I'm just as bad as that bitch at the bottom of the cliff – what does that make you? You want to play judge and jury, well, here's news for you – we're all guilty! Me with the girls, a teenage drug pusher, and you covering up for everything I've done and drugging some poor bitch to death. Just three terrible people on a clifftop, arguing about who's the worst.'

'And now it's down to two.'

'Yeah. Now it's just us, and you might talk the talk, but I don't think you've got the balls to go into the station tomorrow and tell everyone just how much of a terrible person you really are. When it comes down to it, you love yourself too much. Saint Scarlett of the junkies. With her fun runs,' he spat, voice dripping venom all over the words.

'You'll have to see, won't you?' Her voice was shaking, whether with anger or fear it was hard to tell. Perhaps even she didn't know. Maybe she really had no idea if she could turn herself in, but she just wanted to believe she could, in the face of his bile.

'You're not going to do it!' he thundered, but there was fear in all that arrogance, spreading like blood in the water. Maybe he didn't know what she was capable of either.

'Yes, I bloody well am!'

It was quite possible that Craig had never been denied before. That he'd gone from being coddled and excused as a kid to being a pushy and selfish adult. Maybe Scarlett really was the first person, the first woman, to be able to tell him 'no'. That, or the uncertainty was finally too much. She was a liability.

In either case, he couldn't take it.

'What are you doing?' Scarlett's voice was high and sharp as wire. 'Stop it! Let go of me, now! Craig – Craig!'

When it came, her scream cut through the air, spiralling down, down and ending with a sharp smack as her body hit the churning water and the jagged rocks beneath. Then, nothing. No cry for help, no screaming. Just the water sloshing over another piece of debris.

The wind died down just a little and the sound of Craig's heavy breathing was all that disturbed the silence on the clifftop. Then his footsteps squelched back a little, as if he was shocked by what he'd done with his own two hands.

'One last loose end,' he muttered, tonelessly. Then he turned and his footsteps slithered away from the cliff, from the lighthouse and back towards the lane. By the time he reached the gate, he was whistling tunelessly. Either because he didn't care what he'd done, or because the silence was too much for him to bear.

Chapter Twenty-Four

03:00

Four and a half hours into the blackout

My mouth was full of blood and even breathing hurt. Lying there, swayed by the storm around me, I heard it all play out above my head. The pair of them snapping at each other like dogs. Bickering, then scuffling, and finally the scream.

I can't explain how I felt, hearing Scarlett plummet into the sea. Most strongly came the bloody-toothed joy of vengeance. Then fury flooded up from my gut like acid. Anger at Craig, at Scarlett, at myself. But there was also a deep and toxic guilt. A type of hollow sadness for the woman who'd just crashed to her death, because of me.

If it wasn't for me, for what I'd done back then,

to Chrissy, Scarlett would never have become the person she was. Maybe without me she'd have been a great police officer. One of the ones who actually made a difference. Talking to kids like me and changing their paths. Or fighting back against slimy bastards like Craig. Changing things. Making things better. Without me, she wouldn't have been on the clifftop with that monster. She wouldn't be dead, cold and alone in the storming sea. But then, Cat wouldn't be dead either. In taking Chrissy's life, how many more had I ended, or ruined beyond recovery? How many more ghosts would I end up towing around for the rest of my days?

A loud creak interrupted my thoughts. Perhaps the 'rest of my days' wouldn't end up being that long at all. I'd escaped the death that had just claimed Scarlett. But not by much. I was still caught in a nightmare situation. Only this one had nothing to do with any person and more to do with luck. Bad or good, depending on the outcome.

When Craig shoved me off the cliff I thought it was the end. I went from ready to die to fighting to live. Neither decision really did much. It was pure dumb luck that a landslip had left an old, gnarled tree clinging on to the cliff. That I was in the right spot to smack straight into it, biting my tongue and probably breaking at least one rib. Now I could feel the tree shifting. Its roots were stuck in the clay soil but it was barely holding itself there. I could hear the old wood creaking and groaning at my added weight.

Without warning the whole tree dropped several inches. I cried out, scrabbled for purchase as the trunk tilted downwards. My bloody fingernails scraped at the dead wood. It held, swaying slightly as the wind swept around me. The tension in my body made the puncture wound in my shoulder flash with pain. Somehow I had to get my injured body off the tree and try to climb up the cliff. If I waited too long or made a mistake, it would be the last thing I did.

Unfortunately I was lying the wrong way. My feet were closest to the cliff and I was facing the crabbed branches and empty air. A deep dark drop that made my stomach turn over just looking at it. If I fell from this high up it didn't matter what I hit, I'd be dead. Just as Scarlett had intended. I wondered if she'd felt the tiniest bit of regret as she met the same fate she'd attempted to force on me. Though I doubted she'd had time to think much at all.

Slowly, hardly daring to breathe, I inched backwards. The tree bobbed in the wind and I stopped moving, began again. Over and over, with my heart between my teeth. Crawl, freeze, grip, wait, crawl. The closer I got to the base of the tree, the more unstable it felt. I was putting my weight on the anchor point, pushing the roots through the wet earth.

When the tree dropped again I was too scared to scream. I instinctively hugged the trunk, my cheek tight against the slick bark. I thought it would just keep going until it fell completely. My eyes were shut, my heart beating against my aching ribs. Then, finally, the tree stopped slipping. It swayed, but didn't move down.

When I opened my eyes to get my bearings I nearly threw up. I was looking almost straight down now, the white churning foam boiling over the rocks. Vertigo pulled at my brain, making me lurch headfirst. I caught myself on the tree trunk and shut my eyes again, tightly. No more looking.

Dizzy and panicked, I crawled backwards – too quickly. The tree bounced and the weathered wood popped and creaked. I forced myself to slow down. That tree had probably been hanging there for years, dead and scoured by salt wind. If I wasn't careful it would probably crack down the centre. Slowly, feeling more terrified by the minute, I shuffled backwards. Then, finally, I felt my feet touch the cliff.

I was shaking by this time, uncontrollably. With my eyes squeezed shut so I didn't have to look down I flicked my soaking slippers off, one after the other.

With a better grip and now able to feel where I was moving my feet, I slid back even further. But the further I moved, the more the tree shifted. Moving faster only made it worse but I couldn't bring myself to slow down. There was no time.

I was almost upright, both feet in the wet clay of the cliff, when the tree ripped free and fell. I screamed as roots pulled past me, nearly taking me with them. My arms flailed without support. I wrenched myself back, buried my fingers in the wet soil, and the tree slid out of the cliff, tumbling down and carving a deep gash into the cliff as it went. Then it hit the rocks below, with the splintering groan of hundreds of years of growth being destroyed in moments.

My injured shoulder was bleeding again, the only source of warmth. My stolen coat was pasted to me with rain, runoff and clay. Weighing me down. I still had to climb back up to safety and I was exhausted. One wrong move, one cramping muscle and it would all be over. I swallowed a mouthful of bloody saliva and dug my heels into the earth.

The heavy coat had to go. I managed to get my shaking fingers to grip the tab of the zip. It stuck a bit, clogged with mud as it was, but I eventually got it down. I shrugged the coat off one shoulder at a time, trying not to move too much. Finally I pulled it in front of me and let it drop.

I climbed without knowing how far there was left to go. Without being able to see much beyond my own increasingly filthy hands in the dark. Every time I pulled myself up, the clay sagged and broke, sending me slithering down. I made progress but it was slow and terrifying. Handholds broke away and left me

251

clinging on with one hand or one foot flailing in mid-air. My hands were gloved in clay, my clothes thick with it.

Finally, finally, I reached up and felt only empty air. My palm smacked down on soaking wet turf and I tangled my fingers in the grass, dragging myself up. With elbows on the clifftop I hauled myself up, kicking my legs as I did so. I rolled over onto the wet grass, boneless with relief.

The rain had died down a little. It at least felt like drops of water now, rather than handfuls of gravel. I shook my hands and pawed at my clothes, removing clods of clay. I felt weak and drained from being safe on solid ground. The adrenaline of hanging off a cliff was wearing off and I could only now really appreciate how close to death I'd been just a short while ago. How easy it would have been to panic and fall. Maybe Damian's books had taught me something after all. The importance of keeping a clear head.

When I began to feel my trembling legs again I moved to the shelter of the lighthouse. Under the doorway I crouched on the concrete step and wrapped my arms around myself. All I had to do now was wait for the sun to rise. For a new day to begin, taking this awful night away with it. It was all over.

So why didn't it feel that way?

I knew Craig was probably nearing the cottage right now. If he wasn't there already. Scarlett had said they should burn it down and I knew he wasn't above stealing that idea. She was right; both of them had bled there, leaving traces of DNA on the wires and fishhooks I'd rigged. Though I hadn't thought to document what they'd done in a diary as insurance, he couldn't know that for sure. Much safer to burn the place down. Maybe make it look like an electrical fire caused by a surge of power before the blackout. Or a fallen candle dropped by a strange, lonely woman trying to survive a storm.

Still, once he'd done that, he'd leave, believing me dead. This time I could disappear for good. Go somewhere with no ties to Cat or to me. Not that it would matter with no one left to look for me. Come to think of it, there wasn't anywhere left that I had ties to anyway. I felt a pang for Bristol, my home and the place I'd lost the people I cared about. Without them I could go anywhere. It was all the same to me.

But if the cottage burned, that would be me back to square one. I'd have even less than I'd had when I fled Bristol a year ago; no phone, no money and nowhere to go but also no clothes, camping gear or even shoes. My whole life, if it could still be called that, wiped out in a single fire. Where would I go?

Maybe I could try and tell Davy the cottage burned by accident. That I'd escaped the house fire but lost everything. Perhaps he'd put me up for a while. Drive me to the supermarket to buy new clothes. Maybe we'd bond and curl up on the sofa with Robbie of an evening. Maybe he'd never ask me to leave.

It was tempting, sitting there in the ice-cold pre-dawn. That image of domestic comfort: man, dog, roaring fire. The only thing wrong with it was me. I didn't fit.

Sally would be good for Davy. School cleaner by day, girlfriend by night. Part of that cosy picture. Only Sally wasn't real. Inside, she was the same old me. Rotten with guilt and shame, running from one disaster to another. How long could I keep up the Sally act in close proximity to someone as sweet and kind as Davy? How long before he smelled the rot on me, before the cracks started to show in my mask? The nightmares, the drinking, the grief and paranoia? Davy didn't deserve that. No one did.

For a while I sat there and wondered why I'd tried so hard to save myself from falling. It was amazing how tempting death was when it wasn't yawning below me, only a slip away. I couldn't help thinking, wouldn't the world be better off? Would anyone even notice that I was gone? The thoughts flew around my head like the pale moths drawn to the lighthouse window above me.

I felt uneasy, restless. Yes, I was safe from Craig now that he believed I was dead. Yet I didn't feel as if I'd escaped. More as if I'd been left behind, which left me feeling cheated. Craig was done with me, but was I done with him? It had never occurred to me before that I hadn't just been waiting for them to find me. I'd been counting on it. For a fight that still wasn't over, because he was still out there. I still had to do what I'd promised Cat I would – get justice. That meant Craig had to pay too. Not just for Cat's death either. For everything he'd done.

Three people were responsible for what had happened to Cat. Myself included. I'd suffered for a year with guilt and grief, had fought for my life tonight. Was that enough? No. I knew I would never stop blaming myself for Cat's death. As I would never forgive myself for Chrissy's. That left two other people who had to pay. Craig was still out there, and now Scarlett was dead, being tossed about on the waves, her debt to Cat settled.

But what about my debt to Scarlett? Didn't I owe her for the ruin I'd made of her life? For the death of her little sister at my hands?

I hated Scarlett for what she'd done to Cat, but I was angry for her too. More than that, I felt responsible for her. For what she'd become. I was the reason she was so full of hate. I'd killed her little sister and there was nothing I could do to make that right. I was the reason she'd ended up owing

Craig to keep his silence. If she hadn't tried to hurt me, she'd never have hurt Cat, or fallen in with him.

I'd changed Scarlett, changed the whole shape of her life. She'd done the same to me. She was dead at the bottom of the cliff and yet I still felt her burning glare on me. All that rage and hate like a curse she'd left behind. For all that I felt awful for her, I was afraid of her still. Afraid of the image of me she'd held up to my face. She was the one person who really understood just what a terrible thing I'd done. Damian had always tried to shield me from it, and yes, I'd held myself responsible, but it wasn't the same as what she'd done. Scarlett had burned it into me. Now she was gone and I felt like I'd lost something when she died. Like somehow, in those last few moments together, finally face to face with it all out there, we'd balanced one another perfectly. Guilt and blame. Regret and revenge.

Now it was just me and the echo of Scarlett's voice in my head, demanding to know what I was planning to do with my ill-gotten life. What I was going to do for her, for Chrissy. I was the one who'd brought her to that cliff. But Craig was the one who pushed her off it. I think she and I were in agreement for the first time in our lives. Craig had to pay.

So what was I going to do? For Scarlett, for Cat, for the other girls Craig had hurt. For all of them and for my own sense of grief and guilt – I had to go after him. Tonight wasn't over and it never would be. I could feel it deep inside. This was a debt I owed to so many people, myself included. I couldn't walk away. They wouldn't let me. I wouldn't let me.

What I was going to do I had no idea, but it wasn't going to come to me sitting in the shelter of the lighthouse. I got to my feet and faced the track down towards the cottage. My mind was full of names: Cat, Chrissy, Damian, Scarlett. Too many pieces of the same messed-up picture. All of them a part of me. All of them hanging off me and pulling me down, threatening to bury me. Only they weren't holding on to me. They were dead and gone – I was clinging to them. This was the only way to free myself, to let go of them. One way or another, I was going to end this. Once and for all.

Chapter Twenty-Five

04:00

Five and a half hours into the blackout

I hurried along the track towards the cottage. Most of the way was flooded but it didn't slow me down. I was already wet through and barefoot – there wasn't much more that the puddles could do to me. Besides, my mind wasn't on the mud under my feet or the sharp wind that cut through my wet clothes. I was only thinking of one thing: reaching the cottage before Craig got away. I would have run over broken glass to get to him.

I'd been shaking when I pulled myself up the cliff but I wasn't shaking now. I was still, braced by the anger that I stoked with every step. Thinking of Cat, of her cold hand in the river. Of Scarlett and her thin, horrified scream. On the outside I was blazing, my skin hot and tight with rage. My jaw hurt from being clenched. I kept seeing his face in my head and my fingers curled into fists on their own. Yet inside me there was a black hole that felt cold and empty, almost frighteningly calm. The eye of a storm that was tearing everything down around me but was leaving me untouched, for now. I felt that still space yawning open inside me, a cliff over which I would throw myself headfirst, not caring where I was going to land. Or if I would survive the fall.

I had no idea how I was going to beat him. How I could overpower him, what I'd do once I had. My thoughts weren't that focused or practical. I was on fire with fury, but there was fear there too. Of Craig and of what he could do to me. I felt like a cornered animal. I had tried running, I had tried hiding. Nothing had worked. Blood roared in my ears and shadows haunted the edges of my vision. My body was gearing up for the fight of its life. Kill or be killed. For the first time ever I felt like I could do it, intentionally take a life. There was so much rage in me that it didn't leave room for anything like consequences. Not just my rage but Scarlett's. I understood in that moment just how she'd felt about me, how badly she'd wanted to hurt me. I was in awe of her. Such a strange way to feel about a woman who tried to kill you. Who murdered your friend.

But I felt it. How she hadn't ripped me apart with her bare hands that night . . . she had more control than me.

When it came down to it, would I be able to kill Craig? Mentally I told myself I was prepared, but physically? He was bigger than me, stronger, trained. Would my fury make me strong, or betray me? I couldn't see that far ahead. I only saw me getting to the cottage. Maybe the rest would be down to fate, luck, whatever had been saving my skin all night.

The only thing I knew for sure was that once I got to him it would be the end of this. The end of the last year of fear and a debt I'd owed for a decade. One that could never be fully repaid, but that demanded something. A price. Maybe only one of us would be leaving this clifftop. Fewer, if there was any justice in the world. God knows I didn't deserve to live any more than he did.

Still, despite the feelings that consumed me, I paused once I got within sight of the house. It was as dark and lifeless as it had been when I fled it hours before, but that didn't necessarily mean anything. Craig could easily be inside, quietly staging a fire. Perhaps he was even having a moment of guilt over everything he'd done. Unlikely, but I'd been surprised before.

The cottage felt wrong. Ever since I arrived it had made me feel safe and grounded, a sort of pillbox or dug-out in the war between me and everything that was after me. A bolthole that rendered me invisible and protected me against everything I'd left behind. Now that belief was in shreds. It was just a mouldy old house, sadly slipping towards destruction. Tonight it felt like the object at the centre of a curse. A bad energy emanated from it and I felt closer to danger with every inch I moved towards it.

I took a few steps, crouching as I approached. A thick fog was rising as the wind died down and it hung about the lane, making it hard to see ahead. When I got nearer and saw that the track ahead was empty I froze again. The car was gone. Did that mean Craig had already escaped?

My insides squirmed with mixed emotions. Despite myself I was partly relieved, knowing that I wouldn't have to face him again. Face a fight I might not win. At the same time I wanted to get my hands on anything, everything, and rip it to shreds in frustration. He'd escaped me and now I'd never be able to get at him. It had to be tonight. I felt it in every cell of my body. Tonight, in the two precious hours left before sunrise, in this awful darkness where no law existed, that was the time to act. To end this. It felt like Halloween or the small hours when the clubs kick out and it's too early and too late to go to bed. A between time when the normal rules didn't apply and you could get away with anything. Even murder. I knew all about that – hadn't I seen it all before, from both sides?

I was torn, desperate for the car to indeed be gone but also hoping to find it still there, just out of sight. I wanted to hurt him, I needed him to still be here, but I was terrified that he would be. I felt sick as I hurried past the cottage and followed the tyre tracks through the mud. I was frantic with the need to stop him, to lose him, to run in the opposite direction. I didn't know what I wanted anymore.

When the fog lessened I saw the car further down the lane and stumbled to a stop. He'd moved it? Why? And why only a little way down the lane? Had it always been there and the dark was playing tricks on me? No, I'd seen it through the window, run past it as I left. It had been right outside the cottage. I crept closer and realised that it was also now facing away from the cottage, back down towards the village. Craig had moved it, turned it around in preparation for leaving. Did that mean he was inside or that he'd headed back to the cottage?

After long moments of indecision I rationalised that he'd probably moved the car to get it out of harm's way and positioned for an easy escape. If he was setting fire to the cottage, that made sense. He'd need to vanish before the blaze attracted attention.

I was filled with conflicting impulses: to run, to hide, to fight. To simply stand there until nature or Craig did what I didn't have the strength to do. End it all. When I lurched back into action it was towards the car. I needed a weapon, or a way out, but the car was my only hope of finding either.

I cupped my hands on the driver's window and looked inside. The engine wasn't running and there were no lights on, but I could see the keys in the ignition. He must've left them there after he moved it. On the front passenger seat I could see the blocky shapes of a wallet and a phone.

My cold fingers clenched into fists against the window. The urge to simply snatch the keys, to drive away, was so strong I could hardly breathe. Even choking on anger and grief I still had that sliver of fear inside me, stuck like a splinter through my heart. He'd left me with a getaway car. I could be miles and miles away before he even knew I'd taken it. I could save myself.

After all that he'd done and all my resolve, my natural instinct was still to run away. To escape from everything I'd done and act like it never happened. I could almost feel Damian with me, telling me to run, that he'd take care of it all. That he'd deal with it. Only Damian was long gone and I was on my own now. This wasn't like back then, with Chrissy. When Damian could tell me what to do and I could let him decide for me. Where I could tell myself that I would have done the right thing if only he'd let me. This was my decision to make and I wouldn't be able to blame him for holding me back from throwing myself into harm's way if I chose to run.

With a frustrated grunt I tore myself away from the car window and headed back towards the cottage. Not this time. I had to do this, for Cat. Not to mention I owed it to Scarlett, in some weird twisted way. Justice for what Craig had done to her. For what I'd done to her, and Chrissy.

I still didn't have a plan. No weapon and no traps and tricks left. There was just me, dripping wet and striding towards the cottage, veins filled to bursting with adrenaline. I felt like I was on fire. My mind flashed with images of the junk outside the house. The old iron boot scraper might make a reasonable weapon. I could see it in my hands. Feel the weight of it. If I could just find it in the long grass before Craig came out and found me.

When I reached the cottage gate I crouched low to keep out of sight of the windows. The rain had died off but this close to the cliff edge the wind was still a force to be reckoned with. It cut through my wet clothes and flattened the overgrown grasses around me. The sea below was rushing and crashing at the cliff base. I could hear movement inside the cottage, clumping footsteps and the thud of things being rearranged without concern for noise or damage. He was definitely inside.

The ground under my feet was saturated, the clay squelching as I moved. I winced at every noise I made, certain that he'd hear me. What was my plan here? An all-out fight was impossible to win but maybe I could sneak up on him? If it came to a confrontation I doubted very much that I'd be able to get the upper hand. I was exhausted and he'd had time to regroup. Could I really wrestle him to the ground and restrain him with only the benefit of surprise on my side? Or take him down and batter him to death before he could overpower me?

In the dark I couldn't spot the boot scraper, but in casting about for anything I could use I spotted a rusty chain on the ground. It was thick and heavy. A potential bludgeon, or I could try and get it around his neck somehow? On my arrival it had held the front door shut. I'd taken it off ages ago to stop anyone asking questions about my being at the cottage. But I'd left it in the grass, the padlock still attached. I felt for the coil of rusty chain and began to lift it, link by link, to prevent any unnecessary noise. It was heavy and icy cold against my sweating palms.

With the chain in my hands I hurried around to the back of the cottage. The back door stood open. Two boards had been torn off and the mesh was bent so that someone could reach in and unbolt it, but it was still sound. It was also half open. Hardly daring to breathe, I eased it the rest of the way open and crept inside.

The kitchen was a wreck. I wasn't sure if Craig had smashed stuff while looking for fire-starting materials or just because he wanted to. There was broken china and glass all over the floor. He'd torn out drawers and emptied them, scattering cutlery. No sharp knives though. Wherever the knife block had ended up, I couldn't see it. I still picked up a dinner knife, carefully so as not to scrape it on the floor. It was better than nothing if he managed to get the chain off me. I shoved it into the waistband of my joggers.

Picking my way between the sharp shards of china as best I could, I kept my head up, looking for Craig. Inside the house and away from the sea the sounds of movement were louder. He was in the living room, where the fireplace was. A good spot to set a fire if you wanted to make it look like an accident. I approached the door from the side and peered around the frame.

There was Craig, with his back to me. On the table in front of him were the mostly empty gas cylinders for the stove, plus the one I'd been using still. The candles, a bottle of cooking oil, the lighter fluid I used on the fire if the wood was wet, and my paperbacks. Enough to get a blaze going on the wooden table which would spread to the sofas.

He was holding the bottle of vodka I'd just bought. I watched as he twisted the cap off and took a swig, wincing at the taste. It was the cheap stuff after all. Then he poured it over the table and the surrounding area, before smashing the bottle on the floor.

With the chain in my hand I took a tiny step forward. This was it. My one chance to strike. If I could hit him over the head with the bundle of heavy chain he'd go down, hard.

I wanted to hurt him, to stop him. To make him regret ever putting his hands on me, on Cat and on anyone else. There was a ringing in my ears, like the pressure in my skull had increased to dangerous levels. I could feel my throat closing up, my breath trapped in a hard knot in my chest that throbbed with every beat of my heart. My pulse was heavy, slow, almost painful. I tasted blood.

The chain was in my fist and my arm was moving.

Somewhere, through the roaring of my blood and the ringing in my ears, I heard the skid of a match on a box. A tiny yellow flame pushed back the gloom. I had time to take a breath as if to blow it out. I was still moving towards him. Then the flame dropped. It hit the table and sprang into a sheet of fire, chasing every shadow from the room in a sudden burst of light.

Craig turned and I locked eyes with him. In the jagged light from the fire his mouth opened in horror, nostrils flaring in anger as he recognised me. This was the second time I'd risen from the dead. I saw in his eyes that he would not allow a third.

That look and the fire at his back brought the fear out in me. Instinctively my feet began to move, taking me back towards the door. The impulse to run was overwhelming. I couldn't stop myself from fleeing the room, bare feet crunching over glass and china. Even as my blood howled for me to go back, to get him. I heard Craig yelling, heard him skid on the kitchen debris in his wet boots. Then I was out and holding the door.

I'd like to say I didn't think about what I was doing as I forced it shut. That I was overcome by emotion as I passed the chain through the door handle. Wound it tight about the iron downpipe and pulled it taut, driving the dinner knife through the links so they couldn't be pulled apart. I'd like to be able to say that it was rage or fear that drove me. That I was blameless in what happened next.

But that would be giving myself too much credit.

Fear and rage had been at odds in me since I left the lighthouse, too much of one or the other taking hold of my thoughts. But as I gripped the door, it was like everything worked together. I was afraid and I was furious. I was exactly where I needed to be and I knew what to do.

I wasn't caught up in a swirl of emotions. I was at the heart of them, in the calm space. The eye of the storm.

Chapter Twenty-Six

05:00

Six and a half hours into the blackout

During my time at the cottage I'd turned it into a fortress and locked myself in every night. Now I was outside, and my fortress was the ideal prison to keep Craig from escaping. He'd set his fire, and was trapped inside with it. Slowly I backed away from what I'd just done, hardly daring to look at the chain my hands had just wrapped around the door handle, in case the sight of it punctured the eerie calm that had cocooned me.

I jumped when Craig's body slammed into the door. My calm shattered like glass. The chain jangled and pulled tight but didn't give. He was beating at the door, tearing at the remaining planks. But they were nailed on outside and even if he'd been able to get them off, the window wasn't big enough to climb through.

I stepped back, dazed, then took another step and another until I was around the front of the cottage. I flew out of the gate, my feet burning with a dozen cuts from broken glass. I felt sick and exhilarated and shaken to my core. But it was over, it was done. Craig was trapped in a burning house and I was outside, safe and on my way to the one route out of this awful night – the car.

Finally I made it back to where he'd parked it. I quickly climbed in and grasped the key, ready to turn the ignition. Then I chanced a look in the mirror, back at the cottage, and felt my stomach turn over.

The fire was spreading fast, despite all the rain that had fallen during the night. The sofas were old, with lots of stuffing that was probably not fire retardant. What with that and the fuel and the wooden floors, it was clear Craig had no hope of putting it out. I could already see flames flickering through the front windows.

As I sat there, part of me was screaming for me to move, to go back and undo what I'd done. To stop what was going to happen. To take it back before I became a murderer by cold-blooded intent.

The rest of me felt grimly satisfied. More than that . . . relieved. Relieved that it was finally over.

That Craig would suffer and be gone and I wouldn't have to worry about him ever again. After a whole year of watching my own back and feeling ill every time I saw anyone who looked like him, he'd finally be gone. Just like Scarlett was gone.

I still felt sure that he deserved to die. That it had to be here, tonight, that it happened. But how long would I be sure for? A day, a week? How long before the doubts came back? I couldn't stay full of adrenaline and fury for ever. Even now I could feel it ebbing away, like a high that was slowly fading. Cold, sober reality was prickling at the edges of my awareness. It had taken only seconds to decide to trap Craig in the burning house, but the decision would be mine to carry for decades. Just as I carried Cat's death and Chrissy's too. Another death, another secret, another thing to run from.

If I left him to this death, this awful end, didn't that make me the worst of us? Didn't that make Scarlett right all along about how evil I was? Didn't I feel some kind of impulse, even now she was dead, to prove her wrong? To cling to the idea that there was some good in me?

I don't know if that alone would have been enough to make me go back for him. I was thinking about Scarlett, about what she'd said to me, when I heard Craig screaming. His voice was shrill with fear, carrying over the cliffs. For a moment it didn't sound

273

like him. It sounded like a woman, like Cat's screams that night in the abandoned house. Like Nicole shrieking after me as she tried to shake Chrissy awake. Like Scarlett as she plunged from the cliff.

It was like being in four places at once, three memories and one terrible now. I could almost feel Scarlett in the car with me, her eyes burning into the back of my neck. I could hear the voice from my nightmares telling me, *This is your chance to prove me wrong. This is when you show me what you'd really do if you got what you wished for. If you could go back.*

That part of me – I'd hesitate to call it the better part, because it had Scarlett's voice, and anyway, wasn't it just normal to not want to cause death and destruction? It didn't matter what I called it; that part of me won. I tore open the car door and began to run back towards the cottage as if it were Cat caught in that blaze. Or Chrissy. Or both of them. Maybe I was running to save my soul before it burned to a crisp.

When I reached the gate I froze again, though not out of indecision. Craig was at the living-room window, backlit by hungry flames. He'd managed to break the glass but the strong chicken wire stapled into the frame was keeping him inside. He was tearing at it frantically with gloved hands but it wasn't budging. I'd bought the strongest mesh I could afford and used long, thick staples. That chicken wire wasn't coming out. Just as I'd hoped when I installed it. Though back then I'd intended it to keep people out, not in.

There were flames behind Craig, spreading into the hall but also creeping around towards the kitchen – if he didn't move quickly he'd be cut off from the back door.

He grabbed at the wire and pulled again but this time he saw me.

'You! Let me out of here, you mad bitch!'

I flinched at the fury in his voice, at the fear it sent through me. Though it was higher-pitched than it had been before, on the cliff. He was panicking. Tears running down his red face as smoke got in his eyes.

'Open the fucking door!' he bellowed.

I ran around to the back of the house, skidding on the mud. He'd clearly tried to batter his way out after I'd run for it. The chain was pulled tight but the knife was holding firm, if bent. It was twisted into the chain and spearing links together. Panicked, I reached for it but before I could get a grip on the wet handle, the door began to shake, jerking it out of my hand. Craig was thumping at the door, trying to shake it loose of the chain that held it shut. It would only open an inch or so before the chain refused to budge.

'Stop it!' I made another grab for the knife but my finger got caught in the snarled chain. I whipped my hand back with a yelp. Blood bloomed around my nail, which had been crushed. I put it into my mouth and sucked, the blood coating my tongue, mingling with the taste of smoke.

'Open. The. Door!' Craig growled, still shoving and kicking from his side to punctuate his words.

'I can't unless you stop moving it! It's stuck!' But he either wasn't listening or couldn't hear me over his own heavy breathing and the banging on the door.

'Fuck this,' he spat.

The door went slack but I heard him moving away, bumping into things as he went. What the hell was he doing?

'Come back!' I called, still struggling with the snarled chain, but he only got further away. I yanked the knife free and fought to untangle the chain. Easier said than done. It was wet and slippery, the rusted links clinging together in places. Thankfully the fire wasn't yet close enough to heat the metal, but smoke was drifting through the door and into my eyes. My hands were shaking. I could hear the roaring of the flames. Where the hell was Craig? What was he doing?

After several minutes I gave up with a snarl of frustration. The chain was partly undone but all the shoving had pulled part of it into a knot. I couldn't prise the thick links of chain apart and the bolt cutters I'd used months ago were somewhere at the bottom of the cliff, with the rest of the shed. Maybe there was enough give that he could squeeze out?

I almost cried out when Craig reappeared at the door, his face blackened with soot. He must've been trying to find another way out but the fire had forced him back to me. There was blood trickling down his face but he didn't seem to care.

'Get me out of here!' I was close enough that spittle hit my face. He was pushing so hard at the door that a vein was standing out in his forehead. There was not enough give for him to get out, but he had an arm through, reaching for me. Blood, tears and sweat were beading on his skin. Smoke drifted out of the broken window, acrid and suffocating.

'I can't get the chain off – you need to try and put the fire out, or find another way!'

'Bullshit – you're trying to kill me.'

'Well, if I am you're doing a much better job,' I said, dizzy with smoke and panic. Even the ground under my feet felt unsteady, shifting as I tried to stand on it. 'You need to get low. There's too much smoke in there, you're going to pass out and I can't get in there to help you.'

'Like you would,' he said, straining at the door.

Would I if I could? There was a world of difference between standing outside and trying to open a door, and going into a burning house with this man in it. What was he going to do to me if I got within grabbing distance of him, knock me out and leave me to burn?

The impulse of guilt, the urge for redemption that had sent me back for him was weakening. I'd been drawn back by a scream I'd imagined as belonging to someone I wanted to save. Needed to save. Face to bloodied face with him, I couldn't see Craig as anyone but who he really was. The man who'd raped my best friend and dumped her in the canal to rot. The man who'd tried to do the same to me. His voice, the sight of him, the smell of him, stirred the embers of my righteous anger. Looking him in the eye was like holding a gun to the head of that 'better self' inside me. If I could go back and save Chrissy, save Cat, I would. But he wasn't them, he was nothing even remotely resembling an innocent person.

The part of me that hadn't wanted to run back to the cottage, the part that had decided to trap Craig in the first place, the part of me that had marched to the cottage with murder in my mind, curled like smoke through my blood. I stepped back. For a second I was outside myself, watching as I flailed around in the mud, trying to save this bastard. I hated that I'd done it. He'd killed two people and assaulted who knew how many more. He'd tried to kill me. The only reason I was still there was some need to prove myself to be a good person. To make amends, to somehow try and fix my life by doing the right thing for once.

But when had being a good person saved anyone?

Good people – like Cat, Chrissy, even Damian, once he turned himself around – what did they get? Preyed upon, killed in senseless accidents, vile attacks. Scarlett had started off good and what I'd done had destroyed her. Turned her into a monster. Then there was me, and there was Craig. Cockroaches, black holes that sucked the luck out of everyone around them. Well, just because his seemed to have finally run out, that didn't mean I had to go down with him.

The night was almost over and there could only be one survivor. I was a fucking cockroach, but I wasn't going to be the one under the boot. Not tonight. Not for this bastard.

'What are you doing?' Craig's voice leapt a few octaves.

I didn't turn back, just kept walking, or rather limping, towards the track and the car that promised an escape. As I walked I felt myself teetering. My legs were wobbly. I was finally running out of adrenaline. How long before I crashed and couldn't move another inch?

I paused for a moment, but the unsteadiness didn't go away. It got worse. It wasn't me, it was the ground

I was walking on. I felt a weird tremor pass through me, from the soles of my bloody feet and up through my body. A weird, wrong feeling. Like the earth was about to open up and swallow me whole.

Craig was shouting, pleading or cursing, I couldn't hear over a weird rumble, like thunder but slower, more powerful. A deep rolling roar that grew louder and went on and on. Gathering strength and speed like a rock crashing down a cliff. Like thousands of rocks and the cliff as well.

I looked back towards the cottage and immediately started to run. I made it across the track and jumped a drainage ditch, twisting my ankle as I fell and landing on the wet grass. I was scrambling, trying to get up, to move, when I looked back. It was as if someone far below was pulling at the grass like a tablecloth. The whole thing was sliding towards the edge.

The whole cliff was going down.

My heart was in my mouth as the rain-weakened soil sagged and slipped towards the sea. I was frozen, terrified. The collapse was deafening; lumps of earth hitting the waves, stone walls crumbling into one another, the chimney falling in a clatter of slates, and through it all, Craig's screams.

Just as the cottage began to slide over the cliff, the lights flickered on for a moment. Electricity was restored, and against the firelight and the bright, bare bulb I saw Craig silhouetted for a moment, facing the fire to escape the fall. Then the cliff dropped, tearing away completely, and the cottage was gone, taking him with it.

I was shaking, cold and shock gripping my body, but I also felt a weight slip from me as I collapsed on the grass. He was gone. Both of them were dead and gone, lost to the sea. I was free. Not just from Scarlett's vendetta and Craig's need to silence me, but from the last people who'd come close to knowing what I'd done. What I'd have to carry for the rest of my life.

No one but me knew all of it and it had taken a while for it all to come back to me. I was so drunk that night. But I was reasonably sober when I did what I did. I chose to do it, though if I could have gone back afterwards and changed it, I would have. No matter what it cost me. Though, as I'd proved to myself, there was no going back.

It had taken me a while to remember it all properly. To sort the blank spaces and flashes into order. I'd drunk so much and everything happened so quickly afterwards. When bits and pieces started to come back, I never told Damian. I couldn't bring myself to put that on him. Or maybe I just didn't want to see how he'd look at me once he knew. If he thought it was just some awful accident, I could cope with that. We both could. But if he knew that it wasn't

281

all down to bad luck, I couldn't imagine how he'd feel – about me, about any of it.

I was worried, that night, after Nicole and her friends left me there by the fire. What if the pill didn't work? I'd be out fifteen quid and no one else would buy anything from me. I had to make sure that the 'freebie' did its job, that they came back for more. So, after I finished my first drink I opened a few alcopops. I popped a pill or two in one and gave it to Chrissy. Just to make sure she was properly high. I figured once the others at the party saw how good the stuff was, I could up the price a bit and make up the difference. I wasn't thinking of the pills or the stupid drug assemblies I'd zoned out in at school. I was thinking of the knocks on the door – the heavy ones that meant someone was coming in to get what was owed. Of the cupboards that were practically empty, the messages we'd left on Mum's phone that she hadn't answered. The rent that was due from her empty account. I was thinking of how nervous Damian had looked in the flat with those guys and how I needed this to work. We both did.

So I took the pills, not many. Just two, three. I just stuffed them down the neck of the bottle and swirled them around like they were aspirin. Like they were harmless. I'd never seen anyone overdose. I thought those pills were just one up from weed. A bit more serious legally but just fun – they made you laugh, they made you dance and perked you up. They were pale blue and they had little hearts on them.

I should've known better.

Instead I found Chrissy when the other two sent her over to get them drinks. I gave her the bottle and watched her drink it. Then I had few drinks myself to calm my nerves while I waited for her to get high and the others to come back to get more pills. Then I had a few more drinks. I blacked out. At some point the pills must've really kicked in, though I didn't see it. Later, when I realised my pouch was gone, I figured Nicole had to have nicked some off me and taken them herself. Not as many as I'd given Chrissy, but enough that she got sick. Or maybe that was just the booze. The shock of seeing a little girl she'd invited out turning grey and start frothing at the mouth.

I didn't mean for it to turn out like it did. But that didn't matter, did it? It didn't make Chrissy less dead, or less abandoned in the woods. Scarlett had told me she wanted foxes to eat my eyes. What exactly had she seen when they found her sister? Something that broke her. Something that lodged in her and poisoned every part of her life. So no, what I'd intended didn't matter. I'd done it. It was my fault and I had to live with it.

When Damian told me it was just a mistake and not really my fault, I wanted to believe him. I didn't.

But I wanted to. I never told him what I did. Never told anyone. I could hardly stand knowing it myself, let alone seeing it reflected back at me.

Back then I really did want to go to the police, at first. At least that's what I told myself. It was Damian who stopped me, out of fear of the Wests. But really I wasn't sure if I'd have been able to turn myself in. For years I got a chill whenever I saw police or passed a station. Would I have been able to walk inside and tell them I'd killed a twelve-year-old girl? I think I'd have rather gone into the burning cottage to rescue Craig. Damian might've tried to hold me back from confessing, but I was the one who let him. It was all on me.

Just like tonight, when it came down to it, when I walked back to the car and had that phone in my hand; Craig's screams in my head and grief knotted up through me like an invasive creeper. I couldn't do it. I couldn't turn myself in, couldn't finish the job of getting justice. The idea of being arrested, of being trapped and of everyone knowing what I'd done, made me want to die.

I wasn't sure whose car I was about to get into. After checking the boot and finding a bag of women's gym gear, all of it too small for Scarlett, I decided they'd either borrowed or stolen it. Either way I couldn't keep it for long. As long as it got me away from Churchcliffe before sunrise, I didn't care.

I stripped off my wet, filthy clothes and put on some of the gym stuff. I emptied Craig's wallet and overarmed it off the cliff. The phone too. There was a lot of cash in the wallet. Probably because he didn't want to leave a trail by using his cards.

After shoving my filthy feet into a pair of slightly too big trainers, I got into the driver's seat. I let out a long, slow breath and tried to get my heart to stop thundering inside my chest. I was finally all right. I was getting out of there and nothing was going to stop me. The rear-view mirror showed me a dirty-faced woman with lines of pain etched in the filth around her eyes. I wiped my face with a windscreen cloth and pulled a woolly hat over my dirty hair. It'd do.

I nearly screamed when a dark shape landed on the bonnet. It took a second for me to realise what it was. With one hand over my mouth I opened the door and Duzzy leapt inside. He was wet to the skin, bedraggled and pissed off.

'You nearly gave me a heart attack.'

He collapsed on the passenger seat and started to lick himself dry. I slammed the car door and started the engine. The headlights illuminated the flooded track and I eased the car forward, mindful of the deep puddles.

The car wasn't great and the heating took an age to kick in. My breath came out as a white cloud and it wasn't long before Duzzy slipped into the back seat to get away from the draught blasting from the vents. What I was going to do with him I had no idea. I couldn't take him with me. I didn't even know where I was going.

With no streetlights in the lanes it was easy to forget that the electricity had come back on. At least until I reached the village proper. There were already lights on in some houses as people got up and got ready for work. A car passed me on its way out of the village and I pulled the stolen hat down lower. I didn't want anyone to recognise me.

A tractor was idling in the high street, blocking my path. I stuck the car in first gear and waited, desperate to move, to get out of there. Clouds of vapour rose as the tractor's engine strained, manoeuvring it back as it turned. Presumably it was backing into the lane behind the church.

That was when I spotted Davy. He was dressed for work, on his way to sort today's post. He was heading for his van, parked on the other side of the road. He didn't look up as he passed me by and I was partly glad and partly disappointed. I liked him. But like everything else in Churchcliffe, even the cottage, he was temporary. I didn't belong in a place like this, with a person like him. I was starting to realise I didn't belong anywhere. That no one deserved to have me clinging on to them, dragging them down with me. Not even Duzzy.

I leant over and snagged the cat. He mewed as I opened the door and shunted him out, but then went running over towards the other side of the road. Davy must've heard him because he turned, smiling confusedly at the sudden appearance of the cat. He'd seen Duzzy at mine more than once and was probably wondering how on earth he'd made it into town. He bent to stroke the cat and then tried to pick him up, but Duzzy wasn't having it. He twined his way through Davy's legs and jumped onto the church steps, slinking towards the churchyard. At the end of the day, he was a half-wild animal, not the type to trot at heel for gravy bones. Davy watched him go, the tractor finally reversed and I drove away.

Where I was going and what I'd do when I got there, I had no idea. I'd had so many chances to change my destination but at every turn I kept picking the easiest road. Anything to keep myself safe, no matter what it cost anyone else.

I'd need a new name, that was for sure, but I could find one of them anywhere. On a bench or in the paper. I'd invent a new look, find a way to get some cash, quickly, then . . . who knew. Maybe I'd get lost in a big city or hide myself away in a small town. Perhaps one day I'd find someone like Davy who I could bring myself to say 'yes' to. Who I could let in despite everything I'd have to keep hidden from them. Maybe I'd have friends again someday. Whatever I did, my new life had to be different to the two that had come before. This time I had to disappear into a new person and never come up for air. Perhaps one day I'd even become that person for real, whoever she was going to be.

What was I going to do with my ill-gotten life? I didn't know anymore. But I wasn't giving up my freedom. Not out of guilt, or shame, or because it was the fair thing to do. If I was going to live the rest of my life with all these ghosts, I'd at least build my own cage and keep the key to it in my own two hands.

As I drove out of Churchcliffe I didn't look back.

Epilogue

Years after the blackout

It's the tail-end of Christmas Day and all over the estate, celebrations are winding down. The communal bins are piled with bags that are bursting at the seams, scattering wrapping paper and glitter onto the wet pavement. New bikes are leaning against front gates, gleaming wet under the streetlights. It's drizzling, not so much a white Christmas as a grey one. Though it hardly ever snows here. No one really wants it to. No adults anyway. Everyone has to get to work in a day or so, or is old enough that the idea of slippery pavements make them anxious.

At number seven, Rhoda stands at her kitchen sink. She's elbow-deep in greasy water and tackling the piles of washing-up created by a day spent cooking. The radio has reached the depressing end of its Christmas Day playlist. First thing it was all jaunty carols and pop songs. But as she pours congealed gravy down the sink a tear-jerking rendition of 'In the Bleak Midwinter' begins to warble from the radio.

Though her children are both off school, neither of them has offered to help. Mutterings about having a game to play online with friends, and exam stress, excused both of them after dinner. She reflects that whilst it's nice to get out of the school run for a week, to not have uniforms to iron or algebra to attempt to understand, this festive routine is no less stressful. The messes might be more exotic, involving glitter and spilled bubbly, but at the end of the day it is all still work to do. More specifically, work for her to do.

Rhoda pauses in scrubbing an encrusted pan and blinks away the beginnings of tears. This morning she was all smiles, but now the weight of that work – the presents bought and wrapped, the food prepared and the house cleaned and decorated – it's all pressing down on her. It all feels as if it was the setup for a few seconds of joy that haven't quite felt worth it. She's climbed a mountain of peeled spuds and wrapped presents, but the view from the summit is of a long trek down the other side. The cheap bath products she received this morning have lost their mystique now the paper's off and Rhoda's on the depressed side of tipsy. She tells herself she should be happy, and normally she is. There was a time when she never thought she'd have this: a family, her own home, a Christmas with luxuries stacked in every cupboard. She is content, she really is. But sometimes she can't help but miss her independence. Her life before. A life where the only person she had to cater for was herself and if she didn't feel like washing up, she could leave it until tomorrow.

Across the way at number four, someone else is in their kitchen. Maxine Havers isn't washing up but opening several tins of cat food. Unlike Rhoda, Maxine has spent Christmas alone. Her festive meal came frozen and the only presents she's opened are ones she bought herself in the January sales last year and kept safely stashed in a cupboard until she almost forgot what was inside. You'd be forgiven for thinking Maxine is in her sixties, careening towards pension age. But you'd be wrong. Years of cigarettes and anxiety have carved lines into her face, weathered it as the sea ages wood. Extra decades are notched into her skin. Poverty keeps her whip-thin and shabby, while several tots of vodka a day add a shuffling uncertainty to her steps.

The cats at number four are having a good Christmas. A mix of strays and rescues, they come and go as they please and are fed well. The house is littered with blankets and beds to sleep on and Maxine is one of the last people on the estate to still use her old fireplace. In the New Year she'll be out collecting dumped Christmas trees to fuel it. People will stare at her as she carts them home and she will pretend not to notice. For now, though, she's making do with a bag of coal and relying on an electric blanket and neat vodka to keep her warm. The electric meter in the front hall has become greedier and greedier. Lately she hasn't been able to meet its appetite with the little she makes at the betting shop where she works three days a week. They've cut her hours again.

She finishes laying out the cats' dinner and returns to the front room to watch the evening film. On the coffee table are her supplies for the evening: half a bottle of vodka, a glass, a pouch of tobacco and a box of chocolates dutifully dropped off by Rhoda's eldest.

Rhoda is the one neighbour she doesn't actively avoid. Maybe it's just because when she goes out in the sleepless small hours she often sees her across the street, still awake and having a sneaky cigarette in the side alley.

At the entrance to the close, blue lights are flashing. They cast grim shadows from the inflatable snowmen and reindeer scattered around the front gardens. At her window, Rhoda squints out, trying to see if it's an ambulance heading to number four. She's been worried about Maxine. This time of year is hard for people on their own, as the TV reminds her daily. Loneliness kills at this time of year, like the cold. She feels a pang of guilt for being sorry for herself when across the street poor Maxine has no one and nothing. According to her daughter, the woman was pissed at ten in the morning when she dropped the tub of Roses round. Though perhaps she'd only just woken up and was just groggy.

The appearance of Paul's reflection beside hers in the window makes her jump.

'You all right, love?' he asks, still wearing his paper hat from dinner.

'Just trying to get a start on all this before it dries on.'

'Oh, leave it. We'll do it tomorrow.'

'Who's we?' Rhoda retorts, though he does not hear. She contemplates asking for a dishwasher next year. It would be useful but ultimately quite sad to receive one as a gift, she thinks. Like a sign she was giving up on romance altogether, sinking into middle-aged obligation.

Paul puts his arms around her, sensing dissatisfaction. 'It was a lovely dinner. Best yet, I think.'

'You're just saying that because your mother isn't here this year with her incredible everlasting trifle.'

'Don't. Even thinking about it gives me heartburn.

293

Look . . . why don't you go and watch telly, get the kids down and put a film on? I'll do the rest of that.'

Rhoda briefly considers it, touched by the offer. But then she thinks of all the other times Paul has taken a turn with the washing-up and how she had to do most of it again anyway. It is not one of his strengths and she has given up trying to show him how to get it right.

'No, I'll do it – you go spend some time with them. I'll be in later.'

Paul has noticed the lights and is frowning. 'Do you think it's Maxine?'

Rhoda is touched by this strange moment of synchronicity. Sometimes she forgets that she and Paul share the same kind of concerned nature. 'Do you think I ought to go over and check? If it's an ambulance taking her in, she might need someone to bring her some pyjamas or look after the cats.'

Paul has started to put his shoes on, but pauses as the lights grow brighter, the emergency vehicle having manoeuvred around the badly parked cars of friends and relatives that fill the close.

'It's not an ambulance, it's the police. Not sure what they want – I can't hear anyone blasting music. Besides, it's still early.'

'Must be late for dinner,' Rhoda jokes, mostly to herself.

'They're probably out to arrest someone,' Paul says, watching as the blue lights pick out the shape of Maxine, also at her front window, watching them through nicotine-stained blinds.

'On Christmas Day?' Rhoda asks.

'I don't think they take it off, Rhoda. Criminals don't either, I expect. Or it's one of the neighbours rowing – you know how it is this time of year, booze, family and spending lots of money. Recipe for a blow-up.'

'It just doesn't seem right somehow. Imagine getting dragged away from your family by the cops on Christmas Day.' Rhoda briskly upends the bowl of dirty water and it gurgles down the drain.

'They probably deserve it – that many police don't come out for nothing. Besides, if they've done something awful, they've probably broken up someone else's family. Destroyed their Christmases, or changed them for ever at least.'

'I suppose you're right,' Rhoda sighs as one of the kids comes in, carrying an armful of dirty glasses from their room. 'It just depends which way you look at things.'

Acknowledgements

This book was written over the course of a year which was . . . chaotic, to say the least. A move across country, rats in the walls, a month without hot water and a fortnight with no kitchen. Safe to say I ended the process of writing *The Blackout feeling* a lot closer to Megan than I did at the start. Though at least her cottage had a working shower.

I have to say thank you to my family for being there during the last few months. Yes, there were tears, especially when we saw the state of the oven, but saw the state of the oven, but we've made it together. It's only been a few months but this already feels more like home – because you're here.

Thank you to various members of my extended family, especially Auntie Mel and Diane, and Auntie Nicky. Thank you for believing in me, and for being such fantastic, strong, funny women who never give up.

Thanks to Vander as well, for doggedly insisting on buying every book I come out with despite me constantly offering free copies. The best quality a friend can have as far as a writer is concerned!

I owe everyone at Avon for making the process of bringing this novel to publication as stress-free as possible. Despite their understandable concern when I told them I couldn't make it to the Christmas party, as I'd just found out I was moving to Cornwall in a week's time. I promise I'm more organised than that statement would suggest.

That being said, special thanks as always to my editor – or editors in this case. Firstly, thanks to Cara Chimirri for her amazing suggestions and prompts during the planning stages of *The Blackout*. A belated thank you to Rachel Hart for her work with the publication of *The Resort* earlier this year – the success of which has been incredibly heartening – and a second thank you to Rachel, for bringing fresh eyes to *The Blackout* in the editing stage and helping to make it the book it is. Thank you too Raphaella Demetris, for jumping in as well. It was a team effort, but it's been so utterly seamless and for that I cannot thank you all enough. Thanks as always to Laura Williams at Greene and Heaton, my incredible agent who helps to weed out the good ideas from the simply shocking ones that occur to me at 1am. You input on *The Blackout* was as always, invaluable. Further thanks to Kate Rizzo as well for all her amazing efforts on the international front.

Lastly, thank you to everyone who has read and reviewed my previous books. It makes a huge difference and has really helped *The Resort* to reach a wider audience. I hope you enjoy *The Blackout* just as much.

Now read on for an exclusive short story
from Sarah Goodwin . . .

The Breakdown

I loathe the countryside.

It was a mantra on repeat as my poor little car jolted over yet another enormous pothole. Why was it always me who got these properties? The no-hopers and tear-downs. Places forgotten by both time and their owners, left rotting until they were inherited by distant relatives and swiftly disposed of.

The place I'd just been to was at least semi-decent with some lovely period features still hanging on for dear life under seventies DIY décor. Someone with a vision and three hundred grand to spend might just snap it up. I'd done my best to give it a decent chance. It had taken me ages to get some half-flattering pictures and to measure around all the junk. Which was why I was headed home in the dark. The clock on my dashboard said it was ten at night. It was actually nine though, I'd never learned how to change it for daylight saving.

The single-lane road spooled out in front of my headlights. I could only see about five metres ahead at any time because of the way the road twisted, rising and falling as if it had been laid over the bare ground and not planned at all. The darkness was peppered with so many moths and tiny bugs that it had the look of the deep sea on those documentaries. The ones where they go down into the pitch black where toothy, spiny monsters lurk.

My eyes flicked to the speedometer. I was crawling along at twenty-eight but it felt like forty at least. The dark was playing tricks on my eyes. Aside from the swirling moths I occasionally saw flashing eyes in the dense hedgerows. Greenish-yellow glints that were there and gone in seconds. They appeared on the road too. What were they? Frogs? Toads? Disgusting. I thought of my tyres grinding over one and shuddered.

It had been warm when I left the office. One of those golden October days which felt like a last brush with summer. Only it had quickly turned frigid as soon as the sun dipped. I hadn't brought a coat, just my blazer. The heat in the car was taking ages to reach me. My hands felt numb on the wheel, the tip of my nose a knot of ice. Despite the chill I still had trouble keeping my eyes open. It was the road,

302

steadily appearing out of the blackness as if it were being built just ahead of me, out of sight. It was hypnotic. I kept coming back to myself and realising that I'd been somewhere else. Each time I got a nasty jolt as I realised that my lack of attention might have led to disaster. Yet a few moments later I was off again. A cycle of zoning out and snapping back to reality.

Reaching out I fumbled with the radio in the dark. Some noise to keep me focused. I spun the dial too hard to turn it on and the volume shot up. I winced and quickly turned it down, the car drifting sideways as I leant over. I pulled the wheel straight again. The radio was frazzled with static. Probably the trees all around me, that or I was between signals. Annoyed I felt for the CD button and the clicking of the plastic disc took over from the radio, replaced eventually by music. I tapped my fingers on the steering wheel to keep myself alert. The heating kicked back in with a billow of hot, stale air.

Where was the turning? It was meant to be around here somewhere. I'd come this way earlier and was usually fairly good at remembering routes. I had the satnav, but I'd forgotten the little cigarette lighter connection thing so it was basically useless. I'd had to follow the written directions and those were somewhere in my handbag now. Still, I was sure it was up here. I needed to go left at a pub with a white fence. Then I'd be on the road back to the bypass. Back to streetlights and other cars. Back to normality.

But no white fence came. It was just more lane. A hedge on either side, the moths floating and the road jolting along, pothole after pothole. Nothing else. Not even a signpost or an old crisp packet caught in a breeze. It all just looked the same.

I began to feel almost like I was waiting. Not for the fence or a turning or anything so normal as that. But that I was waiting for whatever had caused this weird, endless loop. I had a sense that something had put me here, on this stretch of repeating road. That it was watching me like a hamster in a wheel and that it would eventually reach out and tip me over, just to see what I'd do. To see if I'd react to its presence or even notice it.

I tried to shake it off and put it down to the dark getting to me. The way it does when you're all alone and suddenly all you can think of is every horror film you've ever seen. Every scary story you've ever told. The track on the CD ended and in the beat of silence I held my breath and waited.

That was when I looked down at the speedometer and saw it was hovering just over fifteen miles per hour. I pressed the accelerator and the arrow wavered but didn't move higher. Something felt wrong. I pressed the pedal to the floor, shifted the wheel from side to side and felt the engine trying to do something, but the arrow dropped and bit by bit the car slowly rolled to a stop.

I took the key out. In the sudden silence I could hear my own breathing. It was fast and uneven. My eyes darted to the mirror but it only showed blackness. I turned the key and the headlights came on, the CD booting up. I put the car in gear and eased off the clutch. It didn't move an inch, but the engine spluttered. I revved a bit but after a few tries the engine died. I reached down and popped the bonnet.

With my cold fingers on the door handle, I paused. I could see myself getting out, looking under the bonnet with my phone. Jiggling leads and topping the oil up just in case that fixed it. Whatever 'it' was. But as that image played out in front of me I was frozen. I didn't want to get out of the car. I wanted to climb into the back and hide in the shadows. From what I had no idea. Anything, everything that might be waiting in the dark.

'Come on,' I said to myself, jumping at the sudden noise even though it was me who'd made it. "You're thirty-two. You're not scared of the dark."

The door unlatched. I'd moved my hand without consciously deciding to. Closing it again felt like admitting I was afraid, so I got out instead. My heels were loud on the tarmac as I walked around the car. Something scuttled in the hedgerow, crashing away through unseen grasses. Just a rabbit,

I told myself. Or a fox. Something. Something that was more afraid of me than I was of it.

I lifted the bonnet and shone my phone's torch underneath. I wasn't exactly sure what I was looking for. Everything seemed connected and no steam or smoke was coming out. I checked the levels on my oil and everything else. Nothing was that low. A cold breeze swept over me, rustling the leaves overhead. Something cried out in the dark. A noise like a cat, grieving.

I quickly rounded the car and got back in, almost slamming the door. I had the number for my roadside recovery plan tucked into my visor. I typed it into my phone with shaking fingers. Just the cold. That was all. My eyes strayed to the icons at the top of the screen as the call connected. I had signal. This wasn't a horror film. It was just an annoyance.

"Thank you for calling Anytime Roadside Assistance, an agent will be with you shortly. In the meantime, have you tried our website . . . "

I tuned out the recorded message. If I thought I could get online out here I'd do it. Music played and I looked out into the night, chewing my lip impatiently. Hearing another voice, even just a recording, made me feel less alone. That was something.

A person finally picked up, a woman. I read the policy information from my printed sheet and waited while she found my details.

"Alright, Ms Carpenter, I've got you . . . can you give me the address of where you are?"

I looked out of the windows on either side of the car. It was even darker out there now that I had the internal light on. I could see myself clearer than I could the outside world.

"I don't know where I am. I'm . . . I'm on a lane, I just came from Collier's Cottage. I have the postcode for that."

"How far are you from there?"

"I'm not really sure. I've been driving for . . ." I checked the clock and dug my nails into the steering wheel. "About forty minutes? I don't know how fast I was going though."

There was a short silence. I thought I heard a sigh. "Right . . . so, I need a postcode or a location I can look up so the mechanic can find you."

"Well I'm sorry but I don't know where I am," I said, slightly louder than I intended. "This can't be the first time this has happened."

"OK, I understand." She sighed again. "Do you have a GPS app or any other kind of location-finding service on your phone? Can you download one now?"

"I can't get 4G out here. And no, I don't have anything on my phone that would work without it."

I heard her sucking her teeth. In the background came the tinny sound of other calls, other agents. A call centre full of light and motion. She was lucky.

She had no idea what it felt like to be out here, alone, without even a light on the horizon.

"Can you not just . . ." I waved a hand in the air helplessly, "send someone to roughly where I am and have them look for me? I could honk the horn or flash my lights so they can find me?"

"That's not exactly something we do . . ."

"Well then what can you do? Because it's your job to come and help me."

"I need to talk to my manager."

The hold music was like a slap to the face. I felt equally annoyed and afraid. What the hell did they expect? For me to be able to tell them which two trees I was stranded between? Waiting, I drummed my fingers on my knee and looked at the windows, alert for any movement outside.

"OK." Her voice came back on the line, making me jump. "I need you to try and find some kind of road sign or landmark and then call back to let us know where you've broken down."

"Are you serious?" I breathed. "It's pitch black out there. I was driving for ages and I didn't see so much as a road marking."

"I'm sorry but I can't do anything else from this end," the agent said. "If you find anything that can help us locate you, please call back and—"

I hung up. It wasn't going to do me any good to keep having the same argument. My phone flashed as I went to put it away. Low battery warning. Fantastic. I dug around on the floor and found my in-car charger. It had a built-in connector, thank God. I hooked the phone up and got out of the car. I'd have to find a sign and then come back for it. As a last thought I turned my hazard lights on. There wasn't much point going back the way I'd come. I wouldn't be able to walk back to the cottage and I hadn't seen anything helpful as I drove. No, I had to carry on the way I'd been going.

I began to walk, wishing I'd not worn heels. The autumn night air cut through my sheer tights and nylon blazer. With my arms folded around myself I stumbled along the uneven road. The rustling of the trees and hedges seemed louder now. Maybe the wind was picking up. Even louder was the sound of my own breath and the thumping of my heart. My eyes jerked from side to side as branches snapped and my mind thought it saw things in the shadows.

I was hoping to see a light sooner or later. A house or another car on the road. Even a street lamp which might have a sign on it. Some hint as to where I was. But everything was dark, all across the horizon. Dark but not still. Everything was in constant motion, swaying and shifting.

The trees overhead thinned slightly, letting in some moonlight. I picked my way up the bank and looked out over the fields. Not even a distant headlight.

This was really the back of beyond. I slithered down the slope and continued up the road.

How long I'd have walked if I hadn't seen the owl I had no idea. It came swooping down like a ghost, white and shrieking. I stumbled, automatically crouching whilst also trying to run away. It passed over me, gliding through the air. I knew it wasn't dangerous but the fright it had given me wouldn't let up. I couldn't make myself walk any further. I just wanted to go back the way I'd come, where it was safe. I'd just sit there and wait until another car came past. Or at least until the sun came up.

I hurried back the way I'd come, hardly pausing to look for any signs I might have missed. When I saw the flashing hazard lights I broke into an awkward run and didn't stop until I had a hand on the door. The sound of it closing behind me was the most comforting thing I'd ever experienced. The overhead light was on and I let myself relax just a little. Then I reached for my phone to see how much it had charged. But my fingers found only the dangling end of the charger.

I swept my hand over the passenger seat, the console, leant over and groped about on the floor. My phone wasn't there. It had vanished. No, not 'vanished' – it had to have been taken.

The hair on the back of my neck stood on end. I felt my skin tighten and my body seemed to lock up.

Only my eyes moved, finding the rear-view mirror and checking the back seat. I couldn't see anyone but that didn't mean no one had been there. Someone had definitely taken my phone and whoever it was might be just outside or even crouching out of view of the mirror.

I balled up all the courage I could muster and, with my breath held between my teeth, I turned. There was no one in the back seat. The windows, however, were all impenetrable – reflecting the internal light and my own terrified reflection back at me. I hesitantly reached up and felt for the light switch, plunging myself into darkness.

My eyes weren't adjusted to it and for a moment the air around me seemed thick, purple and white dots clouding my vision. Then the shapes outside the windows resolved into the familiar shapes of trees and black masses of hedge. If there was someone out there they had to be hiding behind something. I couldn't see the shape of a person out there.

With shaking fingers I reached for the lock and clicked it. The doors clunked as the locks engaged and I pressed myself against the back of the seat, trying to make myself small and safe despite having just trapped myself in a glass box. I let out a shaky breath, a cloud of white. It was just as cold in the car as it was outside now, but that was the least of my worries.

Someone was out there and they had my one means of calling for help. I should have called the police when the roadside recovery people couldn't help. They'd have come to find me, wouldn't they? I should have called them, but that was just wishful thinking now. Whoever was out there had my phone and I had two options: wait for them to come and get me, or make it easy for them and get out of the car.

The hazards didn't put out much light and with the flashing it was difficult to see. As my eyes adjusted to the dark I kept thinking I saw a person-shaped shadow. My heart would skip a beat and then the sight would resolve into a tree trunk or swaying hedge. Still I had no doubt that there was someone out there.

Gradually, as no attack came, I convinced myself to move. I reached into my handbag on the passenger seat, hunting blindly for anything I could use as a weapon. I wasn't the type to travel with a manicure set or scissors. Something I regretted at that moment. I checked the glove compartment and business cards spilled out onto the floor. My fingers brushed against a fountain pen – a prize for winning some sales competition. I flicked the cap off and tested the nib with my finger. It was metal and sharp, but wouldn't do much unless I managed to get someone's eye or ear. Still I clutched it tightly in my fist.

Why weren't they doing anything? Was this how

they got their rocks off? Sitting in the dark, scaring people? How had they even found me? It was bad luck I'd broken down here . . . wasn't it? A sliver of cold ran through me at the thought someone might have tampered with my car. It had been sat in the public car park all day, then outside the cottage while I took pictures. Anyone could have broken in and messed with the engine, then followed me at a distance, waiting for me to become stranded.

Maybe someone had driven by while I'd been walking. They'd stopped at the car, spotted my phone and just taken it, then turned around and gone back the other way for some reason. I found my purse in the dark. They hadn't taken that, or the fifty-odd quid inside. No, it wasn't just a thief.

A flashing orange light caught my attention and I nearly cried out in relief. It was a truck. I hit the horn twice, then threw open the door and leapt out, waving my arms. The truck slowed and I saw the logo on the front. Anytime Assistance. They had sent someone!

The truck stopped. I waited by the driver's door until he got out, holding a tablet in a heavy rubberised case.

"Iris Carpenter?" he asked.

"Yes," I sighed gratefully. "Thank you. I was so . . . they said they couldn't send anyone until I called back with a location."

"I got a call saying they hadn't heard from you for an hour and since I was in the area, could I come out and drive around looking for you. I'm not technically meant to be working today, I just live round here. I figured if you weren't local you'd be trying to get to the bypass so I came out this way."

"Oh my God, well, thank you because I've been going out of my mind here. Someone took my phone from the car while I was off looking for a road sign."

He gave me a funny look. "You sure you didn't lose it in the car?"

"No, I didn't. I'm positive."

"Right, well – shall I have a look at the engine?"

I was slightly annoyed that he didn't seem to believe me, but I just wanted to get home. "Sure."

He shone a torch around through the car windows as he approached. I felt my face flush as I realised how messy my car looked. The back seats were piled with printed brochures, boxes of plastic keyrings and other freebies. My handbag had spilled all over the front seat and my business cards were everywhere. I could see him thinking 'how would she find her phone in that mess?' and maybe he was right.

I popped the bonnet again and he looked underneath, plugging his tablet in and frowning at the screen while I hovered awkwardly nearby.

"Alright, so basically," he said, sounding bored by whatever he'd found, "there's a part here that's become clogged up with carbon. The engine's started to overheat and it's been restricted by the on-board system. It'll have slowed right down and then cut the engine entirely to prevent damage. I don't have a replacement but I'll tow you to a garage and they can either exchange it tomorrow when they open, or they might be able to clean and reuse the part which will be cheaper."

"Right, OK. I suppose I'll call a taxi from the garage then," I said, relieved to have a plan, even if it was one that wouldn't see me home for a while yet.

"I doubt it – only one taxi company comes out here and you have to pre-book. They might have a car free but you'll have to wait a while."

"Great, well at least I won't be stuck out here."

"I can drop you off if you like. Or at least take you into town."

"Really? That would be amazing, thank you so much."

"Alright, hop in while I get your car on."

I grabbed my handbag and got into the front of the truck, which was spotless, much to my embarrassment. It was warm though, which was a relief. Mostly I was just glad to be out of the dark and not alone anymore. I was already starting to doubt myself. Maybe my phone had fallen under the front seat and I was just panicking over nothing. I started to put together a mental list of things I needed to get for my car, starting with a spare satnav connector.

The guy got back into the truck and started it up. The radio came on, clearly tuned better than mine and playing a classical music station. I told him my address.

"What I'll do is drop you off then take the car in on my way home. Save some mileage."

"Thank you so much. This is really kind of you."

"It's fine, really."

He was a very careful driver, but I suppose that came with the job. We went the way I'd walked and I nearly swore aloud when, after only ten minutes, we passed the white fence I'd been looking for. The sign for the pub swung in the wind. If I'd only broken down a few minutes later I'd have been able to give a location to the woman on the phone. Hell, I could have maybe gone in for a drink while I waited. The pub was dark now though. It might have been closed for hours.

I was about to ask whereabouts the driver was from, just to make conversation, when his phone rang. He didn't reach for it, but that was no surprise given how seriously he seemed to take driving. But he didn't pull over either.

"Do you want me to get that?" I asked.

"No. It's fine," he said, shortly.

Was it a trick of the dark or had we sped up?

The phone stopped ringing and then went off again. It was the same ringtone I had.

I began to feel a funny twisting in my belly. The phone in the centre console wasn't ringing. The noise was coming from his pocket. A second phone. Maybe his personal one, but though that seemed plausible enough it didn't feel right to me. Not for any real reason. I just felt uneasy.

The phone stopped ringing and I let out a breath. But something still didn't feel right. After a few seconds I realised what it was. We needed to go left at the pub to get to the bypass. He'd gone straight on. An alternate route? The same instinct that had assumed my phone was stolen told me no. This wasn't right.

Forcing myself to sound calm I gestured to the phone in between us. "Would you mind if I borrowed your phone to call my husband? He'll be worrying."

I was expecting him to either say it was fine or make up some excuse. What I wasn't expecting was for him to mutely take the phone and move it to the inside of his door. Out of my reach.

My mouth went dry, my mind moving quickly. He'd been sent to look for me by Anytime Assistance. They would have told him I was alone. Maybe he even had my details and knew I wasn't a 'Mrs'. That there was no one waiting for me at home. He could have come across my car from the opposite direction and taken my phone, then circled back around to find me. I hadn't seen him call Anytime Assistance to tell them he'd actually found me. He could just say he never did. Drop my car off back in the road like I'd broken down there. No one would know I was ever in this van.

I knew something was wrong and he knew I knew. The air was crackling with my fear. Could he feel it? Was he enjoying it?

We rode in silence while I considered my options. We were going too fast for me to jump out. The doors were locked anyway. I could try and talk to him but he didn't seem likely to talk back now that the mask was off. I had to get out of this truck. I had to make him stop.

The pen was in my blazer pocket on the side furthest from him. I slowly moved my hand until I had it, holding it like a tiny knife. My seatbelt was on tight. I'd have to trust that would be enough to save me. All I had to do was get the phone from him and call the police. All I had to do was not miss.

I transferred the pen to my other hand and aimed for his eye.

Read on for a sample of *The Resort*, out now!

Prologue

I love a mystery. That's what this whole trip was meant to be about. Chasing a puzzle, a myth, all those ghost stories and unexplained events. This place has so many secrets. A history of either violence or misfortune, perhaps both, has made its mark on every bit of it.

If ghosts are real I wonder what these ones have seen. What stories they might tell if only I could hear them. Perhaps they could answer some of my questions or spark new ones. Or else whisper their last words to me.

Perhaps they might have warned me.

The ground underfoot is only lightly dusted with snow, not yet frozen. My boots slither in the mud beneath as I try to run. It's pitch black under the trees, and out of the moonlight I can hardly see two feet in front of me. I'm already exhausted from the long walk and my muscles are screaming at me to stop. I have to keep going but fear can only give me strength for so long. It's so hard to make any progress. I'm stumbling, sliding, my legs straining.

Am I still being chased? I can't hear anything over my own blood roaring in my ears. The panicked gulps of air I'm sucking in. I twist and look, catch sight of a shadow between the trees and whip back around with a whimper. Oh Christ. The figure isn't even hurrying after me. As if my escape attempt is completely futile and I just don't know it yet.

The cabins loom out of the early morning mist. The same cabins that only a few hours ago I was happily poking around in. Looking for clues. Now, as I throw myself up the porch steps and slam the door behind me, I wonder what clues I will leave behind for the next person unlucky or stupid enough to come here.

Pressed to the door I flick the latch and brace myself to hold it shut. Perhaps I had enough distance that I wasn't seen coming in here? A moment after that thought I realise that I must have left a trail in the mud. Footprints leading right to my hiding spot. A place so obvious a child could find me, let alone . . .

Straining my ears I listen for footsteps or voices. With my lip clenched between my teeth I count inwardly. I reach ten, then twenty, and after sixty seconds my heartrate slows ever so slightly. Maybe I got away? Surely I wasn't that far ahead. Only a few seconds at most when I looked back before. But then again, perhaps I'm not the only one fleeing the scene? Maybe that figure wasn't striding after me, but slipping away?

I wish I had my bag, the phone in there. The GPS. Anything to help me get out of here, find help. But I put it down to rest my back and that was when I saw the blood. Fresh blood steaming on the ground, peppering the light snow. I feel sick remembering it. The blood and the sounds that man was making. The terror and pain on his face.

Then I hear it. Footsteps on the porch, slow and deliberate. A convulsive shiver runs over me, and despite my instinct to hold the door shut, I back away. There's a creak and a click. For a moment I think I see a black eye glinting between the warped boards. Then, everything is agony.

Chapter 1

Getting to the airport was the usual struggle. I'd been awake half the night worrying I'd sleep through my alarm. The other half of the night was taken up with nightmares that I'd already overslept and that I had gone to the wrong airport by accident. Not exactly a restful start. Ethan, of course, slept like the dead, because it wasn't his sister's wedding we were going to. He had nothing to prove, unlike me.

In the end I woke up half an hour before the alarm went off and decided I couldn't take it anymore. So whilst Ethan slept on I tiptoed around getting into my airport uniform of leggings and a hoodie. In the cheap fluorescents of our bathroom I already looked like death. I'd had my hair cut and dyed for the wedding into a dirty-blonde shag that was meant to look mussed yet cool. Fresh from bed it just looked limp and sad.

I made a tea and drank it looking out at the empty street. Well, empty except for two rats going through a capsized recycling bin across the way. Until a seagull bullied them away and started ripping into a black bag. The Bristolian equivalent of watching the deer emerge and sip morning dew. I picked my cuticles and wondered if I ought to have booked a manicure.

Just before the alarm I crept back to the bedroom with a tea for my husband. He opened wary eyes and then glanced at the time, groaned and accepted the mug. As he lifted one hand to rasp his stubble, he exposed the tattoo on his ribs. A faded flash-art skeleton from his teen years. Both of us had patches of embarrassing ink, but thankfully most of it was easy to hide. I ruffled his mop of dark hair and he said something that sounded like 'fucking destination weddings'.

Our pre-booked taxi was ten minutes late and we hit traffic on the way to Bristol airport because of some kind of vintage car fair happening nearby. Normally I'd have enjoyed seeing so many old-fashioned cars and motorbikes, but not today. Even the sight of an honest to God omnibus didn't make me squeal in delight. Today was not the day for it. Not when we had a strict timetable to follow.

'We should get a stall at that next year,' Ethan said, watching as several ancient VW campers chugged past our stationary taxi. 'Bet they'd love some proper vintage vinyl.'

I nodded, inwardly screaming at the traffic to just please move.

I was practically hyperventilating by the time we got checked in at the airport and headed for security. Ethan had forgotten to take his phone out of his carry-on and we got pulled aside to dig it out and re-scan. At least he'd not worn his Docs. All that lacing and unlacing would have driven me mad. The whole time we were waiting I was watching the multiple giant clocks in the airport and getting tenser every minute. If I was late to the start of Jess's wedding week, I would never forgive myself. I wasn't sure she would either, though she'd never say anything.

Finally, we passed security and reached the far less stressful part of the airport. Though my level of anxiety barely dipped.

'Do you want a coffee?' Ethan asked doubtfully, eyeing my bouncing leg.

'Tea, please.'

It was only after he'd gone that I remembered my water bottle. It was empty, as per airport rules, but I'd intended to get a drink for the flight. One of my fussy little 'quirks', as Ethan called them, was not liking to drink from bottles I'd bought. I'd worked at a supermarket one Christmas and seen rats running all over the flat packs of drinks. Damn it, maybe I could still get a drink before we had to move on. I opened my bag, then realised the bottle wasn't in there. I must have moved it to Ethan's bag when I had to fit the wedding present into mine. At least I hadn't forgotten that. Even the thought of doing so made me feel a bit ill.

Oh well, they'd have water on the plane. They didn't charge for that, right?

I was pleasantly surprised, though, when Ethan returned with two cardboard cups and my water bottle.

'You remembered?' I said, gratefully taking the full plastic flask.

'A husband's duty,' he said, tipping an imaginary hat. 'I got you iced tea because there was a queue for the water fountain. But it's in the bottle because I know you're a fusspot.'

'Even better.' I kissed him on the cheek and for a few minutes we escaped the stressful rush of the airport, sipping our hot drinks in an oasis of calm. Then they announced our gate and we were off again like tired horses on their third race of the day, dragging our bags with us.

The flight to Bavaria was just under two hours. Not that it mattered much because we'd have gone for economy even if it was twenty hours. We couldn't afford anything else. Not yet anyway. My inheritance was still pending and I didn't want to think about what it would mean when the money finally came in. For me and for my relationship with Jess. That money had started to symbolise everything that remained unresolved between us. The rift in our relationship packed full of pound coins.

Desperate not to think about it I plugged my headphones in and put on a children's audiobook from when I was about five. Something to calm me, that familiar story in a voice whose tone and rhythm I knew off by heart. Both Ethan and I liked old things, found them comforting in a weird way. After all, if a piece of uranium glass or a shellac record could survive for decades without a scratch, we could survive anything. He put that in his vows.

'Bugger, I forgot my—' Ethan was saying as I pulled a spare set of earbuds from my bag. 'Cheers.'

'At least you always forget the same things,' I said.

I sipped my iced tea and leant back against the headrest. My sleepless night caught up with me in a rush and before I knew it, Ethan was gently shaking my arm. I struggled upright and he tugged my headphone from my ear.

'We're here,' he said, amused by my confusion. 'You didn't even snore. I've never seen you sleep that deep.'

I nudged his knee with a playful frown. Still soaked in sleep I helped gather our bags and we joined the tail end of the queue to get off the plane. Outside the air was cold and I hugged myself, wishing I'd thought to put my coat on before hefting the bags. I couldn't be bothered to drop everything now and struggle with it. It had been enough of a bother at security, but I was putting up with it instead of bemoaning our lack of checked luggage.

Our flight was one of those little planes they never bother pulling in to the airport. Instead you have to gather on the tarmac and wait for a bus in the morning chill. I just wanted to get into our rented car and go back to sleep.

Eventually we got through the airport and out to the blocky little office in a car park with rows of shiny cars outside, their insides lined in paper. I waited whilst

Ethan went in to sign some final paperwork and then came out to look over our car. It wasn't a great model; no heated seats or fancy sound system. Just a basic-level run-around. We'd even brought our old satnav from home instead of paying out to borrow one. I only hoped our maps were still good. I felt a bolt of panic at the thought of not being able to find the resort. Had Ethan remembered to check the map updates? Was that what was going to undo all our planning?

I checked the time on my phone. We were on schedule. I'd been hoping to be a little bit ahead of ourselves by now. It was very important that we weren't late. Just this once I could not be late. I'd let Jess down enough over the years. This was not going to be one of those times. Everything was going to be perfect for her wedding week.

'We need to stop for fuel,' Ethan groused as we pulled out of the car park. 'They only put a bit in. You better believe they're getting it back with less than a quarter of a tank. That's if I don't push it back into the car park on fumes. Fucking rip-off.'

He chuntered away like any English person on holiday whilst the satnav guided us to a petrol station. I was already struggling to keep my eyes open. Even with all the slightly abnormal normality of another country to watch as it flew by the window. The different logos and sign colours, how the plants at the side of the road weren't quite the same as back home and the way the radio had German announcers and adverts in between American pop songs.

330

At the station Ethan dug a paper wallet out of his bag and handed me some euros.

'Do you want to get some snacks for the journey? Can you grab me a coffee, oh, and some cigarettes?' he asked.

I nodded.

'Don't forget a lighter!' Ethan called after me.

I went in and picked up sandwiches, chocolate bars and crisps. There were coffee machines at the back, but I couldn't work them out. Either they were the most complicated ones I'd ever seen or my foggy brain just couldn't grasp them. My coins kept being returned and none of the options I pressed ended with a cup being dispensed. So I opted to get Ethan an energy drink instead. Unlike me he was happy to swig from the can, but I'd go over it with an anti-bac wipe just in case.

The cigarettes were the worst part, because I had to point and mime to get them and a cheap lighter. The woman behind the counter was obviously trying to be nice about it but I felt so stupid. I should have at least bought a phrase book. I left the shop with my cheeks on fire.

'I have these by the way,' Ethan said, digging two pre-packaged waffles out of the front pocket of his hemp hoodie when I returned to the car. 'They brought them around while you were—' He tipped his head and snored with a whistle.

'You said I didn't snore!'

'I was sparing your feelings. The woman in front of

331

us tried to smother you twenty minutes in, took me and two flight attendants to pull her off you.'

'My hero.'

Ethan grinned and tucked a cigarette behind his ear for later.

I set the satnav with the address Jess sent me. Her wedding was being held at a ski lodge and she was paying for our stay there – room, food, everything. Even my dress and Ethan's suit, which were probably already waiting for us there. All we had to do was get there on time. I would not fuck this up. According to the satnav's estimation we'd arrive with some time to spare. Just not as much as I'd originally planned in. We'd been delayed on landing and then the queues in the airport held us up even longer. We'd lost about an hour. Hopefully we'd make it up on the drive. Otherwise we'd have just enough time to freshen up before the welcome dinner Jess told me about when I rang last week.

I sipped from my bottle and hoped my outfit for the dinner wasn't getting too creased in the bag. Not that I wasn't going to look like a heap of shit next to Jess anyway. I think she travelled with an iron and maybe even a mini-dry-cleaning set. Jess was always called a 'natural beauty'; soft dark hair, big dark eyes and perfect skin without even trying. The kind of woman made for pearl earrings and shift dresses. The kind who looked expensive and professional. I'm the one who changes hair colour like I change my underwear, with healed piercings all over and bad tattoos on my lower back and legs. I'd never seen Jess look anything but perfect and polished. I could barely keep polish on for a day without picking it off. But that wasn't a big deal anyway. Maybe I was just freaking out because this would be our first time meeting face to face since the funeral. This was meant to be her week, her day. Honestly, the fact that I couldn't compete with her on a good day could only help me here.

We were moving over the city's roads so smoothly it almost felt like we weren't going anywhere at all. Before too long I felt my eyelids droop. My forehead met the cold glass of the window and I missed whole stretches of the songs on the radio.

Ethan reached out and turned the volume down, then gently patted my knee. The satnav piped up and told him to take the next left. I closed my eyes, relieved that we were going to make it. This time, I wouldn't let my sister down.

You'll want to stay. Until you can't leave . . .

A group of strangers arrive on a beautiful but remote island, ready for the challenge of a lifetime: to live there for one year, without contact with the outside world.

But twelve months later, on the day when the boat is due to return for them, no one arrives.

Eight people set foot on the island. How many will make it off alive?

A gripping, twisty page-turner about secrets, lies and survival at all costs. Perfect for fans of *The Castaways*, *The Sanatorium* and *One by One*.

'Because he chose you. Out of thirteen girls. You were the one. The last one.'

Lucy Townsend lives a normal life. She has a husband she loves, in-laws she can't stand and she's just found out she's going to be a mother.

But Lucy has a dark and dangerous secret.

She is not who she says she is.

Lucy is not even her real name.

A totally gripping, edge-of-your-seat thriller with twists and turns you just won't see coming. Perfect for fans of *Girl A* and *The Family Upstairs*.

**It was a safe haven . . .
until it became a trap.**

Mila and Ethan are on their way to at a luxurious ski resort when the car engine suddenly stops and won't start again.

Stranded, with night closing in, they make their way on foot back to some cabins. But when they find the windows boarded up, they have the eerie sense they shouldn't be there.

With snow falling, they have no choice but to break into one to spend the night.

**In the morning, when Mila wakes, Ethan is gone.
Now she is all alone.
Or is she?**

A totally gripping and spine-tingling psychological thriller. Perfect for fans of *The Hunting Party* and *The Castaways*.